JONNIE JACOBS

joins the ranks of today's most celebrated mystery authors with the outstanding debut of the Kate Austen mystery series!

* *

"*Murder Among Neighbors* is a fun read . . . it's definitely worth a visit to Ms. Jacobs' neighborhood."
—*Mystery Forum*

"The clues are by the page full. Kate Austen . . . could be habit forming." —*The Contra Costa Sun*

"*Murder Among Neighbors* is a terrific debut filled with twists, surprises and engaging characters. May clever, gutsy, sexy Kate long continue to cope with the ills of our times: fallible husbands, school bake sales and murderers."
—Gillian Roberts, author of *With Friends Like These . . .*

"A first rate mystery." —*Rendezvous*

"Jonnie Jacobs is a decidely fresh voice in mystery fiction. *Murder Among Neighbors* is a really enjoyable debut—one can only hope to see a lot more from both Jonnie Jacobs and her irrepressible character."
—Susan Rogers Cooper, author of *Funny as a Dead Comic*

"Amateur sleuth and single mother Kate Austen is as warm and appealing as her neighbors are deadly in this debut novel . . . Jacobs skillfully blends murder, motherhood and suburban intrigue, then spices it up with humor and romance for a delicious read."
—Jaqueline Girdner, author of *Tea-totally Dead*

MURDER AMONG NEIGHBORS
A Kate Austen Mystery
by Jonnie Jacobs

* *

Don't miss Jonnie Jacobs's newest Kate Austen mystery
Murder Among Friends
now on sale wherever hardcover mysteries are sold!

JONNIE JACOBS

MURDER AMONG NEIGHBORS

ZEBRA BOOKS
KENSINGTON PUBLISHING CORP.

ZEBRA BOOKS are published by

Kensington Publishing Corp.
850 Third Avenue
New York, NY 10022

First Kensington Hardcover Printing: September, 1994
First Zebra Paperback Printing: August, 1995

Printed in the United States of America

Walnut Hills is your basic affluent suburban community—quiet, insulated and a tad self-righteous. Located over the hills, just east of Oakland and Berkeley, it's close enough so that those of us who live there can easily hop in to buy freshly baked baguettes and Peet's coffee, and on occasion even journey across the bay to San Francisco for an evening of opera and four-star dining. But distinctly remote enough from the exigencies of urban living that we don't have to worry about some nut cases snatching our purses or our kids, or pulling knives on us for smiling at the wrong time.

There is plenty of free parking, a lovely bike trail—with an adjacent path for horses—and more city parks than stoplights. Our schools have service clubs rather than gangs, our local gas stations are trusting enough to let you pump before you pay, and the weekly crime report—printed in the local paper right next to the gossip column—typically logs nothing weightier than complaints of an after-hours party in the park or a call regarding some prepubescent kid trying to swipe a Bic lighter or can of Coke from the local 7-Eleven.

In other words, it's not the sort of community where you'd expect to stumble over a murder. And Pepper

Livingston was certainly the last person you'd ever expect to go and get herself killed.

The Livingstons' house is next-door to ours, although that isn't the way it sounds. There's over an acre of property separating the two houses—the Livingstons' acre plus—so we don't exactly call out to each other as we pick up the morning paper. In fact, from our front steps you can see only the far corner of the Livingstons' porch and a couple of upstairs windows. Densely planted rhododendrons and an orchard of walnut trees obscure almost everything else.

Ours is a modest house, the sort of place realtors love to call "quaint." It was, in fact, originally the carriage house for the estate which later became the Livingstons' local residence. Personally, I've never thought their place was all that attractive, though it certainly is impressive, with its lush grounds, wide circular drive and Georgian pillars. Pepper called it "comfortable." But it wasn't, she told me the day I met her, nearly as nice as their house in the Napa Valley. Andy and I had scrimped and saved to buy our place, and some months it was touch and go whether we'd be able to make the mortgage payment on time, so I couldn't begin to understand the kind of money the Livingstons had.

I knew Pepper because we were neighbors—believe me, an acre or two between houses is nothing in this town—and because our daughters went to the same nursery school and sometimes played together. We shared a car pool and an occasional cup of coffee—rather, I had coffee; Pepper drank tea, herb tea—but we weren't really close. Pepper was busy running the Benefit Guild and playing tennis at the country club, while I baked brownies for school parties and wiped messy noses on class field trips. I have been known to sneer at all that monied life, but the truth was, I would probably have changed places with her in a minute. Until the day she died, that is.

Pepper was killed sometime around midnight, so whether she died on the fifth or sixth of May no one knows for sure, but her body wasn't discovered until the morning of the sixth. I had just dropped my daughter Anna off at nursery school, and as soon as I turned onto our street I saw the police cars—five of them—parked in a neat line at the far end of the Livingstons' driveway. No sirens, no flashing lights, no half-open doors signaling a hasty exit.

At first, I thought maybe Pepper was organizing some fund raiser for the police department—that's the sort of thing she did—but when I considered it further, I didn't see why she needed to meet with the bulk of the force simply to discuss her plans. Besides, her daughter Kimberly had a cold, which was why I hadn't taken her to school that morning, and somehow I couldn't imagine Pepper playing host to a group of policemen while Kimberly whined and sniffled in the background.

The whole time I was cleaning up the breakfast dishes and washing out the sink, I was also peering out the window to see if I could catch a glimpse of any activity.

Nothing. Absolutely nothing.

What they were all doing in there, I couldn't imagine. In the back of my mind I was trying to figure out the most socially appropriate way to broach the subject with Pepper later that afternoon. I knew the minute the police left I would be on the phone grilling her; I just wanted to be able to do it with some class.

Finally, because the waiting was making me antsy, I drove to the cleaners to pick up Andy's suits, which I'd had cleaned so that if he ever "found himself" and decided to come home to us, they'd be there waiting for him. It was either that or pack them up, along with his monogrammed shirts, twenty pairs of Italian loafers and maybe his prize record collection, and ship the whole mess off to Goodwill—which was something I'd considered doing on more than one occasion.

What stopped me was Anna, who thought her dad was nothing short of terrific. And maybe some small, feeble hope that it might still work out right.

"It's not you, Kate," Andy had explained the evening he announced he was moving out. "It's me. I have to sort things out, figure out where I'm going and who I am." I thought it was pretty clear who he was—my husband, Anna's father and regional sales manager for Voice Mail USA, but that was apparently not what he meant.

Maybe it was the prospect of turning thirty—although my thirtieth birthday a year earlier hadn't fazed him in the least—or maybe it was looking in the mirror one morning and finding his thick, sun-streaked hair was no longer quite so thick . . . or sun streaked. Or maybe it was the fact that I was pregnant again.

Whatever the reason, he had quit his job, taken half of our meager savings, and was now jaunting around Europe, trying to put meaning back into his life.

When I was honest with myself, which was less often than I liked to admit, I knew I'd seen it coming for a long time. Probably even before Andy himself. And I knew that the disenchantment wasn't totally one sided. Andy is a sweet guy, and a lot of fun, just so long as your wants and needs happen to coincide with his. It had taken me a while to figure that out.

By the time I returned from the cleaners, only a couple of police cars remained in Pepper's driveway, but they had been joined by some new, unmarked cars and a gray van which I recognized as belonging to a local news network. My curiosity finally got the better of me.

Very nonchalantly, as though I'd just happened to look up and notice a touch of unusual activity in the neighborhood, I moseyed over to the Livingstons'. In the driveway, a policeman was leaning against the fender of his car, writing in a notebook. He was short and stocky with thinning hair and a heavy black mustache. Like a cop in some TV sitcom.

"Is everything okay over here?" I chirped, knowing full well it was a dumb question. The police don't hang out in front of your house all morning if everything is just fine. Even in Walnut Hills there are other things to do.

The man looked up and glared in my direction. "Who are you?"

"Kate Austen. I live next door." From where we were standing my house looked even smaller than it was, but I thought the fact I lived in the neighborhood would give me some credibility. "That's our place over there."

"You know the Livingstons?"

"Yes. At least I know Pepper. I've only met Robert a few times."

The man played with his mustache a moment, combing it with his fingers and then brushing the ends flat. Finally he looped a thumb through his belt loop and shook his head sadly. "I'm sorry you gotta hear it like this ma'am, but there's been a homicide here. Your friend is dead."

I waited for him to smile at his truly tasteless joke, but he continued fingering his mustache instead. "Someone broke into the house during the night."

"There must be some mistake," I sputtered, trying

to ignore the queasy feeling in the pit of my stomach. Terrible things didn't happen to people like Pepper. Even minor inconveniences fell much more often at my doorstep than hers.

"No mistake, I'm afraid. Be sure to lock your doors and windows up tight," he warned as he climbed into his car. "Until we catch this weirdo, no place is safe."

I nodded numbly and moseyed back home again, not at all nonchalantly.

It's funny the things that go through your head at a time like that. I couldn't focus on the dead part. I kept thinking of that mane of silver blond hair, the long polished nails, the wide mouth capped with perfect, white teeth. Pepper drove a candy red Mercedes convertible, and that was the image that stuck in my mind—gorgeous Pepper behind the wheel of her snazzy little car, dashing off down the street as if she hadn't a care in the world.

Before I got to know her, when all I saw was the picture on the society page and the array of delivery trucks that stopped daily at her door, I thought she was your basic pampered princess, which on one level she probably was. How many people, after all, hang around the house folding laundry, or whatever, dressed in a silk jumpsuit and heels? Or have their mechanic make house calls? But Pepper was also a surprisingly nice person, at least most of the time. Very straightforward, with none of the cattiness which is typical of so many of the women in this town.

Not that we were exactly chummy. Our lives were too different for that. Our expectations, our experiences, even our husbands.

Once, a few months after they moved in, we invited Pepper and Robert over for a barbecue. Andy, in faded shorts and thongs, was mashing burgers and gulping beer when Pepper and Robert arrived bearing a bottle of fine French wine—to my mind sheer show-manship when you live in California—and an arrange-ment of flowers which probably cost more than the en-tire evening meal. After a few false starts, Pepper and I settled into a comfortable pattern of mommy-talk. But Andy wasn't so lucky. He was deep in the role of back-yard host, poking at the barbecue fire and glibly show-ing off his knowledge of baseball trivia while Robert, in gray flannel slacks and a blue blazer, balanced precariously on one of our aluminum lawn chairs and tried to engage Andy in a discussion of tax-exempt bonds.

The evening was a disaster, and we never attempted anything like it again, although the Livingstons did in-clude us in several of their large holiday parties. We went at my insistence, and always left early at Andy's.

Pepper's was a charmed life, I thought, sometimes with envy. But that was before I realized that nothing is as simple as it first appears, and everything has its price.

My conversation with the policeman left me shaken, and after I dragged myself home, I plopped down at the kitchen table where I began absently picking at the glob of dried orange juice and corn flakes left from Anna's breakfast. I was still sitting at the table some-time later when the doorbell's sounding and Max's barking shook me from my daze. I opened the door cautiously, letting Max inch his fuzzy brown nose through the crack before I even peered out. Hadn't I just been warned to keep my doors and windows locked up tight?

"Officer Jenkins," the man at the door said, holding his badge out for me to examine. "May I talk to you for a moment?"

At first I thought it was the same policeman I had spoken to earlier, but on closer examination I saw that although the resemblance was truly amazing, Officer Jenkins had less hair and more belly.

"Sure," I told him, "just a minute. Let me get the dog out of the way first."

Max wouldn't hurt a flea, but he's been known to crawl into any available lap, all fifty pounds of him. And he's very free with his kisses. That's his Airedale parentage we've been told. He's got some other kinds of dog in him too, but the exuberant terrier spirit dominates. He's a charmer, a fluffy teddy bear of a dog but also a handful.

I locked him in the kitchen and then led Officer Jenkins to the living room, where I kicked a path through the assortment of Barbie-doll clothes spread across the floor.

"Can I get you anything. Coffee? Soda?" I wasn't sure what proper etiquette called for. My experience of talking to the police was pretty much limited to those times I mumbled at them under my breath as they handed over a ticket.

"No, thanks," Jenkins said, dropping his ample body into the green armchair I was itching to replace.

I took a seat across from him, on the couch, perching on the edge like a guest at a formal tea. Jenkins pulled out a notebook and clicked his pen. Then he took his time looking around the room.

"Is this about Pepper Livingston?" I asked, offering him my polite, hostess smile.

He looked surprised. "How did you know about Mrs. Livingston?"

"I was talking to one of the other policemen a little while ago. Over in front of her house."

"Oh," he said, clearly disappointed. Maybe he thought he'd stumbled onto the killer already, exposed through her unthinking, but incriminating, slip of the tongue. Again clicking his pen, he asked, "Did you know her well?"

"We're friendly, and our daughters go to the same preschool, but we don't, uh . . . didn't exactly travel in the same circles."

Jenkins scratched something in his notebook, then looked back at me. His face drooped, like bread dough before it's begun to rise, and his lids barely opened. "Is that a ficus over there?" he asked, pointing to the large pot in the corner.

"Yes, it is." Had they found ficus leaves at the scene of the crime? Irrationally, my heart began to pound.

"It's beautiful. I can't seem to keep the darn things alive myself."

I relaxed and again smiled. "It's mostly luck. You have to have the right light, room temperature, that sort of thing."

He nodded and cleared his throat. "When did you last see Mrs. Livingston?"

"Yesterday afternoon, about two o'clock. She dropped my daughter off from school." That was less than twenty-four hours ago, I thought with a chill. We had stood talking by the side of the car. I had touched her bare arm, making some comment about skin that tanned rather than freckled, and promised to buy a ticket to the Guild Wine Festival.

Jenkins made another quick notation. "How often do you water it?"

"Water it?"

"The ficus."

"I don't know, once a week I think, when I water the other plants."

He admired the tree for a moment, then shifted his gaze back to me. "Were you home last night between the hours of ten o'clock, P.M., and two o'clock, A.M.?

I nodded.

"Did you see or hear anything unusual?"

I tried to remember. "No, not really."

"You're sure? No screams, shouting, loud noises?" He asked the questions as if he were reading from a script.

"No. I went to bed about ten, but I'm a light sleeper. I'm sure I would have heard anything like that."

"What about unusual activity in the neighborhood? Anyone going door to door selling window-cleaning services or magazine subscriptions?"

"Only salvation."

He stared at me blankly.

"No," I told him. "There hasn't been anything out of the ordinary." I noticed that Jenkins had closed his notebook, clipping his pen to the front cover. My time was almost up. "How did it happen?" I asked, trying hard not to sound like the nosy busybody I really was.

"Looks like someone got in through the kitchen window." He shifted in his chair, settling in more comfortably. "An open window, it's like an engraved invitation. People just don't realize."

I mumbled concurrence.

"Looks like she was strangled. Some kind of rope or cord, if I had to guess." Officer Jenkins appeared to find talking about the murder more interesting than investigating it, and his voice lost its monotonous quality. "It happened in the bedroom. Her body was lying across the top of the bed, but she was dressed in her nightgown and the covers were mussed as though she'd been asleep. Probably woke up when she heard a noise, then went to investigate."

Not exactly the way I would choose to go, but preferable, I suppose, to being hacked apart with a knife.

"Looks like some jewelry was taken, and maybe some other stuff, but nothing big. Stereo, VCR, TV—

they're all there. Until the husband's had a chance to go through her things we won't have a complete list."

"Robert. And Kimberly, the little girl. They're all right then?"

He nodded, then leaned back, resting his arms on his belly. "Apparently the husband was out last night. Didn't get in until after one. Slept downstairs so as not wake his wife and that's why he didn't discover the body until this morning. It was the little girl, actually, who found her."

All of a sudden it finally hit me, the dead part. I thought of Kimberly rushing to snuggle with her mother in the early morning and finding instead a stiff, unresponsive corpse. She might have shaken Pepper lightly, like Anna does when I'm pretending to sleep, and then finally, with growing frustration and fear, gone to get Robert. "Something's wrong with Mommy," she would have whimpered. "I can't get her to wake up." In spite of the deep breath I forced into my lungs, my eyes filled with tears and my throat ached. How could you explain to a five-year-old that her mother has been murdered?

Officer Jenkins leaned forward, tugging at his mustache. I got a whiff of cigarette smoke and mint mouthwash. "You all right, ma'am?"

"It's just such a shock."

He nodded. "Well, if you think of anything . . ." He tucked his notebook back in his pocket and looked around the room. "Be sure to keep your doors and windows locked."

It must be the official line, I decided; it was the second time that day I'd been similarly warned.

We were at the front door going through the "Thank you . . . oh, anytime" routine when it struck me. "Did you say the prowler came in through an open window?"

"Yeah, in the kitchen."

"Why would Pepper leave the kitchen window open?"

He shrugged. "It was a warm night."

"Yes, but they have air conditioning."

"Maybe she liked fresh air. Or maybe she just forgot to shut it."

He wandered off to his car, and I went to pick up Anna. It wasn't like Pepper to forget to lock a window. In fact, I was surprised she'd opened it in the first place. None of the Livingstons' front-facing windows had screens—they ruined the effect of paned glass, Pepper had explained to me—and Pepper was finicky about bugs. On more than one occasion I'd watched her, dressed to a tee in her AnnTaylor finery, walking about the family room swatting at flies, even as we talked. "I don't know which is worse," she told me once, "the live ones buzzing in your ear, or the dead ones squashed on your wall."

I thought of that same Pepper, now dead, and shivered.

2

The phone was ringing when we walked in the door, and Anna rushed to answer it. In my preparenthood days, when I thought one simply told one's children what was and wasn't allowed, I used to curse parents who let barely intelligible youngsters field incoming calls. But having children teaches you a thing or two, and I'd finally realized that some battles are simply not worth fighting.

"It's Daria," Anna said, handing me the phone and wrinkling her nose at the same time. Daria Wilkens was probably my best friend in Walnut Hills. Not that we had one of those intensely intimate, soul-mate friendships you sometimes read about, but Daria was the first real friend I made after moving here, and the threads of our lives were entwined in ways too complex to unravel. Anna thought Daria was too "geeshy," and while I wasn't sure I understood the meaning of the word, I did sometimes understand the sentiment. Not that it mattered. You take your friends the way they come, blemishes and all.

"I just heard. It was on the radio."

"You mean about Pepper?"

"Of course I mean about Pepper. What else would I have heard?"

"I don't know, maybe something about famine, threat of war, the budget deficit, that sort of thing."

"I don't think this is anything to joke about." She sounded shaken, and I immediately regretted my flippancy.

"You're right, it isn't."

"What have you heard? The news didn't have much." The fact that Daria had heard the news at all was something of a surprise. Usually she listened to those dignified classical stations—the kind where announcers speak in soft, cultured voices, delivering only public service announcements and an occasional, tasteful commercial. I didn't think these stations covered news, much less messy, morbid stuff like murder.

"I haven't heard much," I told her, shooing Anna off to the other room. "There were a bunch of police cars in front of the Livingston place this morning, and then a policeman came by a little later to talk to me."

"What did he want?"

"Just to ask some questions. How well did I know Pepper? Did I hear or see anything unusual last night? That sort of thing."

"Did you?"

"Hear anything? No."

"You're sure?" The sharp tone in her voice made me feel guilty, as though I should have been listening for cries of help instead of selfishly sleeping the night away in a comfortable bed. "What about Max? He didn't bark or anything?"

"Max only hears sounds that interest him, like the doorbell and the creak of the refrigerator opening."

"So what do they think? Any suspects yet? Any leads at all?"

"Hey, I spent ten minutes talking to an overweight officer with bad breath who seemed more interested in how I kept my ficus green than in finding Pepper's killer. I don't know any more than you do." I shivered and kicked at a piece of loose linoleum with my foot. "Be sure to keep your doors and windows locked."

"Huh?"

"That's what the police keep telling me. Makes me feel like I'm six years old."

"Oh, God, I hadn't thought about that. This prowler could have broken into *your* house last night instead."

"Only if he was blind or truly crazy. Who would choose to rob us and walk away with maybe a new blender and a pair of Kmart cufflinks, when he could go next door and fill a treasure chest?"

"Still, it wouldn't hurt to be careful, especially now that you're there all alone."

"Except for Anna."

"You know what I mean." Andy and Daria's husband, Jim, were old friends; that's how Daria and I met in the first place, so she feels somehow responsible for Andy's leaving and worries over me like a neurotic parent. She can't understand why I don't spend my days in bed, weeping.

Sometimes I wonder that myself, but it's a hard act to pull off when you've got a four-year-old. Besides, there's only so long you can hold onto What-Might-Have-Been. And only so long you can delude yourself about What-Actually-Was.

"You know what I find most upsetting?" I said. "Kimberly. What goes through a little girl's mind when her mother is murdered?"

"Well, if she's anything like Pepper she'll handle it just fine."

The comment was insensitive, even for Daria, who was inclined to see things the way she wanted, no matter what the truth was. As fond as I was of her, there were times when she drove me crazy with her self-serving certainty and her steadfast unwillingness to admit to shades of gray.

"Surely you don't mean that?"

She appeared to think about it for a moment. "Actually I do, but I didn't intend it to sound as crass as it did."

Anna was pulling on my shirt and whispering in my free ear that she was hungry. "Got to go," I told Daria. "I'll keep you posted."

"The minute you hear anything."

"The very minute."

"Are you sure you're all right over there?"

"Of course."

"I've got a meeting tonight, but tomorrow night I'll bring over take-out Chinese and we'll have dinner. Okay?"

As soon as I was off the phone I scooped Anna up in my arms and hugged her tightly, trying hard to blot out visions of Kimberly, who no longer had a mother to hold her. And when Anna asked for some chips, I didn't hesitate. In fact, I set the whole bag on the table and didn't say a thing about her finishing her yogurt first.

How would I explain what had happened? I debated coming right out and telling her what little I knew, but in the end I couldn't make myself utter the necessary words.

"Look," I said instead, "you got a postcard from Daddy."

Munching on a handful of chips, Anna studied the picture of the Eiffel Tower, then asked me to read the card.

" 'Dear Anna,' " I read. " 'Today I visited a castle that was so large you would have been able to sleep in a different room every night for a whole month. But you would have had to go pee in a pot and then carry it outside and dump it in the woods. Poop too. Aren't you glad you don't live in a castle? I miss you. Love, Daddy.' "

She laughed. "Is that really true?"

"People who live in castles today have bathrooms, of course, but in the olden days they didn't." I started to explain the particulars of chamber-pot use, but Anna interrupted.

"When is Daddy coming home?"

"I don't know, honey. I don't think *he* even knows."

I watched the smile fade from Anna's face. She missed him terribly, and that pulled at my heart in a way Andy's leaving never had. What would happen when the novelty of postcards and exotic foreign stamps wore off? How would she feel if he decided not to come back? I wondered if these were questions Andy had even considered.

Yet, Andy did love Anna. And he'd been a good father most of the time. One look at the two of them horsing around together and you knew there was something there. That's why I'd thought he would have been pleased about the prospect of a second child.

We'd talked for years about having another baby someday. And while we hadn't actually planned on it just yet, I'd assumed *someday* covered a lot of territory. For Andy, however, *someday* apparently meant *maybe, but probably not and certainly not now.*

When the little pink dot showed up on the pregnancy test strip, I'd been surprised, but more pleased than not. And the more I'd thought about it, the more pleased I got. Our someday had arrived.

Andy met my announcement with a blank stare. "Jesus, how did that happen?" he asked.

So much for sharing the joy. "Is that important at this point?"

"It's just that I thought you were being careful is all."

I had been careful, most of the time. But either I hadn't been careful enough or most of the time didn't cut it. Either way, I was pregnant and secretly thrilled. I'd figured Andy would come around too, eventually, though by the time he'd left, he hadn't. There was always the chance he might still. But if he didn't, then what?

Whenever I tried to think it all through, rationally, I'd discover that reason only got you so far. Having a baby when you might be on the verge of divorce didn't seem like the smartest thing a person could do. Nor did it seem particularly wise to have a baby, even if you were going to stay married, when only one of you really wanted it. That's where logic took me. But how could I not give birth to this child who'd already taken hold of my heart?

I gave Anna a quick hug. "Off with you now," I told her.

Later we would tack the card up on the bulletin board in her room, along with the other cards Andy had sent over the last month, all of them addressed to Anna. Occasionally he'd add a P.S.—"Say hi to Mommy for me"—but not very often.

I watched her trudge off to her room, the card from Andy in one hand, the bag of chips in the other. I gave in to a moment of remorse, then put the whole thing out of my mind and went into the other room to compose a note to Robert Livingston.

The finer points of good breeding have always eluded me, and I find writing even the simplest thank-you note something of an ordeal. My note to Robert was proving to be even more taxing than usual.

Hi, heard your wife was murdered. So sorry. Hope she died quickly and painlessly. Let me know if there's anything I can do.

It wasn't the sort of letter even Miss Manners could have written easily.

A truly charitable person, I thought, would convey her sympathy in person. But I was chicken. If I couldn't find the words to put on paper, how would I ever know what to say to his face? Then once again I thought of Kimberly, her trusting innocence and quick, wide smile, and tore up what must have been my tenth draft. So what if I stammered and stumbled on my words, it was a small price to pay for compassion. I checked on Anna and then dragged myself next door, secretly hoping Robert was otherwise occupied.

The Livingstons' doorbell plays a melody I've never been able to identify, even though I could now hum right along without missing a beat. I was still following the notes and practicing my opening remarks when Robert answered the door, looking as though he were just about to step out for an evening at the club. He is one of those middle-aged men who would be right at home on the pages of *English Country Living.* Classically handsome features, bright blue eyes, and a full head of hair, graying slightly around temples. The very image of gentility. I've never felt particularly at ease around him, but that's probably because rich, powerful men always make me uncomfortable.

"One of the policemen told me what happened," I said. "I wanted you to know how truly sorry I am."

Robert stood framed in the doorway without moving. I wasn't sure he'd even heard me.

"Is there anything I can do? Run errands for you? Watch Kimberly?"

He smiled then, ever the gracious host. "That's very

kind, but I think we have things pretty much under control here."

He did not look like a man who had recently lost his wife. Not that I expected hysterics, or even puffy, red eyes, but I thought it wasn't unreasonable to expect a hint of emotion.

"Well, let me know if you think of anything," I told him as I turned to leave. "I imagine it's such a shock that right now you don't know which end is up."

He smiled again, a thin, stiff smile and thanked me for stopping by.

Back home I took on the task of explaining to Anna that her friend's mother had been killed. I told her Kimberly would need our extra love and kindness, and Anna nodded solemnly, but I wasn't sure how much she really understood. Then I filled Max's water dish, did a load of laundry and stuck Anna's untouched bowl of yogurt back in the refrigerator. The chips had clearly been the bigger attraction.

Later that afternoon Robert called, hesitant and apologetic, to ask if I could watch Kimberly for a few hours. "There are some things I have to take care of," he said, as he dropped her at our front door. "Are you sure you don't mind?"

He wore the same tan slacks he'd worn earlier, but he had traded the cashmere sweater for a dark blue blazer. Impeccable.

"No problem," I said. "Anna will be happy to have some company."

"I'll come get her as soon as I can. It shouldn't take more than a couple of hours." His smile was perfect, friendly but controlled.

Then, just as I was reinforcing my opinion of him as cold and unfeeling, he knelt down and took Kimberly in his arms. "I won't be gone long," he said gently. "You'll be all right here with Kate and Anna?"

"Will you hurry home, Daddy?"

"As fast as I can. I love you, sweetheart."

Kimberly wrapped her arms around his neck, and as he kissed her one last time I caught the sorrow that passed over his face and wondered that I had ever found him intimidating.

The girls built a Play-Doh city that covered the entire kitchen table, and then helped me make brownies, licking bowl, beaters and spoon as thoroughly as Max would have. When they went out back to play in the sand, I worked on the pen and ink drawing I'd begun earlier in the week. Art had been my passion for as long as I could remember, but it had been years since I'd made a serious effort to produce anything. In the last month, though, since Andy's departure, I'd happily rediscovered an artistic energy I'd thought had deserted me for good.

Several hours later, pleased with how well my drawing had gone, and almost smug in my sense of accomplishment, I turned on the evening news. Pepper's death was the lead story. With an odd mix of fascination and revulsion, I watched as the camera panned the length of the street and then closed in on the Livingstons' house. Finally, while the reporter wrapped up her summary of the morning's events, a close-up of Pepper's face flashed on the screen.

But these weren't the pictures that stuck in my mind when I flipped off the set. What I saw, and couldn't turn away from, was a vision of Pepper's last moments.

As though I were watching a film, I imagined her tucking Kimberly into bed for the evening, kissing her forehead and whispering the magic phrases of their nightly ritual. In bed herself sometime later, from the floating warmth of slumber, some strangeness, some odd sound or sensation, must have woken her. She lay there in the dark, listening to the pounding of her own heart, certain her imagination had run wild, but unable to go back to sleep just the same. At some point she must have gotten out of bed, but whether she did so in a moment of panic or in the resigned way people do when nighttime fears begin to take hold, I couldn't decide. Whichever it was, the intruder was suddenly there, standing in front of her. The unthinkable had become fact. What went through her mind when she saw him there, felt his breath on her face, his hands against her skin? What had she felt in that moment of terror? I couldn't begin to imagine. But I couldn't stop reliving those moments either, as if by witnessing the unspeakable, it might become bearable.

3

It was almost eight o'clock when Robert rang my bell again. I had fed the girls and given them both a bath, in the Jacuzzi with lots of suds. They were upstairs in Anna's room listening to a tape of Shel Silverstein poems, whispering to one another in serious, pensive tones.

"Sorry I'm late," he said, thrusting his hands into his pockets.

"It's fine." I stepped back, opening the door wider. "Would you like to come in for a minute?"

He hesitated, then nodded and followed me into the living room.

"Can I get you something to drink? Beer? Wine? Some coffee?"

Wearily, Robert plopped down on the couch and ran a perfectly manicured hand across his hair. "You wouldn't happen to have any scotch in the house, would you?"

I found a bottle at the very back of the cupboard, still in its Christmas wrapping. "You're in luck. Do you want water with it?"

"Just straight, with ice." When I returned with the glass, he was leaning back against the cushions, eyes closed, but he sat up when he heard me approach.

"Thanks," he said, with a lopsided, self-effacing smile, "I think I need this."

He took several long gulps of scotch and gazed at his feet. In the bright indoor light I could see the dark circles under his eyes and the waxy pallor of his skin. Like an elegant host at the end of a long evening, his manner was impeccable, but the sparkle was clearly gone.

We sat in awkward silence for a moment while I racked my brain for suitable topics of conversation. Everything that came to mind was somehow connected with Pepper, and I was reluctant to mention her name.

"What a day," he said at last.

I nodded and murmured agreement.

There was another moment of heavy silence, then Robert sighed. "If only I'd been home last night, Pepper would still be alive."

Or you might both be dead, I thought to myself. Robert might be a formidable match at the negotiating table, but he wasn't the sort to send an intruder scurrying for the door.

He drained his glass and held it up, questioningly.

"Same as before?"

He nodded, and I went to replenish his drink.

"Do you want to talk about what happened?" I asked as I handed him the fresh drink. I still wasn't sure if it was better to talk about Pepper or not. But Robert had initiated the subject, and the truth was, we could hardly sit across from each other, with Pepper murdered less than twenty-four hours earlier, and talk about the Oakland A's.

Robert stared into his glass, then swallowed hard and looked up. His gaze drifted to the window behind me. "I didn't find her until this morning," he said slowly. "I got home late last night. Didn't even bother to go upstairs, I just slept on the couch in the den. Pepper is usually up before I am, but this morning the house was strangely quiet. When I saw Kimberly sitting on the bottom step sucking her thumb, I knew something was terribly wrong." He paused, and when he continued his voice had a throaty rasp to it. "Pepper was lying diagonally across the bed with a big gash on her cheek. Her head was twisted sideways at a funny angle. I could tell she was dead even before I touched her."

A shiver worked its way down my spine, all the way to the tips of my toes. "The police said some jewelry was taken."

He nodded. "But it wasn't any of her good stuff, just the everyday jewelry she kept in her dresser. Her wallet was taken too. The bedroom was messed up, but it doesn't look like anything else is missing. Nothing obvious anyway. The funny thing is, Pepper doesn't even keep her good jewelry in the safe, she just stores it in a shoe box in the closet." This last was accompanied by a half-smile which I found oddly touching. "She was a remarkable woman," he said, emptying his glass.

"Can I get you another?"

"I probably shouldn't." There was a short pause. "But I will, thanks." Robert had a way of looking directly at you when he spoke, which I found both flattering and a little discomforting.

"How about something to eat too? This isn't exactly L'Étoile, but I could make you a sandwich or an omelette."

"An omelette sounds wonderful."

He followed me into the kitchen and sat at the table munching pretzels while I diced mushrooms and grated cheese.

"The policeman who was here today said the killer . . ." I paused and glanced at Robert, but the word didn't seem to phase him. "That the intruder probably got in through an open window."

"Yeah, that's what they say."

"It doesn't sound like Pepper, forgetting to close the window."

"No, it doesn't." Robert stretched his legs out in front of him and brushed at a piece of lint on his knee. "But she's been distracted lately, worrying about the Wine Festival and all. She was probably making a mental list of things that still needed doing and the window just escaped her mind."

He watched me break the eggs into a bowl. "Don't you drink?" he asked, gesturing to my glass of Calistoga.

"Sometimes." Then, because it sounded rude, like maybe I was faulting him for downing scotch instead of crying over a dead wife, I explained that I was pregnant. I hadn't told anyone except Daria because I wasn't sure what I was going to do about it, and my throat grew tight when I said the words.

Robert's eyes drifted to my middle. "Only six weeks," I explained.

"The beginning of a new life. It must be very exciting."

Under the circumstances, it was hardly that. In fact, I was trying hard to ignore the whole thing in the hope that it would miraculously disappear. Following the advice my mother used to give me when I complained of a stomachache.

Robert leaned forward and adjusted the band on his gold Rolex. "Unfortunately, that was an experience we missed." I must have looked perplexed. "Kimberly is adopted," he explained. "You didn't know that?"

Not only had I not known, I would have sworn that Pepper participated as enthusiastically as the rest of us in the discussions of pregnancy and childbirth that are inevitable among mothers of young children. But now I felt like a callous jerk. Probably she had listened and nodded, and thrown in a general "God, yes" or "Me too," while the rest of us jabbered on.

"No," I told him. "Pepper never said anything."

"It was a big disappointment to her. She didn't give up, even after we adopted Kimberly. There was a part of her that still held out hope, although she knew it was very unlikely." He took a pretzel and broke it into tiny pieces. "It was me," he said with a twisted smile. "Lazy sperm. So lazy they're almost comatose."

The words sounded so funny coming from reserved and refined Robert, that I almost laughed. Instead I scooped the omelette onto a plate and set it in front of him, struck by the fact that the man was not at all what I'd expected.

While he ate, we talked about our daughters and debated the relative merits of ballet lessons and gymnastics. I offered to lend a hand with Kimberly, and he explained that his sister would be coming up from Los Angeles to help out for a few days. Although we chatted easily, there was something vaguely disquieting about the whole experience, as though we had forgotten that Pepper was not simply away on a short holiday.

Finally Robert looked at his watch and sighed wearily. "I guess I should be going."

We found both girls sound asleep on the floor of Anna's bedroom, surrounded by a herd of stuffed animals. Robert hoisted Kimberly easily over his shoulder without waking her. "The sleep of the innocent." He chuckled. "It always amazes me."

At the door I turned on the porch light. "Please let me know if there's anything I can do."

"You know what I keep thinking, Kate? What if she was still alive when I got home? Maybe if I'd gone up to check on her I would have been able to call the ambulance in time to save her."

"You can't do that to yourself. Chances are, it wouldn't have made any difference anyway."

He fixed his eyes on the daddy-longlegs making its way up the side of the door. "There's always the possibility it would have, though. And the terrible thing is, I'll never know." Then he caught my eye and his lips curled into a weak smile. "Thanks for the drinks and dinner. And the company. I wasn't sure how I would ever get through this evening."

He was halfway down the driveway when I thought of something else. "What about the alarm?" I called after him. "Wouldn't an open window have set off the alarm?"

"Those two windows in the kitchen aren't on the alarm. The previous owners remodeled after the system was in place. We always talked about adding them on, but we never did." He gave a kind of half-laugh that came out more like a hiccup. "I guess we should have."

Watching him head off to confront whatever demons he would find lurking in the recesses of his mind that night, I was filled with sadness. Not just for Pepper and Robert and Kimberly, but for all humanity— frail and vulnerable, and yet instinctively resilient.

In the middle of the night I woke up when I thought I heard a sound. The doors and windows were all secure, and when I peered outside everything seemed as it should be. But I couldn't go back to sleep, so instead I lay there in the dark, staring at the vast nothingness around me, and tried to figure out how anyone would be able to track down Andy in the event I was killed.

* * *

We rarely argued, but the night before Andy left we had a terrible fight. I was at the sink scraping bits of roast lamb and potato into the garbage—the remnants of a special meal I'd prepared in hopes that it might somehow cause Andy to have a last-minute change of heart—while he sat at the kitchen table sorting through his plane tickets and passport.

"Do you think you'll miss me?" he asked.

What kind of man announces he's leaving his wife and then asks if she will miss him? "That's a stupid question," I told him, in a voice that made clear just how stupid it was.

"I take it that's a yes." His tone was almost playful. "I'll miss you, Kate."

"Look, you're the one who's leaving. Nobody is forcing you to go."

"You still don't understand it, do you?"

"No, I don't." Although on some level I probably understood better than he did.

Andy had the misfortune of being too good looking, of having had it too easy his whole life. People liked him, adored him in fact, and he had a gift for being in the right place at the right time. While the rest of us were getting whacked about a bit, learning a lesson or two from the school of hard knocks, Andy was gathering life's pleasures by the bushelful. And he didn't want the fun to end.

Out of the corner of my eye I saw him get up and walk over to stand behind me. Silently, he began kissing the back of my neck and running his hands down my arms. I tried to twist away, but he pressed against me. His hands moved down to my thighs and then up to my belly, where they traced slow, warm circles through my jeans.

"Stop it," I said, turning away.

But he didn't listen. One hand began working on the

buttons of my shirt while the other unzipped my pants.

"I said, knock it off."

"Come on, Kate. You know you'll like it. For old time's sake if nothing else."

All the sadness and regret I'd felt earlier coalesced into a ball of anger that settled in the pit of my stomach. "Get away from me, Andy."

"You won't have another chance for a long time, Kate."

My hands were wet and greasy, but I managed to turn slightly and elbow him hard in the abdomen. "You're sick," I said, keeping my back to him.

"Geez, I was only trying to be affectionate."

"No you weren't. You were trying to take what you wanted. You never think of anyone but yourself."

Andy reached across to the silverware drawer, which I had just opened, and slammed it shut. "You know what your problem is? You don't know how to have fun. You're so fucking serious, worrying all the time about the details of living, that you forget to actually live."

"Believe it or not," I said, pulling the drawer open again, "life is not one big picnic. Most people realize that along about the time they stop wearing diapers."

"Most people lead boring, confined lives."

I dried my hands and sat down at the table. It was worth one last shot. "Do you honestly think taking off to frolic around Europe for a couple of months is any way to sort things out? Sure it will be fun, but so what? You can't spend the rest of your life running away from responsibility and everything that doesn't amuse you."

But Andy was not in the mood for such a discussion. "At the moment," he said, pushing back his chair, "I'd say it's certainly better than the alternatives."

He pounded up the stairs and slammed the bathroom door hard, so that the clay dinosaur Anna had made in nursery school rattled on the window sill above the sink. Later that night when I got into bed, Andy was already asleep, lying with his back toward me and clinging to the edge of the mattress. If he'd tried to shift any farther, he would have fallen onto the floor.

Sometime in the middle of the night I woke up and reached my hand across the empty expanse between us. Soon I would have the whole bed to myself, every night. No warm body anywhere, no soft breathing. I slid over so that I could curl my body around his and kissed the back of his shoulders very lightly. Without rolling over, Andy took my hand in his.

"I really do love you, Kate," he whispered. "I'm just not sure that's enough."

Maybe not, I remember thinking, but it's a beginning. And for Anna's sake I thought he should at least try to make it enough.

Pepper used to go to the nine o'clock exercise class at the club. She wore those skimpy—but expensive—leotards that fit like a second skin and matching satiny tights. At the end of her workout her hair was always tastefully mussed and her face had just the right amount of shine to it. No question, she had looked terrific, like an ad for Reebok or some high-fiber cereal.

Andy and I didn't belong to the club—some months we could barely afford the mortgage on our house—and in any case I preferred jogging to exercise class, forgoing firm thighs and a flat stomach for a healthy heart. And style for comfort. Sweat pants and an old tee shirt of Andy's are my standard attire. And I don't glow, I sweat. By the end of my run I look a mess.

I was almost home, eager for a cold glass of water and a warm shower, when I saw Mrs. Stevenson standing in her driveway and motioning to me. An older woman, a widow of many years, Mrs. Stevenson lives across the street about three houses down. She's lived in the neighborhood longer than just about anybody else and still refers to most of the houses by their previous owners' names. We live in the old Williams place, even though the couple who had the house before us were named Bothello. They'd only lived there two years and that apparently wasn't sufficient time to earn a place in the annals of neighborhood history.

Mrs. Stevenson held a pair of pruning shears in her hand, and I thought she probably wanted to complain that Max had gotten out again and been trampling her flowers. I would apologize, offer to pay for the damage and promise to be more careful in the future, but I didn't want to be drawn into a prolonged discussion of everything wrong in the world, so I kept jogging in place while I spoke.

"Good morning, Mrs. Stevenson. Has Max been causing trouble again?" At the sound of his name, Max, who bounces along beside me most mornings, let out a polite woof and sat down.

"Goodness, no. I haven't seen hide nor hair of him except when he's running with you." She leaned over to address the dog, and her voice had that high-pitched, sugar-coated quality people sometimes use with animals. "You've been a good boy lately, Max."

"But you wanted to see me?"

"Yes. I have a problem. Well, it's not really a problem but a situation. And I don't know quite what to do."

Still breathing heavily, I nodded and kept on running in place. Listening to a recital of society's ills was a piece of cake compared to letting yourself get sucked into solving someone's problems.

"It's about that woman who lives in the old Crocker place. The one who was murdered yesterday."

I stopped hopping from foot to foot. "Pepper Livingston?"

"Yes, that's the one. There was a policeman who came by and asked me if I heard anything the night she was killed—I didn't. I'm a very sound sleeper, which is unusual for a woman my age. Anyway, I didn't think

about the car until after he left, and now I don't know
whether it's important or not."

"The car?"

"The one that parks in front of my house. I first noticed it because of the way it pulls in behind the oleander. I've seen it there a couple of times in the last week
or so, but no one ever gets out. It just pulls up and
stays there, sometimes fifteen or twenty minutes,
sometimes for an hour, and then drives off."

"And you think it might be connected with Pepper's
death?"

"That's what I don't know. It's not a place most
people choose to park. You have to pull way in off the
road to get to it."

The oleander, a large bush covered with pink flowers, was located near the corner of her property. The
Livingstons' house was diagonally across the street. It
would be an ideal, unobtrusive spot for casing the
place, but then cars parked along the street all the
time.

"You never saw anyone get out?"

"Never."

"Could you see into the car?"

"No. It had tinted glass, I think, or maybe the light
was just wrong. I never really looked because it didn't
seem to matter."

"What kind of car was it?"

"One of those four-wheel-drive things everybody
has these days." She thought about it for a moment.
"An Apache I think."

"An Apache?"

She nodded.

My knowledge of cars was limited, but I was pretty
sure there wasn't any such vehicle. "You mean Isuzu?
Or maybe Acura?" There were plenty of odd-sounding
names out there.

"No, it was an Apache, like the Indian."

"A Cherokee?"

She smiled. "That's it. I knew it was an Indian name."

"What color?"

"Dark."

"Blue? Black? Gray?"

"Yes, something like that."

"I don't suppose you got the license number?"

"No, I didn't think about that until now. Is it important?"

"Probably not," I said, recalling Mrs. Stevenson's penchant for finding disaster in every nook and cranny. "But if you see the car again why don't you try to get the license number, just in case."

Mrs. Stevenson nodded seriously. "This whole thing is very upsetting. There's never been anything remotely like it in this neighborhood before. But times are changing, I said that to Mrs. Lucas just the other day. What with all the drugs and guns and immigrants . . ."

Pleading an appointment I couldn't be late for, I excused myself and jogged home with Max following at my heels. Inside, I kicked off my shoes and contemplated the kitchen, which was a mess. Even by my standards. Shower first, then the kitchen. But after I had something to drink.

A few minutes later I was standing at the sink downing a glass of orange juice and listening to Max lap water from his dish, when the doorbell rang. My first inclination was to simply ignore it, but Max had already run into the hallway and begun scratching at the door, dripping water from his chin onto the hardwood floor. Besides, it was too early in the day for anyone to be concerned with saving whales, spotted owls or starving children, and the Jehovah's Witnesses had given up on me long ago. Dismissing a salesman, I thought, would be easier than contending with Max's incessant barking.

With my most menacing, what-the-devil-do-*you*-want scowl firmly in place, I opened the door, not even bothering to rein in Max. Strangers who ring my doorbell, especially at nine-thirty in the morning, do not receive a warm welcome.

"Mrs. Austen?" The man on my doorstep shifted from one foot to the other and stifled a yawn. "I'm Lieutenant Stone. With the homicide division."

No uniform this time; no paunch or receding hairline either. What with his blue oxford-cloth shirt, open at the collar, and brown, slightly scruffy loafers, Lieutenant Stone looked more like a head-in-the-clouds history professor than a cop. A decidedly attractive one at that.

"I'd like to ask you a few questions. About Pepper Livingston." Reaching into his shirt pocket, the lieutenant flipped open an official-looking ID which I didn't even bother to examine. I was too busy thinking about how dreadful I looked, and probably smelled.

"Actually I'm kind of in a hurry right now," I explained, concealing myself as best I could behind the opened door. It was true that I had a meeting at the nursery school in a little over an hour, but had my hair been cleaner and my clothes less ratty, I would probably have been more accommodating. Murder is, after all, a far more fascinating subject than the school's need for a new slide. And it wasn't every day that a good-looking male showed up on my doorstep. "Maybe you could come back later."

"It won't take long." Lieutenant Stone was already stepping through the doorway and I realized that I did not really have a choice.

Moving aside, I forgot to hold onto Max, who immediately nudged against the detective's thigh, leaving a large wet splotch on the front of his trousers.

"Sorry," I said and grabbed the dog's collar. "I'll lock him up."

"Don't bother." Stone reached down and tickled Max behind the ears. A second, smaller spot appeared near the first.

My scowl had faded the moment I opened the front door, and now, as I led the way to the living room, I tried for my utterly gracious, somewhat provocative smile. "Can I get you anything? Coffee or some soda?"

"Thanks. I'd love some coffee."

The lieutenant peered into the living room when I gestured in the direction of the couch, nodded politely and then followed me into the kitchen, taking a seat on the far side of the table, away from the gluey mound of Cheerios that Anna had left behind before going to nursery school.

I had hoped to run a comb through my hair and maybe dot a little blusher on my cheeks while the water boiled, but that was now clearly out of the question.

"Cream or sugar?"

"Just black."

Max perched eagerly next to Stone, waiting to see what fine morsels might happen his way. "Come here, Max," I said, opening the back door and silently praying that for once in his life Max would obey.

"He's not a problem."

"He has very bad manners."

"No worse than some of the people I deal with." The corners of Stone's mouth turned up ever so slightly. Then he rocked back in the chair and ran a hand through his hair, which was dark and thick, and a bit longer than I would have thought befitted a police officer.

While I fixed the coffee and set out some of the muffins I had baked for the nursery school meeting, Stone gazed out the window into the garden. He seemed, not pensive exactly, but immersed in some private rumination. I wondered if he was studying the layout of the Livingstons' house or merely taking a moment to watch the birds peck at the feeder. Finally I handed him a mug, one of the remaining few without a chipped rim, and sat down across from him, wishing fervently that I had opted for exercise classes and colorful leotards instead of running and grubby sweats.

"Thanks." He stared into his coffee, taking his own sweet time about getting down to business. Finally, he asked, "You were home Wednesday night?"

"Yes."

"Did you see anything unusual?"

"I already spoke to Officer, uh, Jenkins I think was his name. He talked to me yesterday afternoon."

Stone nodded. "I know, but this is the way we do things, so humor me, okay?" His voice had the calm, easy drawl of someone accustomed to taking charge. "Did you hear anything?"

I shook my head.

"I don't mean just screams. How about cars, footsteps, thuds, anything at all?"

"Nothing."

"What about your husband?"

"He's . . . he was out of town that night."

Stone took a long, slow sip of coffee and then reached for a muffin. "Good coffee."

"Thanks."

"So, tell me about Pepper Livingston."

"There's not much to tell. She was one of the movers and shakers of the Walnut Hills social set—president of the Benefit Guild, social chairman at the club, director of Sunshine House, head of the Save Our Hills

Action Committee, that sort of thing—and from what I hear, a wonderful hostess. One of those people always on the go, yet never frazzled or annoyed."

"Quite a lady."

"She was one of the most composed and polished women I've ever known." These were qualities I noticed in others because I lacked them, despite years of effort. With me it was usually speak first and think later, but even when I remembered to think first it didn't make much difference. Some women were simply born with the right instincts, and some were not. "But she wasn't all fluff," I continued. "She took her responsibilities seriously."

One of Anna's Barbie dolls was lying, unclothed, on the counter off to my left, and I was considering how best to move it to a less conspicuous location. I found it somehow unsettling to have a naked woman, even one only eleven and a half inches tall, stretched out between Lieutenant Stone, whom I found quite attractive, and myself.

"And everyone loved her."

"Well, not loved maybe, but they admired her."

Stone sat up straight and frowned. "Mrs. Austen, I am not asking for a character reference. I'm trying to get a handle on a murder. Do you understand the difference?"

I nodded and nonchalantly tossed the morning paper over Anna's Barbie.

"Now, the husband says you were one of Mrs. Livingston's best friends—"

I interrupted. "That's not really true. We were friendly, but that's different than being friends."

Stone's mouth grew tight. "Look, Mrs. Austen, I'm tired, I'm under a lot of pressure and—"

"Kate. Please call me Kate." The words just popped

out, and I was embarrassed. This wasn't exactly a social call.

He nodded but didn't smile. I suppose if you investigate murders for a living you don't do a lot of superflu-
ous smiling. Still, his manner softened just a bit.
"Okay, Kate. I'm under pressure. The investigation is
going nowhere fast, and I'd really appreciate any help
you can give me. You knew Mrs. Livingston; I didn't.
So help me out here."

I took a sip of coffee and thought hard. "Pepper
wasn't the most diplomatic person in the world. Some
people thought she was pushy and maybe a little
snooty, but that's hardly grounds for murder—particularly in this community."

Stone reached for another muffin. Still no smile, but
I thought I detected a flicker of amusement in his eyes.
"What about this Sunshine House she was involved
with?" he asked. "Isn't that the place that runs pro-
grams for troubled kids?"

" 'Kids on the edge,' that's what Pepper called
them."

"They're a pretty tough group. Did she ever bring
any of them to her house?"

I laughed. "Hardly. She was a founding director
and member of the board, but I don't think she ever
set foot in the place herself." Pepper's civic minded-
ness had its limits.

"Had she mentioned noticing anything unusual recently—strangers, odd phone calls, that kind of
thing?"

I tried hard to remember, but drew a blank. "Not
that I recall."

Stone slouched down in his chair and chewed grimly
at his lower lip.

I really did want to help. I wanted Pepper's killer to
be properly punished; I wanted our town to be safe

again so that I wouldn't get goose bumps every time I heard the wind rustling the leaves; and most of all I wanted Lieutenant Stone to appreciate what a clever, cooperative and remarkable woman I was. But there was nothing I could tell him.

I stood up and started for the stove. "More coffee?"

Stone shook his head. "But thanks."

I sat down again, and in the process turned my chair slightly so that my better side faced Stone. "It's strange that the kitchen window was unlocked."

"Why's that?"

"Pepper didn't usually open those windows," I explained, "only the ones at the back and on the far side of the house where there are screens. And she wasn't the sort to go up to bed without checking first."

"There's no sign the window was forced, and even the most careful people sometimes make mistakes." He broke off part of the muffin and fed it to Max who swallowed it in one bite and then resumed his attentive watch. "She apparently took a Seconal that evening maybe a couple so that might account for her unusual carelessness."

"Seconal?"

"A sleeping pill, it's one of the—"

"I know what Seconal is." It was just that I couldn't believe I'd heard right. And this, I thought somewhat smugly, in a woman who took some Chinese herb concoction for headaches and scoffed at me for drinking caffeine!

With a weary sigh, the lieutenant looked out the window again in the direction of the Livingston house. "You're the only neighbor close enough to have seen or heard anything that night. You sure you didn't?"

I shook my head sadly. "I'm not being much help, am I?"

"It's not you, it's this case. There's nothing." He

reached for yet another muffin, his third. He looked to be a bit older than I was, maybe in his late thirties, yet his abdomen was flat and taut, like that of a younger man. Not your standard three-muffin physique.

"You mean no fingerprints, that sort of thing?"

"No fingerprints, although they're vastly overrated as an investigative aid. No one who saw or heard anything that night. No reports of strangers casing the neighborhood."

"What about footprints or . . . blood?" I asked pertly. "Surely there has to be something." I'd read just enough about criminal investigations to think I knew what I was talking about.

"Look, Mrs. Au—Kate—I'm the detective here. I'm asking the questions, okay?"

"But you're also trying to get a handle on a murder, remember? And you asked for my help."

"I didn't mean that kind of help."

"How am I supposed to know what might be useful to you if I don't know anything about the case?"

He appeared to consider my argument for a moment; then he stopped scowling into his coffee and looked at me. "If I tell you what we have, which in this instance means what we don't have, would you be willing to go over there this afternoon and have a look—before they clean things up. You might see something that we missed. The husband hasn't been much help so far. Couldn't even give us a description of the missing jewelry."

The thought of poking around the room where Pepper had been murdered, where her lifeless body had sprawled across the bed, did not appeal to me, but I thought it was the least I could do. And I did want to know what they'd found.

"Okay. Deal."

"The physical evidence is minimal. A few bloodstains, which have been identified as Pepper's. She was struck in the face with something that had a hard edge to it. Some hairs, which are also Pepper's, and a bit of fresh mud on the carpet. No unusual tire marks, no footprints, no carelessly dropped monogrammed handkerchief. There's really nothing but a small fragment of fabric, a heavy silk, the kind in good ties. Looks like yellow and black and maybe a little burgundy. We're not even sure it's connected with the murder. It was caught in the joint of the brass headboard."

"That's it?"

"Pretty much. Looks like entry and exit was made through the window. Front door was locked up tight. If I had to guess I'd say it was some drug addict or two-bit burglar who assumed the house was empty and then panicked when he found it wasn't."

Stone picked the last muffin from the plate and took a bite. My stomach was full from just watching.

"What do you want me to look for?"

"Anything unusual or different. You knew Pepper; you might notice things we wouldn't."

I knew Pepper, but not as well as everyone seemed to think. And I'd only been in her bedroom a couple of times. Once to admire a new chaise longue and armoire, and another time to retrieve a pair of tennis shoes Anna had left there. It was a spacious room, bigger than our living room, and, like the rest of the house, decorator perfect.

Lieutenant Stone eyed the empty plate, then said, "Tell me about the husband. Did he and Pepper get along?"

"She never said much about him—no gushing about how wonderful he was but no complaining either. He's an executive with North Coast Bank, does something like managing money for rich clients. Always very cordial but in a starched sort of way. In fact, until last night, I'd always considered him to be slightly pompous."

"Last night?"

"We had dinner."

Stone leaned across the table. "You had dinner with Robert Livingston last night, the night after his wife was murdered?" He sounded surprised, as though we'd been dining at The Blue Fox.

"It was only an omelette."

"Just the two of you?"

"The girls were upstairs."

"And your husband was still out of town."

"Yes."

I could see the wheels churning, concocting some elaborate scheme. Perhaps Robert and I had conspired to bump off Pepper so that we could enjoy an illicit affair, covering our tracks by pretending to be strangers.

"It's not the way it seems," I said. "Before yesterday I had hardly spoken to him. But our daughters are friends, and I offered to watch Kimberly for a bit. When he came to pick her up he stayed for a drink. It was late, so I fixed him something to eat."

That seemed to satisfy him, maybe because the idea that I might kindle unbridled lust was beyond belief.

"Did he seem upset?"

"What kind of question is that?"

"One that merits an answer."

"Of course he was upset, his wife was just murdered."

"Upset, how?"

"You know . . . sad." The bottom of my foot itched, and I tried scratching with the tip of my other shoe. "Actually. I'm not sure Pepper's death has truly hit him yet."

"So he wasn't distraught."

Although I had found myself surprisingly comfortable with Robert last evening, I had to admit feeling slightly put off by his composure. But maybe expecting hysterics from a middle-aged banker was asking too much. "No, not really distraught. Why, he isn't a suspect is he?"

"Not really, but in theory the husband is always a suspect in a case like this. And he has no alibi. Supposedly he was at the office, but no one else was there to corroborate his story. Besides, something about his manner doesn't sit right with me."

"That's just Robert," I told him breezily. "He's not the sort of guy to drop over for a beer and a bit of gossip." I watched Stone brush the crumbs from the table onto his hand and then deposit them on the now empty muffin plate.

"Well, I guess that's about it." Standing, he handed me his card and said, "Don't forget about checking the Livingstons' bedroom."

"I won't."

Max had fallen asleep at the lieutenant's feet the moment the muffin plate was empty, and he didn't budge now, even when Stone moved the foot his head was resting on.

"Thanks for the coffee. And the muffins."

"Would you like another? You know, to take with you?"

He smiled then, for the first time all morning, and it was a wonderful, boyish grin that made the lines around his eyes crinkle.

"That would be great."

I put two muffins in a plastic bag, then walked with him to the door. If Mary Nell was still on her diet and I didn't eat any, there would be just enough muffins for the meeting.

"I'll be in touch," he said.

Hidden by the drapes, I watched until he climbed into an older model Ford and drove away. Then I raced upstairs to take my shower and noticed, for the first time, a large glob of toothpaste smack in the middle of my left breast.

"Kate, we'd just about given up on you." Susie Sullivan flashed me one of her perfect smiles, then added, "Though of course we knew *you* weren't busy with the Guild Wine Festival. That's where the others are—there are always so many last-minute details to be taken care of."

I ignored the jab and pulled up a chair. Besides Susie, only three other advisory board members were present. Not a sufficient number for making any momentous decisions, but at least there would be enough muffins.

"Sorry I'm late, the police wanted to ask me some questions."

"The police?" A look of dismay, which she didn't even try to disguise, crossed Mary Nell's face. But then Mary Nell was often dismayed. She and her husband moved here from Kansas last fall, and though the transfer was a promotion, she made it clear this was not a move which pleased her. I couldn't see how anyone would prefer Kansas to California but then, as Mary Nell was fond of reminding me, I have never been to Kansas.

"About Pepper."

"Oh God, I forgot. You two are neighbors, or rather, *were* neighbors." Cindi Hanson reached for a muffin as she spoke. "What did they want? Who do they think did it? Do they have any leads?"

Cindi speaks a mile a minute, in a tight, clipped

voice, and often jumps from subject to subject so that she's hard to follow. But she sometimes answers her own questions, or ignores them and rattles on about something else, so I waited for a moment before speaking.

Four faces, including Cindi's, watched me eagerly, so I told them what I knew. When I had finished, Mary Nell said, "This is just so terrible. How does something like this happen?"

"Simple," replied Sharon. "You take a cord, pull it tight across the throat . . . and *voilà*—you've killed someone."

"That's disgusting. Anyway. I meant why. Who would want to kill Pepper?"

Susie examined her nails, which where long and frosted in iridescent pink. "I can think of quite a few people."

"That's not funny," I told her.

"Who says I was being funny? Pepper never thought about anyone but herself. You never had to work with her, so you don't know what a pain in the ass she could be."

I didn't know if this was intended as another snub or simply as a statement of fact. The Benefit Guild, the country club, and other such trappings of upper-crust life were much beyond my reach. True, Anna went to Walnut Hills Montessori, which was *the* preschool for parents who wanted to give their child an edge in life— you need the right connections to even get on the waiting list—but that was only because Daria was a good friend of the director, and when Daria takes it upon herself to be helpful, she goes all the way. Outside of school, I almost never crossed paths with any of the other mothers.

"Maybe Robert got tired of supporting her extravagant lifestyle," Cindi offered, and then giggled.

"Pepper sure could go through the money. I once heard Robert arguing with her about it." Susie took a short breath and looked around the table. "He's such a sweet man. I don't think Pepper ever appreciated what a gem of a husband she had."

"Is that the same as wealthy?" Sharon asked.

Susie glared at Sharon momentarily and then lifted her hair off her neck, letting it fall forward over her shoulders. "I wonder how he's holding up? I'll have to call him. Or maybe a short visit would be better." Susie was in the final stages of divorce number two and well into the search phase for husband number three. It was clear that Robert had now been added to her list of potential candidates.

"I don't know him well, of course," Mary Nell said hesitantly, "but he always seemed very nice to me. The kind of man who'd be happy to give his wife whatever she wanted."

"Pepper must have had plenty of her own money, you know, family money. I don't see why she had to bleed poor Robert." It was poor Robert already. Susie didn't miss a cue.

"I wouldn't count on it," Cindi commented.

"On what?" I asked.

"On Pepper having money of her own." Cindi looked around to make sure everyone was listening. "I think Pepper was full of shit. She certainly didn't go to Smith as she claimed, and I doubt that she grew up on Long Island either, at least not the same Long Island I grew up on."

"What makes you say that?"

"She knew a few key names, but none of the local lore. Whenever I'd catch her in some inaccuracy, she'd change the subject or make some cute remark about having a mind like a sieve. Besides, she had a tattoo on

her butt, and Smith women do *not* have tattoos. Anywhere."

By the time we'd spent half an hour talking about
Pepper, and eaten all the muffins, we decided it would
be silly to make any school decisions with so few of us
present. So we picked a date for the next meeting and
adjourned. On the way out Mary Nell caught up with
me and said, "Can I talk to you for a moment?"

"Sure." We sat on one of the long wooden benches
in front of the school. "What's up?"

"It's about Pepper."

I waited.

"I don't want to be a gossip or anything . . ."

That was one thing Mary Nell could never be accused of. "Get on with it," I said.

"Remember the Patersons' party last week where
. . ." And then she looked embarrassed. "I guess you
weren't able to make it that night."

Especially since I hadn't been invited. "Right, you
know how busy things get this time of year."

She nodded. "Well, when I went upstairs to use the
phone—I wanted to make sure Danny was okay with
the new baby sitter—I found Pepper spread out on the
Patersons' bed. At first I thought she might be asleep,
or drunk, but then I saw she was just lying there, staring up at the ceiling. It was kind of embarrassing really. I didn't want to intrude, but I did need to use the
phone, so I asked her if everything was okay. She
looked at me like I had two heads. 'Everything okay?
That's a good one. How about nothing's okay, everything sucks.' Then she got sort of hysterical, half
laughing, half crying, and started pounding the pillow
with her fists."

Mary Nell was opening and closing the clasp of her
purse as she spoke, but I couldn't tell if it was finding

Pepper so distraught or having to repeat Pepper's language that made her uneasy.

"Did she say what was bothering her?"

"No, and I wouldn't dream of prying. But I've never seen her like that. She's usually so cool. I mean was."

"Well, we all have our moments." Although I wasn't actually sure Mary Nell did.

She set her purse down on the bench between us and folded her hands in her lap. "Pepper was nice to me, nicer than a lot of the women around here. And now I feel so bad that I didn't do something to cheer her up." Her voice got all shaky, and I was afraid she might become hysterical herself. "I've never known anyone who was murdered before," she confided. "Things are different in Kansas."

"Murder isn't exactly commonplace in Walnut Hills either."

"No, I guess not." But she didn't look convinced. "Oh, by the way, I have something for you." Retrieving her purse, she pulled out a photograph and handed it to me. It was a picture of Anna and Kimberly, with me and Pepper standing behind them. Mary Nell was always taking pictures and making copies for people. If there were ten people in the picture, she made sure she got ten copies. "It's from the Easter party. I've been meaning to give it to you for weeks. I made a copy for Pepper too. Only now it's too late to give it to her." Then she reached into her purse again, pulled out a little white handkerchief edged with pink rosebuds and dabbed at her eyes.

5

While Anna played near the wading pool, I sat in the shade under the mulberry tree, sketching a clump of blue and yellow iris. I had filled the pool that morning so the water could warm in the sun, but Anna chose not to set foot in it anyway. Somehow, she had talked me into letting her bring outside my entire collection of plastic bowls, funnels and strainers, and now she sat on the grass beside the pool in her new pink bathing suit, happily pouring water from container to container and chatting with herself in a language I couldn't make out.

I had always assumed I would have children, even as a girl when no boy would be my partner at dancing class. But it wasn't until I had Anna that I stopped being able to imagine my life any other way.

To this day I can recall, so vividly it takes my breath away, the sensation of holding her for the first time—a tiny, warm bundle with bright blue eyes and breath that was soft and moist against my cheek. After all the hours of Lamaze training and the months of talking nonstop about "the baby," you'd think I would have known what to expect, but nothing had prepared me for the rush of love I experienced when it finally dawned on me that the tiny, soft form in my arms was, indeed, real.

Andy was there too, taking pictures and grinning like a cat with its own secret supply of warm milk. In those first few weeks after we were home, he continued to take pictures, sometimes a roll a night, and he would make reprints to send to friends and relatives, even people we hadn't seen in years. It was about six months later when she finally became real for him. I think that was when it dawned on him that Anna was not some new toy which could be conveniently stashed in the closet as soon as the novelty wore off. And I know it scared him. As much as he loved her, which I'm certain he did, it terrified him to think his life had so irrevocably changed.

Now there was another tiny, warm bundle growing inside me. Another pair of eyes to gaze with wonder into my own. Another mouth to laugh at my silly antics. I tried not to think in those terms of course, but it wasn't easy. And every time I looked at Anna I got a hard lump in my throat.

There was a date circled on the calendar—my self-imposed deadline. The day by which I would have to decide.

I'm not sure what I was waiting for really. A sign from the gods perhaps, or a fortune cookie with a particularly insightful bit of advice. Or maybe part of me was still hoping that Andy would waltz back into my life, reappearing as the man I wanted him to be rather than the man he was—generous, fun loving, not a mean bone in his body, but definitely not the sort of man to willingly embrace the demands of familial life.

Daria said Andy's only problem was that he got stuck at eighteen and refused to budge. But of course her perspective is slightly skewed, given that Jim has been forty since the day he was born. A mellow, kind-hearted forty I'll concede, but you'd never catch Jim spending the night camped out in the rain with hundreds of others just to buy tickets to a Stones' concert. Or planning his own birthday party at the Santa Cruz Boardwalk, then showing up in a black tux with fifty helium balloons tugging at his wrists.

It always struck me as funny that Andy and Jim were friends in the first place, but then men's friendships are very different from women's and the two of them shared an interest in golf, which seemed to outweigh everything else.

Although I'd heard about him for years, I never actually met Jim until after we bought the house in Walnut Hills. He and Daria had us over for dinner one night, before we'd even moved in. Jim grilled steaks, mixed margaritas, fetched chips and jumped up with a smile on his face every time Daria said "Honey, would you . . ." but he'd never get out more than a sentence or two before he'd grin, shuffle his feet and grow quiet again. And although he laughed heartily at all the appropriate intervals, I wasn't sure he really found anything very funny.

"Jim's not what I expected," I told Andy as we drove home that night.

Andy laughed. "Don't be fooled by that shy manner; he can be as wild and reckless as the best of us."

While I never saw anything the least bit wild about Jim, I'd grown quite fond of him. There was an unaffected steadiness about him which I found reassuring. A steadiness which was decidedly lacking in Andy.

"What are you drawing, Mommy?" asked Anna, coming up to peer over my shoulder. "It's pretty. It looks just like the flowers in the garden."

She clapped her hands and several drops of water

fell onto the page, smearing the pastels. The corners of her mouth fell, and she started to cry. "Oh, no. It's ruined."

"It doesn't matter, I was just playing around." I hugged her and gave her an Eskimo kiss, which usually makes her laugh, but she continued to whimper. "I'll do another one tomorrow," I promised, "just for you. Would you like that?"

She nodded and the tears finally stopped, but she looked as though they might start again at any moment.

"Let's go see if Kimberly wants to play, shall we? There's something I'm supposed to do at her house this afternoon, but it won't take long. Afterward, Kimberly can come back here with us. I'll buy ice cream cones." The prospect of examining Pepper's room filled me with enough trepidation that I felt as in need of such a treat as the girls.

I had met Robert's sister, Claudia, only once before, but she welcomed me as though we were old friends. "Kate, it's been ages," she said as she gave me a quick hug. "I'm so glad to see you again." Then, growing suddenly solemn, she added, "I only wish it were under different circumstances."

Despite a strong family resemblance through the eyes and mouth, Claudia and Robert are about as different as two people can be. Whereas Robert is slight, with almost delicate features, Claudia is tall, big boned and angular. She's at least twenty pounds overweight and not at all refined. Looking at her, you would think she was someone's maiden aunt rather than an anthropologist who'd "gone through"—Pepper's words—four husbands and several lovers. Adventure fascinated her far more than money, and although she and Robert were on good terms, she was quick to distance herself from his affluent lifestyle, which I think she found morally offensive.

Following her into the kitchen, I explained that Lieutenant Stone had asked me to look around. "Do you think Robert would mind?"

"Not at all." She called Kimberly and then gestured to the stack of bills and papers on the kitchen table. "I'm trying to help out," she explained, "but I think I may just be adding to the confusion."

She gave each of the girls two big cookies and a can of soda, then threw in a bag of chips too, and sent them out back to have a picnic.

"How's Robert doing?" I asked when we were alone.

Claudia shrugged. "You know him," she said. "He's a hard one to read. From outward appearances he seems to be holding up remarkably well, though I don't see how he's going to manage on his own."

I nodded agreement. I couldn't see Robert making peanut butter sandwiches without crusts, or taking time off from work to drive the car pool. I wasn't sure he even knew the name of Kimberly's school.

"I just wish I could stay longer. Unfortunately it's the end of the term. There are papers to grade, and I have three graduate students taking their orals next week."

"What about Pepper's family?" I suggested. "Would any of her relatives be able to come stay for a while?" I'd never heard her talk much about her family, although she'd once mentioned a brother she hadn't spoken to in years.

"Apparently not. I asked Robert that same question last night, and he passed it off so quickly I asked him a second time just to make sure he'd heard me." Standing, Claudia walked to the window to check on the two girls. "Kimberly tells me she's never even received a birthday card from her other grandparents, so I guess theirs is not exactly a close family."

"No, it doesn't sound that way."

"I never really got on with Pepper, we're different sorts of people. But she was good for Robert, and he adored her. This is going to be hard on him." She gave a resigned, little laugh. "Though of course he'd never admit it. If you ask me, he puts too much weight on propriety."

I offered again to help out, and she promised to relay the message. Then, rather reluctantly, I headed upstairs to the bedroom.

Even in the bright afternoon light, with Claudia puttering around downstairs and strains of girlish laughter drifting in from the yard, I experienced a moment of panic. Less than forty-eight hours earlier a maniac, a cold-blooded killer, had walked these same steps, perhaps stopping at the landing as I did to gather his bearings. What had he been thinking that night? What had he been looking for?

The bedroom door was closed, and I opened it cautiously. I'm not sure exactly what I was expecting—a scene from *Friday Night Massacre,* or maybe something more clinical, like the silhouette of a body outlined in red paint across the spread—but it looked pretty much like any ordinary empty bedroom. Messier than Pepper liked, but even in its present state neater than my own.

The dresser drawers had been dumped, their contents heaped in an almost orderly fashion next to the chaise, and the clothes in the armoire were in disarray. But an arrangement of fresh daisies still adorned the chest under the window, the two club chairs in the corner looked as though they had been readied for a house tour and a framed photograph of Kimberly smiled up from the bedside table. Nothing about the room suggested murder.

Once, many years earlier, my own apartment had been burglarized, and although the thieves took very little—there was little worth taking—they knocked all my pottery onto the floor and slashed the upholstery. But that was San Francisco and this was Walnut Hills. Maybe better class neighborhoods attracted more genteel thieves. And more deadly, I thought with a shudder.

For half an hour I forced myself to study the scene, going through drawers, shelves and boxes, searching for some sign of the killer. I closed my eyes to picture the room as I had last seen it, then opened them abruptly, looking for The Big Clue. Nothing. I wasn't even able to find the rough spot in the bedpost where the silk threads had snagged.

It was a stupid exercise. Was I supposed to somehow uncover a bloody, sharp-edged object the police had overlooked? Or maybe the killer's driver's license, complete with photo and home address? And even though I was sure she would want me to help find her killer, it felt wrong to be poking about Pepper's empty room, fingering her silk nighties and cashmere sweaters.

I was getting ready to call it quits when the girls came upstairs and stood in the doorway. "Are you cleaning Mommy's room?" Kimberly asked.

"No honey, not really." Although that clearly would be something I could offer to do. I made a mental note to mention it to Claudia when I went downstairs. "The police asked me to look through a few of your mother's things."

Kimberly's eyes filled with tears. Kneeling, I wrapped my arms around her and hugged her tightly.

"I miss her," she whimpered.

"I know you do. She loved you so much, Kimberly. Don't ever forget that."

"But I'm never going to see her again, am I?"

"Not in the way you used to. She's with you, just the same, though. I'll bet if you close your eyes you can see her now—smiling at you the way she did, so proud. If you try hard enough, I'll bet you can carry on a conversation, just the two of you."

"But it's not real. It's all pretend. And when I open my eyes there's nothing."

Suddenly I had an idea. I didn't know what the police needed still from the bedroom, but I knew that Pepper kept some of her out-of-season clothes and other items she didn't use every day in the guest room. "Would you like some things of your mother's?" I asked. "Things just for you, to keep in your room?"

Kimberly nodded, and a single tear rolled down her cheek.

We crossed over to the guest room at the end of the hallway, and I opened a bureau drawer filled with purses. "How about one of these?" I asked.

While Kimberly made her selection I looked for something else she could have. The closet was full of winter wools, all zipped up tight in garment bags, and an assortment of satin and beaded evening gowns. Finally I found a box of scarves and was starting to dump it out on the bed when I noticed a shiny, white plastic case at the bottom of the box. I knew exactly what it was the minute I saw it, because my own diaphragm came in a case just like it. And there next to it was a tube of Ortho jelly, rolled up neatly from the bottom.

Intent as I was on whisking these particular items from the girls' questioning eyes, it took a moment to sink in. Why would a woman who wanted another child, a woman with a husband who was practically sterile, have a diaphragm? And why would she keep it hidden away instead of someplace convenient like the bathroom or her dresser drawer? Unless, of course, Pepper was sleeping with someone other than Robert.

While Kimberly examined the scarves, I wondered if I should mention my discovery to Lieutenant Stone. It wasn't quite what he'd had in mind when he'd asked me to look around, but it might be important to the investigation. And it would give me an excuse to talk with him again, something I was surprisingly eager to do.

When I got back downstairs, I found Claudia studying her reflection in the hallway mirror. "What do you think?" she asked, turning her left ear toward me and pulling the hair back away from her face.

"You mean the earring?"

She nodded.

"I like it. Is it new?"

"It was Pepper's. The police found it in the upstairs hallway. Just the single earring. The intruder must have dropped it when he was making off with her jewelry."

"I thought it looked familiar." In fact, I could remember admiring it once before. It was unusual looking, a triangle of pounded silver overlaid on gold and edged in bronze. The kind of thing I never manage to find in stores, only on other women.

Claudia turned back to the mirror. "I don't usually wear large, dangly earrings because I'm so large myself." Here she laughed self-consciously. "But maybe I should. There's a fine line between looking exotic and looking silly."

"Pepper didn't usually wear large earrings either, and you certainly don't look silly."

She removed the earring and set it on the library table under the mirror. "Well, one earring won't do me much good anyway. Did you find that incriminating bit of evidence up there?"

For a minute I thought she knew about the diaphragm and I glanced sharply in her direction, but then I realized she was speaking generally. "Nope, not that I really expected to."

She nodded. "It was good of you to try nonetheless. Say, does the name Tony Sheris mean anything to you?"

"No, why?"

"Pepper wrote a lot of checks to him. Two or three hundred dollars at a time. I thought maybe he was tied in with the school or something."

"No, I don't think so." But the name did sound vaguely familiar. "Wait a minute. She had a gardener named Tony, I think. I remember because she told me I should talk to him about doing our place too."

Frowning, Claudia turned and walked to the table where she'd spread out her paperwork. "That must be it then, although I must say, he certainly wasn't cheap. She's paid him quite a bit just in the last couple of months."

"I guess that's one advantage to having a small yard, I can do the whole thing myself."

"I'll go you one better," Claudia said with a chuckle. "I live in a condominium, and the African violet on my kitchen window sill satisfies *all* my gardening instincts."

A little after six that evening, Daria arrived at the front door loaded down with Chinese food from Mr. Woo's.

"Now tell me," she began, even before she took off her jacket, "what's been happening? Do you think the police have any suspects yet?"

"No suspects. No fingerprints even. Apparently there wasn't any physical evidence at all."

While I got out bowls, chopsticks and paper napkins, I told her about my conversation with Lieutenant Stone, carefully leaving out the part about his exquisite gray eyes and magnificent smile. There are some things you don't share, even with a good friend. "To show you how desperate they are," I said, "the lieutenant asked me to look over Pepper's bedroom for any clues they might have missed."

Daria was emptying the cartons of food into bowls, and she turned to look at me, almost sending the asparagus chicken onto the floor. "What did you find?"

"Proof that neatness is an overrated virtue."

She looked puzzled.

"I didn't find anything. The killer might have been a sicko, but he was a tidy one. The room was hardly disturbed, and there was certainly nothing there to identify the killer."

"Pretty smart."

I wasn't sure if she meant me or the killer. "Yeah."

She smiled and handed me a bowl of rice. "You should have called me; four eyes are better than two."

"Even a dozen eyes wouldn't have made a difference. You want wine or soda?"

"You actually have to ask that question?"

In fact, I didn't. Opening the fridge, I found the bottle of chardonnay left from her last visit, and poured a glass while she went to tell Anna that dinner was ready.

"She wants to finish watching 'Sesame Street' first, is that okay?"

"Sure, she only eats rice and pot stickers anyway. Let's go ahead and start though, I'm starving."

Fascinated, I watched as Daria rolled moo shu pork into a pancake and then took a dainty little bite, somehow managing to avoid having juice dribble down her chin or shredded cabbage land in her lap. Daria is one of those women who refuse to yield to the little imperfections the rest of us take for granted in life. Her hair is never dirty, her clothes never spotted, her windows never grimy. And no weed ever had a chance in her garden.

"I did learn something interesting, however," I announced.

"What's that?"

"I think Pepper might have been having an affair."

Daria choked and reached for her glass, taking several large swallows. She even managed that with flair.

"Whatever makes you think that?"

I told her about finding the diaphragm and about my earlier conversation with Robert.

"That's all?"

"That's enough, isn't it? It's not likely she'd take Polaroid pictures of the two of them actually doing it. Besides, I also found the original pharmacy box, from January of this year, so I know it wasn't something she kept as a memento."

"January? That was almost six months ago."

I nodded, not exactly wowed by her powers of arithmetic.

Daria was still coughing, but she sat back now and breathed deeply. "Do you have any idea who it was?"

"Not a clue. I was as shocked as you, I mean I didn't even *suspect.*"

"Well," she said smoothly, "knowing Pepper, I guess we shouldn't be too surprised."

"What's that supposed to mean?"

"Pepper always thought she was such hot stuff. She probably seduced men for a hobby."

There's always been an element of envy, I think, in Daria's relationship with Pepper. On occasion I may fantasize about living in a fancy house and jetting off to exotic places, but it's so far beyond the realm of possibility that I'm not disappointed with what I have. The situation with Daria was different. She and Jim were certainly well-to-do, but his dentist's income hardly qualified them as members of the monied elite. I had an idea Daria resented being on the fringe of a life she secretly coveted.

"Pepper's certainly not the first," I reminded her. "We never suspected Lisa either, or Joan. We think everyone else leads the same dull lives we do."

"Not dull, satisfying."

"Yours may be satisfying; mine, at the moment anyway, is dull." And far from satisfying.

"Well, having an affair is certainly not the way to liven it up."

From out of nowhere, a picture of Lieutenant Stone flashed through my mind. Hands in his pockets, lips curved in a half-smile so that the laugh lines at the corners of his eyes crinkled. "Weren't you ever tempted?" I asked, more eagerly than I intended.

Because of her position as owner of an art gallery, Daria often mixed with interesting and glamorous people. I figured that somewhere along the line, over a glass of champagne, or in the barren loft of some yet undiscovered artist, there had to have been a flicker of unexpected chemistry. But apparently she was better at ignoring these things than I was, because she shook her head emphatically.

"Never," she said. "But then I'm spoiled."

This was an annoying habit of hers. Whenever the rest of us complained about lazy, insensitive husbands, Daria would lean back and listen, lips pursed in a discreetly self-satisfied manner. And then, when there was a lull in the conversation, she'd drop some nugget about Jim's gentleness and devotion. "Not that he's without fault," she'd add demurely, but of course that is exactly what she did mean.

"You know what a sweetheart Jim is," she continued now. "I can't imagine finding anyone else who'd come remotely close."

I nodded, confirming that Jim was indeed a rare and wonderful man, then tried to steer the conversation back to the question at hand. "Do you think I should mention the diaphragm to the police?"

"Why would you do that?"

I shrugged. "It might be important. Maybe Pepper was blackmailing her lover, so he killed her."

Daria scowled. "You've been watching too many bad movies. This Lieutenant Stone asked you to look for murder clues, not pry around in Pepper's private life. Besides, you don't know anything for sure, and spreading rumors is . . . well, it's tacky and quite beneath you." My ambivalence must have been obvious, because she continued, "Think about poor Robert then, don't you imagine he has enough to worry about already?"

She was right about that. I pushed at a red chili with the tip of my chopstick, recalling Mary Nell's words from that morning. "Did Pepper seem troubled recently?"

"No, not really. She was busy with the Wine Festival, and that made her testy on occasion, but I wouldn't say she was upset. Chris took in their mail and fed the cat when they went to Hawaii last month. He said she was practically euphoric, couldn't stop talking about what a wonderful time they'd had."

Chris was Daria's sixteen-year-old son, the one the other boys respected, the teachers praised, and the girls adored. At least that was how Daria saw it.

"She told *me* she was glad to get back home," I said,

standing to reach for the carton of rice from the counter. "Want anything more?"

Daria shook her head. "I never understood why you two were such good friends. You're usually not impressed by all that phony stuff."

"I wasn't impressed—I just liked her. And it wasn't all phony."

Daria gave me one of those don't-be-such-a-simp glares and changed the subject. "You sure you didn't hear anything that night?"

"Of course I'm sure. You think maybe I heard screams, ran to the window, got a good look at the killer and have been keeping it a secret?"

"You might be scared, being alone and all, your life in turmoil."

"It's okay, Daria. Really, I'm fine. And if I saw anything that night I would certainly have said something." Hoping to forestall the it's-okay-to-be-sad pep talk I sensed was imminent, I stood up and started clearing the table.

"Any word from Andy?" she asked.

"He sends postcards to Anna, sometimes I rate a P.S."

"I just don't understand how he could do this to you."

I shrugged. The funny thing was that on some level, I could.

"And I was so fond of him too," Daria lamented.

"The worst part is having to figure out all over again, what to do with my life. I thought that was all behind me."

Before I met Andy, my life had no direction. I drifted from job to job, man to man, day to day, all in a kind of murky bleakness. But marriage changed that. For the first time I knew who I was and where I fit in. Or thought I did. But now things had come full circle and I found myself once again at an impasse. Only this time I had a child to worry about, possibly two, and the thought of being a secretary had lost whatever appeal it once had.

Daria poured herself a second glass of wine and looked around the kitchen, as if she might find there in the blue and white patterned wallpaper or chipped Formica some sign that my prospects weren't as hopeless as I thought.

"I've got an idea," she said, growing suddenly animated. "Why don't you come work for me? The pay won't be anything to write home about, but it would be a great way to ease back into the routine of working *and* you'd be involved in the art world."

"It's nice of you to offer, but—"

"Nice nothing. We're terribly shorthanded at the moment, and it's going to be even worse this summer when Paul takes off for Alaska. I don't know why I didn't think of this before."

"But what about Anna?" I was ready, maybe, to start *thinking* about the direction of my life, but I wasn't sure I was ready to leap into a full-blown change just yet.

"You can work while she's at school, maybe find a sitter for a couple of afternoons a week. I don't need anyone full-time, but I do need someone I can trust. You'd be a such a help, and you'd enjoy it too, I know you would."

"I don't know," I told her hesitantly, "my hours would have to be quite limited."

"Fine. You want to start Monday?"

What the heck, it *was* a good idea. A great idea in fact. "Sure, Monday it is."

She stood up and hugged me warmly. "This is going to be such fun," she said, her voice rich with affection. "Paul and Mandy are lovely people, but we're hardly chummy. I'm going to really enjoy having you around."

"Business and pleasure don't always mix," I reminded her.

"Not to worry. A friendship like ours can weather almost anything."

Daria rinsed the dishes while I cut up Anna's pot stickers and two tiny pieces of chicken which I tried my best to disguise. And when she left I stood in front of the mirror and smiled at my reflection. Maybe this was going to be one of those turning points life is supposedly full of. In the years to come I would look back on this moment and laugh at how easily it had all fallen into place.

6

Walnut Hills Community Church is a massive, modernistic structure of concrete and glass. From the outside it looks more like a power station than a house of God, but it won an award for architectural innovation the year it was built. The list of parishioners reads something like a local version of the social registry, and the church is a hub of community activity, so even those who worship elsewhere frequently find themselves attending recitals, scout functions and political meetings there. Pepper, of course, had not only been a member of the congregation, but of the steering committee as well, and her memorial service probably came close to topping the list of the year's best attended events.

The church was already nearly full by the time I arrived, the air filled with the soft buzz of discreetly subdued conversations. Robert sat in the front pew next to Claudia. He looked remarkably serene, as though he were only peripherally involved in the day's events. Like someone attending the wedding of a distant relative. There wasn't even a hint of the raw emotion I'd detected, although fleetingly, a few evenings earlier. I spotted Daria and Jim several rows farther back and had started up the aisle in their direction when Candice Blackford signaled to me.

"There's room here, Kate," she said, scooting over and patting the smooth, polished wood of the pew. Candice is the high school principal and ex-wife of the town mayor. She's short, dumpy, gray-haired, and exceedingly outspoken. But everyone loves her, even the students she places on probation.

"Quite a turnout, isn't it?" she said, as I slipped in next to her. "I'm sure Pepper would have been proud."

Because I wasn't sure whether she was being sarcastic or serious, I merely nodded.

"Do you think they'll ever find the killer?" She sneezed and then, without waiting for an answer, continued. "I've heard, unofficially of course, that the police have practically nothing to go on. The city council is furious, what with the bad publicity and all. They want the case wrapped up right away. They're putting on pressure to bring in outside help, but Ness won't hear of it."

Ness was the chief of police, a longtime resident of Walnut Hills who reminisced at every opportunity about the good old days when the town had only one stop light, one bank and no one ever had to worry about locking the door. He was also a vocal supporter of Save Our Hills, a group which caused the prodevelopment city council considerable grief.

"Can they make him get outside help?"

"Not technically, but you know how these things go."

Only vaguely. I wanted to hear more of Candice's unofficial information, which was probably more complete and up to date than what anyone but Ness himself was privy to, but just then the organ began a slow, dirgelike march, and the pastor walked to the pulpit where he stood gazing solemnly at the assembly before him.

The room was warm, hot actually, and I could feel perspiration gathering under my arms and along the back of my neck. My gray wool jersey, the only thing in my closet remotely appropriate, was much too heavy for late spring. The other women, I noticed, were all stylishly dressed in lightweight silk or linen, the colors muted and subdued without being drab. I wondered whether each kept a special funeral wardrobe in constant readiness, or if some had run out to Nordstrom in search of the perfect outfit the moment news of Pepper's death hit the papers.

The organ music ended, and there was a long moment when the room was absolutely still. Finally the pastor spoke, addressing first Robert, then the assemblage of friends who had come to show their respect for the remarkable woman who had been cut down in the prime of life. The man had a fleshy face, a wide mouth and long teeth that reminded me of a horse's. Looking at him made me uncomfortable so I peered around the room instead.

A surprising number of faces were familiar, even when I didn't know the names. Without thinking about it, I started playing a mental game, trying to catalog people I recognized. Some were from the nursery school, some from my art class, some from my association with Pepper and Daria. There was the woman who jogged at the same time each morning that I did, another who walked by my house most afternoons with a matched pair of wolfhounds. Across the aisle from me, seated next to an overweight, bald-headed man, I spotted the blonde who drove a pink Cadillac with the license plate SEXY GAL.

The minister was busily listing Pepper's contributions to the community, when I caught another familiar face at the back of the church. Only this one I couldn't quite place. He was young, maybe in his early twenties, with smooth skin and closely cropped blond hair. He sat at the end of the last row, hunched forward, listening intently as the minister praised Pepper for her devotion to good causes. I knew I'd seen the young man before, and he obviously knew Pepper in some way, but I couldn't for the life of me think what the connection could be.

"Look to your left," I whispered to Candice, "last row. Do you recognize that young man?"

If anybody knew, it would be Candice, who seemed to have a far broader knowledge of the community than her ex-husband. Certainly if the young blond had gone to school locally she would know him.

"No, he doesn't look familiar at all. Why?"

"Just curious. I'm sure I've seen him somewhere, but I can't think where."

It was time then to bow our heads in prayer so I had to stop staring, but my mind wouldn't let go. It was like trying to recall the name of a song or an old classmate—I'd think it was there, almost on the tip of my tongue, and then suddenly there was nothing and the process would start all over again.

After the service, the mourners lingered under the giant oak in front of the church, each unwilling to be the first to leave. Out of the corner of my eye I watched as Robert shook hands, patted shoulders and nodded somberly.

I was looking around for the young man with the familiar face when Daria and Jim joined me a few minutes later. Daria, in dark green silk, looked sensational, like the hostess at a successful opening, but Jim looked terrible. His skin was pasty, and his whole body seemed to droop.

"How you doing, kiddo?" he asked, giving me an affectionate hug.

"Pretty well." Better than you, I thought. Either half the teeth in Walnut Hills had suddenly needed serious attention, or the idea of murder was even more upsetting to Jim than to the rest of us. Then I remembered that his brother had recently lost a wife to cancer, and I guessed that Pepper's service had somehow stirred those memories.

"Any word from Andy about when he's coming back?"

Jim has yet to acknowledge that Andy might not be coming back at all, or that he might come back to a bachelor apartment in the city. "No. He writes Anna but not me."

"What's it been now, a little over a month?"

I nodded.

"He'll be back soon, just you wait and see. Andy's not the type to be alone for long."

"We're going to go pay our respects to Robert," Daria said, adjusting the heavy strands of gold at her neck. "Want to come with us?"

I shook my head. "I talked to him the other day. There are only so many times you can say you're sorry and sound sincere about it."

Jim swallowed hard, and I could see his Adam's apple bobbing in his throat. "I have to get back to the office, honey. Maybe you could just write him a little note."

"It won't take long."

"I don't know. He probably just wants to be left alone."

Daria slipped her hand into Jim's. "Nonsense, this is the way things are done."

Looking even glummer than he had, Jim adjusted

his tie and ran a hand through his hair. "Well, we'll have to be quick."

"Kate, you want a ride tomorrow?" Daria asked. "You know how tight parking is at the Gardens."

With all the commotion about Pepper's death, I'd completely forgotten about the Guild Wine Festival. "I don't know, it seems almost disrespectful to go partying so soon after Pepper's death."

Daria gave me one of her don't-be-such-a-dope looks and said Pepper, who had worked so hard on this affair, would want it to be a success. "It benefits a good cause, don't forget. Last year we raised almost seventy thousand dollars for community services."

She was right, of course. I relented and gratefully accepted her offer of a ride.

"Come on, honey," she said to Jim, leading him off in Robert's direction. "We'll just say a few words and then leave."

Turning to go myself, I ran, quite literally, into Lieutenant Stone, who looked as hot and uncomfortable as I felt. But every bit as attractive as I'd remembered.

"What are you doing here?" I asked. My heart was doing a little hop-and-skip number so the words came out uneven and more sharply than I intended, but Stone seemed not to notice.

"It's part of the job," he said, with a lopsided grin. "I'm detecting."

It took a moment to make the connection. "You think the murderer came to Pepper's memorial service?"

"Possibly."

Nervously, I scanned what was left of the crowd.

Stone looked amused. "He's not going to be wearing a sign that says Killer. He probably won't even look deranged or vicious."

The idea that the killer might actually have been in the church, might still be lingering about, turned my stomach sour.

"Was that your husband?" Stone asked, mopping his brow with a handkerchief.

"Who?"

"The man you were just talking to, the redheaded guy."

"No, he and his wife are friends."

He waited, looking at me. "Your husband still out of town?"

I guess when you're trained to be skeptical, to focus on details that appear suspicious, you find them everywhere. I could see that Lieutenant Stone was beginning to find Andy's absence puzzling. Maybe he even thought Andy killed Pepper and then skipped. That would make me an accomplice or a dope, and I didn't like to think of myself as either. "He's in Europe," I explained. "He's been gone for over a month." Pretty hard to kill someone when you're six thousand miles away.

"Long trip."

"We're separated." Sort of, I added silently. It was the first time I'd actually used that word, "separated," and it seemed to hang in the air calling attention to itself. It reminded me of the first times I'd said "my husband" and "my daughter," only on those occasions I'd let myself dwell on the significance of the words.

Stone nodded and then rocked forward slightly, cutting the distance between us in half. "That's rough," he said. Not sympathy exactly, but a statement etched with kindness. He threw me a quick, curious look, then straightened and shoved his hands into his pockets. "Did you get a chance to look over Pepper's room?"

Decision time. I hadn't yet made up my mind what

to tell him. In fact, since I hadn't expected to run into him, I'd sort of put the whole thing out of my mind for a while.

"I checked the bedroom and looked through her things," I explained, feeling my way as I went, "but I didn't find anything that would help you identify the killer."

Something about my manner must have given me away because Stone grew suddenly stern.

"Look," he said, "if you found anything that gave you pause, you'd better tell me. This is murder, not some nice little parlor game."

His tone irritated me. I was well aware that murder wasn't a game. Pepper was my friend, after all, not just some corpse the way she was to Stone. But that was also the problem. Her affair might have nothing to do with her murder, yet if I told Stone about it, there would be a big hunt to locate her lover and a lot of people would be hurt, including Robert.

"We found her jewelry," Stone said. "And her wallet. They were in the Dumpster at the end of the street, in front of that house that's being remodeled."

I knew the house. I even knew the Dumpster, it blocked my view of traffic on the cross street, but I didn't understand what he was getting at. "Well, that's something at least," I offered.

"Yes, it is. It means burglary wasn't a motive."

"How's that?"

He looked at me through half-closed lids. "You don't break into a house and steal something, only to toss it in the garbage on your way out."

"Maybe the thief was after more than costume jewelry. When he found out what he'd taken wasn't her good stuff, he got rid of it."

"How do you know about that?" he asked sharply.

"Robert told me."

I couldn't read the expression on Stone's face. Something between irritation and displeasure. But he passed it off quickly. "Look this stuff may not compare to the crown jewels, but it's not the sort of thing you pick up at Kmart either. All told it's probably worth a couple thousand. Besides, the credit cards and money were still in her wallet, nearly three hundred dollars cash."

"I see." Slowly, I *was* beginning to see. And it left me weak in the knees. "You think someone was actually out to get Pepper?"

"Could be. And he went to the effort of making it look like a burglary in order to throw us off."

"But why would anybody want to kill Pepper?"

"If I knew that, I certainly wouldn't be standing here talking to you." Catching my eye, he smiled then. "Pleasant as your company is."

My heart, which seemed able at this point to take a discussion of Pepper's death in stride, danced another little jig when the smile registered. The magnetic quality to it made rational thought almost impossible. Still, I tried to weigh my choices. I certainly didn't want Pepper's killer to go free.

"Are you . . . when you handle an investigation, following up on leads and so forth, are you guys . . . well, discreet?"

"We try to be, but murder's a messy business. Sometimes a few of the niceties get overlooked. Why?"

Not exactly a ringing endorsement for discretion, but probably the best I could hope for. I took a deep breath and let it out slowly. "I think she might have been having an affair."

The notion was clearly not as shocking to Stone as it had been to me. "Any idea who with?"

"No. I didn't even know about it before yesterday." Then I explained about discovering the diaphragm and about my conversation with Robert the night after her death.

Stone peered at me curiously. "Yesterday you told me you hardly knew the husband, and now you're saying he went into graphic detail about his sex life?"

"It just sort of came up. Anyway, I'd say it was more biological than sexual. And hardly graphic."

A hint of a smile played at the corners of his mouth and his soft gray eyes crinkled. "You do good work."

It had been a long time since anyone told me I did good anything, and the words sent a pleasurable, prickly sensation across my skin. "Do you think it means something in terms of the case?"

"Hard to tell, but at this point we'll take whatever we can get." Stone took off his jacket and slung it casually over his shoulder. "God, it gets hot out here, doesn't it?"

I agreed, it did.

"Do you have a key to the Livingstons' house?" he asked suddenly.

"Me? No, why?"

"People sometimes give a neighbor a key, for emergencies or when they're on vacation, that kind of thing."

"No, she never gave one to me."

"How about any of the other neighbors?"

"I don't know. She wasn't particularly friendly with any of them. In fact, if it hadn't been for Anna and Kimberly, I probably wouldn't have known her myself." Then it hit me why he was asking. "You don't think the killer got in with a key, do you?"

"It's a possibility. You said yourself it was odd that the window was unlocked. We didn't find any footprints or broken branches outside, and there was very little mud on the carpet despite the fact that the sprinklers had come on that evening. Besides, if you want to

kill someone, it's kind of an iffy proposition to hang
around waiting for an unlocked window. Most likely,
the window was just something to throw us off. Like
the missing jewelry." He squinted into the sun. "Any
idea who does have a key? The husband thought the
housekeeper might."

"Connie?"

"You know her?"

"She works for me too." One afternoon a week for
me, three full days for Pepper.

"She has a key?"

She had a key, but there was no way Connie could
have killed Pepper. A lesbian and ardent feminist,
Connie's loathing of men bordered on dementia. She
refused to be in the house when workmen were present, and once even balked at opening the door for the
UPS delivery man. The flip side of this was her equally
zealous belief in the kinship of women, all women.
Men were the oppressors, women the oppressed, it was
just that some of us failed to recognize how truly ex-
ploited we were. Maybe I could have been persuaded
that Connie was capable of murder, but never the
murder of a sister, even one as different from herself as
Pepper.

"You're wasting your time there," I told him. "I'm
sure Connie had nothing to do with Pepper's death."

His eyes narrowed. "We'll look into it all the same."

I shrugged. I didn't envy the cop who drew the duty
of questioning Connie.

"Anyone else?"

"Possibly. There were always workman of some sort
over there."

"What about just recently?"

"Well, they had their windows cleaned, and their
carpets. And she had a painter working upstairs. But
the Livingstons have a very elaborate alarm system."

He groaned. "The husband says he can't remember whether or not the alarm was set that night when he got home."

"Can't remember?"

Another groan. "I have a feeling the guy may have stopped off for a drink or two after leaving the office."

"It had to have been on," I told him. "Pepper set it every evening before she went upstairs."

Stone shifted his jacket to his left shoulder and loosened his tie. He frowned at the grass for a few moments, then asked, "You going to this wine thing tomorrow?"

"I don't know, I guess so. I bought a ticket so I might as well use it."

"Maybe I'll see you there."

"You're going?"

A sheepish grin crossed his face. "Part of the job."

I was beginning to think the city council might be right in wanting to bring in outside help. How could the police hope to catch the killer if they spent their days sitting in church and sipping wine at the Gardens? But then again, there weren't many real leads for them to follow.

Heather was on the phone when I got home, wrapping the cord around her finger and giggling, while Anna sat on the floor eating ice cream out of the carton with a tablespoon. Embarrassed, Heather hung up quickly, brushed the straight blond bangs from her eyes and started to explain. "It was Chris. I just needed to check on a history assignment."

I could remember what it was like to be sixteen. When an hour on the telephone went by in a flash, when talking to your boyfriend seemed like the only thing that mattered.

I flopped down in a chair next to Anna and took a spoonful of ice cream for myself. "I don't mind your talking on the phone," I explained to Heather, "just as long as you remember you're being paid to watch Anna."

She nodded, her hazel eyes suddenly serious.

"And I think it's probably better if you put the ice cream in a bowl first."

"Oh, sure." It seemed to take a moment for the words to sink in. "I'll do it that way from now on."

Taking the carton from Anna, I replaced the lid and stuck it back in the freezer. Given the small amount of ice cream remaining, and the fact that it was practically soupy, I guessed that Heather and Chris had found more to talk about than history.

When I sat back down, Anna crawled into my lap and gave me a big, sticky kiss. "Heather played Old Maid with me," she announced proudly. "And I won every single time."

Anyone who was willing to play cards with Anna, who had her own very precise rules, deserved a star in my book. What the heck, I thought, history assignments were sometimes very complicated, and a dirty bowl was only one more thing to be washed.

"Any chance you're free tomorrow afternoon?" I asked Heather. Now that I knew Stone would be there, the Wine Festival had new appeal.

"I'm sitting for the Livingstons tomorrow, uh . . ."—she looked suddenly flustered—"I mean I'm watching Kimberly for Mr. Livingston." She hugged herself and looked out the window toward their house. "It's going to seem so strange to be in that house now that Mrs. Livingston is dead."

I nodded. Murder was disturbing enough to an adult; I couldn't imagine what it must be like for a young person. "Mr. Livingston is going to the Wine Festival?"

"No, to something in San Francisco."

"If it's okay with him, would you be willing to watch both girls together? You could use our house if you'd like." I was pretty sure Robert would agree. We had done this sort of thing before, and it was probably easier for Heather when her charges had each other to play with.

"Sure. That would be great. No phone calls. And I'll remember the bowls."

After I cleaned up the table, the floor and Anna, I sent my daughter to her room for quiet time.

This murder business was beginning to get to me. I felt a kind of raw sadness that wouldn't go away. I walked around the house, picking up stray socks and old newspapers, and glancing every so often at the expanse which separated our house from the Livingstons'. Finally, I got out my easel and some brushes and went out into the garden.

The setting was one which had captured my imagination from the first day I saw it, and now, with Pepper's death, it took on a special meaning. Setting my things down next to the old log that Anna and Kimberly used as a horse, I began my own personal farewell to Pepper. Maybe the act of painting would soften the gloom that hung on me like a second skin.

Quickly, I sketched the arbor, thick with yellow climbing roses, the old bench with the lilac bush beyond. The crabapple was no longer in bloom, but that was one of the nice things about painting. I could remake the world into anything I wanted. In early spring the tree had been a mass of greens and pinks— at least fifty shades of each. That was the way I would paint it now, from memory.

My hand flew across the page, making light, feath-

ery strokes. In my mind I was reliving a day in late
March when I'd caught a glimpse of Pepper sitting on
the bench with a book in her lap. She'd been wearing a
print dress and one of those big straw sun hats with a
blue ribbon around the crown. I'd been ready then to
ask if I could sketch her, but before I'd had a chance
the gardener arrived and she wandered off with him to
examine a lemon tree damaged by the frost.

Humming softly to myself, I was lost in thought
when it hit me. The gardener! That was the face at the
memorial service. Only he looked different now, which
was why I'd had trouble placing him. Before, he'd had
long hair pulled back into a ponytail. And of course,
he'd dressed in work clothes, usually worn and a little
dirty.

What had he been doing at Pepper's memorial service?

It was hardly an "invitation only" affair, but for
some reason I couldn't explain, even to myself, his
presence struck me as unusual.

My hand had stopped moving and rested in my lap,
clutching the pencil tightly. Pepper treated her help
well, and judging from what Claudia had told me, she
certainly paid her gardener handsomely, but she
wasn't the sort to become chummy with them. When
she'd found out that Connie and I sometimes had coffee together in the middle of the afternoon, she'd been
horrified. "This may be a democracy," she told me, in
a tone which suggested she wasn't altogether happy
about the fact, "but that doesn't mean you have to
treat people who work for you like friends." The fact
that I actually considered Connie to *be* a friend, only
distressed her more. I couldn't imagine that she'd ex-
changed more than a "Good afternoon" or a "Don't
forget to spray the aphids" with her gardener in the
whole time he'd worked for her.

But maybe he'd been fond of her, regardless. Or maybe he was the sort of gentle soul who was profoundly touched by death. There were any number of logical explanations, but none of them quieted the uneasiness I felt. In fact, the more I thought about it, the odder it seemed. Unable to continue drawing while my mind moved in circles, I went inside and called Claudia.

"How are you all doing over there?" I asked.

"Kate, how nice of you to inquire. We're fine."

"Is there anything I can do for you?"

"Nothing at the moment—thanks. I'll be sure to call if there is."

I hesitated a moment before asking, "What was the name of that gardener again, do you remember?"

"Tony something, Sherman, Sharp, Sheris, that's it, Sheris. Why? Did you change your mind about hiring him?"

"No. I thought I saw him at the memorial service, and it seemed odd, that's all."

"Well, Pepper had a way about her. Lots of people admired her." I could sense that Claudia found this baffling.

"Thanks. And don't forget to call if I can help out."

As soon as I hung up, I pulled the phone book off the shelf and turned to the *S*'s. There was only one Sheris listed, a W. Glen Sheris in a neighboring town. I tried the number, but the woman who answered didn't know any Tony. "We have a grandson, Teddy, but he's only nine months old," she said. "My son and my husband are both Walter Glen."

Even if I'd found him, I wasn't at all sure what would come next. I had planned to say I was interested in finding someone to look after my garden, and that Pepper had given me his name. I thought maybe if I could get him talking about her, I might learn something useful. But he was hardly going to admit to killing her—that suspicion *was,* I finally conceded, what underscored my uneasiness—and I certainly couldn't grill him about attending her service.

Still, it was worth a few more calls. I tried information for all the major East Bay cities and finally, in Berkeley, found a listing for Tony Sheris. "Is that the Sheris on Dwight?" I asked. The telephone company won't give out addresses, but I've learned that if you ask the right questions you can sometimes get what you want anyway.

"No, this one's on Blake. Two-three-five-three."

Bingo. Again I dialed, rehearsing my story.

"You have reached a number which is no longer in service. If you feel you have reached this number in error . . ."

I hung up, drained of the elation I'd felt only moments earlier. I'd tell Stone the next afternoon at the Wine Festival. Or maybe I'd just forget the whole thing. Attending your employer's memorial service, even if you happen to simultaneously disconnect your phone, hardly made you a criminal.

By the time I went to bed that night, though, I knew I would do neither. First thing the next morning I was going to drive by the Blake Street address myself, just to check it out. At least that way Stone wouldn't think I was a complete imbecile.

I went to sleep thinking how impressed Stone would be if I managed to uncover an important lead. Right around the time I drifted off, he was telling me how incredible I was and soundly planting a commemorative kiss, which lasted a full minute at least, on my lips.

A little after six the next morning a pair of icy feet pushed against my back.

"Move over, Mommy, you've got the warm spot."

I slid over and then turned so that Anna could curl against my chest. She squiggled and squirmed and inched backward until everything was adjusted to her satisfaction; then she patted my hand and fell back to sleep. I stayed awake, though, enjoying the soft warmth of my daughter and concocting elaborate schemes to explain the behavior of the Livingstons' gardener. By the time I got up I was almost convinced there was, indeed, nothing to explain. Still, I intended to drive into Berkeley that morning.

Because I was already feeling guilty about having to drag Anna with me, I made waffles and hot cocoa for breakfast, and poured extra syrup on her plate. As I predicted, Anna was pleased. Wrapping her arms around my waist, she buried her face in my sweatshirt.

"I'm glad I was the egg chosen," she declared solemnly.

"The egg?"

"Yes. You know how I started out as an egg? Well, if some other egg had been chosen then I wouldn't be alive. And then I would miss you terribly."

A remarkably sophisticated, if self-canceling, concept. "I'm glad you were the egg chosen too," I told her. Then, in the interest of both fairness and biological accuracy, I reminded her that she should also be happy she was the sperm chosen. "It takes both to make a baby don't forget."

"I know, but the egg is more important, right?"

"They're both necessary."

"But the egg is the leader."

A budding feminist. I started to explain and then gave up. "We're going to take a drive to Berkeley this morning," I told her, tweaking her nose. "So run along and get dressed." I changed into a clean sweatshirt and got out the map.

We found the place on Blake without any trouble. It was one of those two-story, stucco apartment houses built in the late 1950s. Boxy and drab, it had probably looked uninviting even when new. The effect now was downright dismal, though given its proximity to the university, I was certain the rent was anything but cheap.

The mailbox listed a Sheris in apartment 206. Standing on tiptoe, I peered through the mail slot to see if Tony had any letters. Empty. I was expecting maybe one from Pepper, begging for mercy? Or a ten-thousand-dollar check drawn on a Swiss bank, with a little Post-It attached saying something like, "Good job, Tony"? Actually, I was so pleased with myself at establishing his identity and finding out his address, I hadn't bothered to think much beyond that, except to convince myself there was something unusual about his connection with Pepper.

The elevator was at the end of the building, diagonally across from the mailbox. Someone had scratched the words "out of order" in the paint on the metal doors, but I wouldn't have trusted it under any circumstances. Instead, Anna and I took the stairs, which smelled of urine and stale grease, but at least appeared to be intact.

"Don't touch anything," I warned her. "And be sure to keep your fingers out of your mouth until we get home and wash your hands."

She nodded and kept her arms rigidly fixed to her sides until we got to the top landing, where she reached out and ran her hand along the length of the grimy railing.

"Anna!"

"Whoops." She looked truly penitent. "I forgot."

With the kind of deep sigh that is second nature to mothers, I reminded her to keep her hands away from her face, then rang the bell. A few minutes later, I knocked on the door, loudly. Just then a pudgy man with curly hair and a scraggly black beard emerged from the apartment to the left.

"I'm looking for Tony Sheris," I said. "Do you know him?"

The man was busy locking his door, and glanced in my direction only momentarily before turning his attention back to that. He had that intentionally disheveled look so many Berkeley residents like to cultivate, and the aloof, somewhat apathetic expression which went with that look.

"He lives here, doesn't he?"

"He a friend of yours?"

I didn't hesitate. "Yes, he is."

"He pulled out day before yesterday."

"Moved?"

"That's what I said, didn't I?"

"Where'd he go?"

The man shrugged and pocketed his keys. "All's I know is he's gone. We wasn't exactly close."

I'd read about declining test scores and poorly prepared applicants, but I hadn't imagined things were this bad. I could only hope the young man was a member of the Berkeley fringe and not actually a student at the university. "Did Tony live alone?" I asked, grabbing at what seemed to be my only chance of finding him.

"Never saw anyone else looked like they lived there."

The man began edging toward the stairs, and I followed after him, as closely as I dared. "Was it a sudden departure?"

He looked at me blankly.

"Had Tony been planning to move or was it a spur-of-the-moment decision?"

"How the fuck should I know?"

I glanced quickly at Anna, who was walking uncharacteristically close to my side.

"Sorry," he muttered. "But like I told you, him and me didn't talk much."

"Was there anyone in the building who *was* friendly with him?"

Another shrug. "He kept to himself mostly."

We were at the bottom of the stairs. I knew he wasn't going to hang around and answer my questions forever, but I gave it one last shot. "What was Tony like?"

The man eyed me with suspicion. "I thought he was a friend of yours."

"A friend of a friend, actually."

For a moment he chewed on his mustache, then apparently decided my reasons for being interested in Tony didn't really matter.

"He was just your average guy. Quiet, kind of a loner, though I did see him with a girl a couple of times. He fed a lot of the stray cats in the neighborhood, fed 'em and talked to 'em. They could probably tell you more than I can." He laughed at his own cleverness. "That's about it."

"What about the girl, does she live around here?"

"Nope, at least I haven't seen her. Wasn't a girl really, more like a woman. Good looker too. Sleek blond hair and a tight little behind. Some guys have all the luck."

Pepper? It could have been her, but I couldn't imagine why she would visit Tony at his apartment. I couldn't imagine her getting all hot and heavy with a guy like Tony either. He was too young, too meek, too bland. I wasn't sure what her type was, but I was pretty certain what it wasn't.

As I led Anna back to the car I tried to stifle my disappointment, consoling myself with the thought that it had been a stupid idea anyway. From now on I was going to leave the detective work to the police.

"Why does that man want to live there?" Anna asked as we pulled away.

"He needs to live somewhere."

"But that place smells."

I delivered a brief lesson in economics and the realities of living—I didn't want Anna to grow up thinking the rest of the world was like Walnut Hills—but I agreed with her that the place was indeed pretty bad. Then I put all thoughts of Tony and Pepper out of my mind and concentrated instead on choosing something to wear to the Wine Festival that afternoon—something stylish and sophisticated . . . and maybe a little sexy.

The Benefit Guild Wine Festival is a fundraiser held each year at the Diablo Gardens, part of an old estate now owned by the city and leased out for parties, weddings, concerts and, with increasing frequency, the making of movies. Restaurants and caterers donate the food, wineries the wine. Members of the Guild bake the desserts. The profits, which are sizable, go to support local charities and services for the community.

As fundraisers go, it's pretty good. A number of local artists exhibit their works, and there are usually several bands. The real draw, though, is the food and the chance to sample wine from a large number of wineries. Since I had sworn off drinking until I was no longer pregnant—however that event happened to come about—I left Jim and Daria to wend their way around the tasting tables while I headed for the desserts. I'd learned from experience that it was one of the first to run low, the Guild ladies preferring, on the whole, to plan parties rather than bake for them. If I spent time savoring marinated chicken wings and polenta with salsa, the best desserts would be long gone by the time I went for them.

"Be sure to sample my fudge," Daria called after me. "You've never tasted anything like it."

Promising myself an extra long run the next morning, I loaded my plate with chocolate brownies, miniature éclairs, lemon cheesecake and a piece of Daria's fudge. Then I grabbed a handful of sugar-coated almonds and moved out of the way.

I was headed for a quiet, shady spot when Lily Peters caught my arm and pulled me aside. "Ah've just had the most awful experience," she drawled in that honey-coated Southern voice of hers. "Ah just can't believe it."

It's hard to tell when Lily is really upset, because she habitually overreacts and sounds breathless even when she says good morning. When I'm around her I feel as though I should be ready to whip out the smelling salts at a moment's notice. Instead I held out a brownie.

She bit her lower lip and shook her head. "No thank you. Ah believe ah'll save dessert for later."

Her face was red and splotchy as though she'd swallowed the wrong way and been coughing hard. The rest of her, though, looked as gorgeous and polished as ever. Lily never goes anywhere unless her makeup is perfect and her outfit is fully accessorized. She has one of those beauty contestant hairdos that hangs in soft, shoulder-length swirls around her face and never looks mussed. She brushed at one of those loose *S*-shaped curls now, and looked at me.

"Ah'm still shakin'," she gasped.

"What happened?"

"Larry and I were standing in line over at the Frog's Leap table. They make a wonderful cabernet if y'all haven't tried it. We were talking about something totally boring, the drought I think, when ah noticed Burt McGregory standing in front of us with some other man, laughing."

"Mmm." I frowned at my cheesecake thoughtfully.

Lily shuddered. "That man makes my skin crawl."

I was pretty sure she meant Burt McGregory, the developer who wanted to build on the ridge line, and not Larry, who was her husband.

"You worked with Pepper on the Save Our Hills Action Committee, didn't you?" she asked.

"I stood in front of Safeway holding a petition, but that's about as far as my involvement went." And Pepper had had to twist my arm to get that. I'm simply not a doer.

"Then you don't know what a slimeball that man is."

Actually I'd heard him called worse. "What did he do now?"

She took a deep breath and exhaled slowly. "Well, the other man made some snide comment about the opportune timing of Pepper's death. Can you imagine? *Opportune*. What a horrible word to use about some-one's death. And then McGregory said, 'Maybe this will put an end to that damned petition of hers. The woman's been a thorn in my side from the start.' "

Here Lily stopped to close her eyes and shudder before continuing. "Then he laughed again and said, 'I ought to find the guy who did it and offer him a re-ward.' " Lily turned to look at me. "Can you believe it?"

"Well, he certainly wouldn't win the Miss Manners award for good breeding, but his animosity toward Pepper is hardly news. And you said yourself he was a slimeball. People like that live in a different world."

"But still, to speak like that about someone who is dead. Someone who was mur-murdered. It makes me nauseous."

I could see that it was indeed making her sick, or at least somewhat unwell. She looked as though she might, at any moment, fall over in a heap. But she pulled herself together and continued.

"I was at the last town council meeting," she said. "The meeting where Pepper made that wonderful speech and the council decided to postpone the vote till next month. After the meeting, I saw McGregory grab her by the arm and call her"—here she lowered her voice and held a hand to her mouth to shield inno-cent bystanders—". . . a royal bitch. He told her she would regret the day she took him on. Wouldn't you'd think that now, given what's happened, he'd feel some remorse?"

"Maybe *he* killed her."

Lily's hands flew to her mouth. "Oh no, I never thought about that."

And here I'd believed that's what she'd been sug-gesting.

"Do you think he did?" she asked with a nervous glance toward the Frog's Leap table.

"Probably not. This isn't exactly Chicago, and it's quite a jump from slimeball to murderer." Besides, McGregory had always struck me as the brag-and-bluster type, all show and little substance. I couldn't imagine that when it came right down to it, he felt passionately about much of anything, except maybe his twenty-two-year-old wife, Lynette.

Larry came over then with a glass of wine for Lily, with a business associate he wanted to introduce her to, so I headed back to refill my plate, promising myself that the following round would be nothing but celery spears and fruit salad. I made a quick sweep of the faces near me, hoping to catch a glimpse of Stone. Then, angry with myself for even thinking about him, I started toward one of the bands.

This man on the brain stuff was not my usual style. I left that sort of thing to women like Susie Sullivan who seemed constitutionally unable to ignore an attractive male. Sure, now and then I'd admire a firm derrière in a pair of tight jeans, or a set of biceps which seriously tested the stretching power of lightweight jersey, but since I'd married Andy, since I'd met him in fact, I hadn't actually spent much time thinking about other men. Not that I had found myself *thinking* about Stone exactly, and certainly not in any substantive way, but something about him affected me nonetheless.

Just as I neared the knoll where a female singer was trying to dazzle the small crowd gathered around her, I saw him. He was standing off by himself, a glass of seltzer in hand, like a director surveying a scene which wasn't playing the way he'd envisioned it. At that same moment, he noticed me and started in my direction with a smile. There was a dangerous fluttery feel-

ing in my chest that even my deliberate deep breathing
wouldn't quiet. But what the heck, I was allowed a few
harmless fantasies, wasn't I?

"This is quite a shindig," Stone said with a sweep of
his free hand.

I agreed. It was, in fact, an amazing undertaking for
a group of rich, pampered housewives. It surprised me
every year.

"And a great selection of wines. Too bad I'm on
duty." Frowning, he raised his glass and inspected it,
then took another swallow of seltzer. "What about
you? You're not sampling any of the wine?"

"I'm on a diet." It was the excuse I'd been using for
the last month. It had always worked just fine, but this
time I was holding at least six hundred empty calories
in my hand, right out in the open.

Stone glanced at my plate and gave me a funny
look. "Interesting diet."

He was standing close enough for me to detect a
faint, fresh smell, as though he'd just stepped out of
the shower. Close enough for me to feel a silent charge
pulse through the warm spring air between us.

"Did you find out who Pepper was seeing?" I asked,
stepping away slightly.

He shook his head. "Not yet. Crime detection is
slow, tedious work. I've got men working on it
though."

"But discreetly?"

"Very discreetly."

I had just begun to tell him about Tony and my visit
to Berkeley that morning, when a tall, willowy blonde
in a very short, black skirt came up to us.

"Mikey," she cooed. "This is the last sort of place
I'd expect to find you."

"Work," he said, smiling blandly.

"Oh, sure." She gave him an odd, cryptic look.

"You expecting someone to walk off with a case of pinot noir?"

"You never can tell."

She was pretty, in an all-American sort of way. Straight, shoulder-length hair parted on the side, cute nose, even white teeth. I disliked her immediately.

With a glance that managed to concede my presence while not actually acknowledging it, she took a slow, theatrical sip of wine, then leaned forward and planted a delicate white hand firmly on Stone's chest. "You do amaze me sometimes," she said slowly. "You really do."

I shifted awkwardly from one foot to another while she continued to eye him with amusement. Finally, with a toss of her head, she was gone.

"Mikey?" I asked when she was out of hearing.

"Short for Michael."

"Is that what people call you?"

"Only Barbara." His expression was grim, but I couldn't tell if it was the name or the woman that did it.

"Who is she?"

"My wife."

Boom. So much for fantasy, not that it really mattered either way, I thought. "She's very pretty," I said brightly.

Stone looked amused. "Soon to be ex-wife."

"Oh."

Just then Daria and Jim joined us, drawn, I'm sure, by Daria's unwavering curiosity. The minute I'd stepped into the car that afternoon she'd been all over me about the good-looking man I'd been talking to outside the church yesterday. When Daria calls someone attractive—or generous or talented or kind—my antennae go up immediately. Unless she is talking about her own family, these words usually signal an ulterior motive. The fact that Stone was a police officer and not some secret admirer did little to suppress her curiosity, and I knew that she was now anxious to meet him in the flesh.

"Kate," she gushed in her most sparkling manner, "we forgot to set a meeting time. How late do you want to stay?"

"Whatever you two want is fine with me."

She smiled at Stone and waited for me to introduce her, which of course I did, though reluctantly.

"Lieutenant Stone is investigating Pepper's death," I explained.

"It's still hard to believe," Jim muttered, kicking at the grass with his toe. "That kind of stuff just doesn't happen in Walnut Hills."

"Unfortunately," Stone replied, his mouth tight, "murder happens everywhere."

Craig Foster passed by just then and gave Jim one of those male-buddy shoulder punches. "How ya' doing? Spent all of Tuesday night's riches yet?"

"I'm banking it, so the next time you guys try to bleed me I'll have an edge."

"Just remember," Foster chuckled, "if my car hadn't been blocking your Beemer, you'd have pulled out at midnight the way you wanted, and you'd still be in the hole."

Jim turned back to us and tugged at his ear. "Poker," he said, looking a tad sheepish. "One of my weaknesses."

Daria smiled blandly and then fixed her gaze attentively on Stone. "How's the investigation coming along?" she asked, with a cute little tilt of her head. When she puts her mind to it, she can be utterly charming.

"About as well as can be expected."

She flashed him a perfect smile. "Oh? Any suspects yet?"

Stone smiled back. A congenial, good-natured, aw-shucks kind of smile. "I'm not at liberty to discuss the case, but I admit it's not the easiest one I've worked on."

"I should think not." She tucked a strand of shiny auburn hair behind her ear. "These random violence things must be very difficult to solve. Something like looking for a needle in a haystack."

"They are, but sometimes we get lucky." His eyes were softly mocking. "Sometimes we even get smart."

Jim looked up and shoved a hand into his pocket. "I guess you're getting a lot of heat on this one. All that publicity and stuff. Does that help or make it worse?"

"In the short run it's hard, particularly when politics get involved. But in the bigger picture it sometimes helps. There may be a witness who knows something but wouldn't come forward without all the coverage."

Daria frowned. "Certainly by now anyone with pertinent information would have contacted you, don't you think?"

"Hard to say."

Her frown deepened. "Pepper was a dear friend of mine. If there's anything I can do to help out, be sure to let me know." Reaching into the genuine alligator purse that had been a birthday gift from Jim, she handed Stone her business card. "Feel free to call me at work or at home. Anytime." She flashed him another of her award-winning smiles, then looped her arm through Jim's and sauntered off.

"Why do I feel like I've just been standing in front of a hot oven?" Stone asked me when they left.

"Daria has that affect on people sometimes."

"Doesn't it wear you down?"

"She's not always like that," I explained, offering him a truffle.

He picked it off my plate and took a small bite, letting the chocolate melt in his mouth before swallowing. "Truly amazing, this diet of yours." He plopped the rest of the candy in his mouth and licked his fingers.

"I thought of something else."

"Mmm."

"About Pepper."

Guiding me by the elbow, Stone led me to an empty patch of grass away from the crowd. I tried not to think about the warm spot where his fingers touched my skin.

"Shoot," he said.

"It may be nothing." He nodded. "But at Pepper's service I saw a young man sitting at the back of the church, by himself. He looked familiar, yet I couldn't place him. Then when I got home, I started sketching the garden between our house and the Livingstons' . . ."

"You draw?"

My artistic abilities were not the issue, but I nodded.

"I would love to have some talent in that direction. I can barely manage a stick figure with enough toes and fingers to be certified as kindergarten level." He shifted his weight. "Do you paint too?"

"Yes."

"Oil? Watercolor?"

"Look, do you want to hear what I found out or not?"

"Okay. You saw a familiar face, and then in the garden you remembered who it was."

"How did you know?"

"Brilliant deductive powers, I guess."

"And do you know *who* it was?"

"The gardener?"

So much for my great investigation. "Then you know about him already?"

"Know what?" His voice grew suddenly serious. "I'm sorry. What did you want to tell me?"

I described my excursion to the apartment on Blake Street that morning. "It's odd, don't you think?"

Stone nodded, seemingly lost in thought. "It's probably just a coincidence, but we'll check it out all the same. Did Pepper ever mention this Tony to you?"

"Once. She thought I should hire him to prune the ivy along the back fence. She said he was a good worker."

"How long had he worked for them?"

I tried to think. "She used a gardening service at first, but she was never happy with them. They were the mow-blow-and-go variety. Tony must have started working for them around last Thanksgiving. I know he wasn't there last summer."

Stone looked perplexed. "Mow-blow-and-go?"

"Mow the lawn, blow the leaves and go. Pepper wanted somebody who took an interest in the garden."

"I see. And Tony fit the bill?"

"Apparently so."

His shoulder nudged mine. "Maybe I should deputize you. Seems you seem to come up with as much as we do." I knew he wasn't merely humoring me because he'd taken out a little notebook and written down Tony's name and address, but there was a glint in his eye which was most undetectivelike. I looked away quickly.

"Still," he said after a moment, "I wish you'd stop playing cop. If you have something you think might be important, tell me about it and I'll look into it. Someone who has killed once finds it easier to kill a second time."

"Are you saying that somebody might try to kill me?"

"If you go poking around where you're not wanted, yes."

I couldn't make up my mind whether to be angry with him or not. I don't like to be patronized, but I'm quite willing to be cherished and protected. And I definitely prefer being alive to being dead.

"You want anything more to eat?" Stone asked, tugging at his tie.

"Maybe some fruit salad."

"Why don't you go grab a table over there by the rose bushes, and I'll get us some food."

Most people who attend the festival like to stay on their feet, drifting from station to station in order to sample the whole range of wines available, so I had no trouble finding a vacant table. I cleared the mess left by the previous occupants and sat down to await Stone's return.

"Fruit salad," he said, setting two heaping plates on the table. "And pasta salad, ribs, and shrimp on a skewer. This is a crazy place to come if you're watching your weight."

"You're right." Actually, I *would* have to start watching it soon, whether I decided to stay pregnant or not. With Anna I'd gained forty pounds, and even after she was born people stopped me on the street to ask when the baby was due. I didn't intend to get myself in that fix again. "Do you think you'll be able to find the killer?" I asked, between mouthfuls.

"If it was actually someone she knew, our chances are a lot better than they were when we were simply looking for a burglar. Your friend Daria was right about random killings. They're the worst."

"What will happen if you don't find the guy?"

There was a moment of silence before Stone said flatly, "Absolutely nothing. It happens all the time."

"You're kidding?"

"I wish I were. If you're smart enough, it's fairly easy to get away with murder."

There was a bleak quality to his voice which I found disconcerting. "You're not very optimistic about this case are you?"

"Let's just say I'm trying to be realistic." He stood and collected our empty plates. "I guess I'd better be moving on. Let me know if you think of anything else."

I nodded, watching him. I was trying to sort through what I knew about Pepper, to search my memory for the single tidbit of information which would make all the pieces fall into place, but instead I fixed on those blue-gray eyes of Stone's. Eyes that seemed to speak a language of their own.

"Why are you getting a divorce?" The words were out of my mouth before I knew it, but they'd been on the tip of my tongue ever since Barbara had waltzed through earlier in the afternoon.

The half-smile on Stone's face faded. "She got tired of being married to a cop, I think. Or maybe it was just me she got tired of." He stacked the remaining cup onto the pile in his hands and replaced his chair carefully so that its back just touched the table.

"Any children?"

"No. We're fortunate in that respect I guess." He didn't sound particularly pleased about it, though. "I was on the force in San Francisco. It's different there than Walnut Hills. It's like trying to build a castle with dry sand. Nothing holds. Half the time I wouldn't get home when I said I would, and when I was home, my mind was a million miles away. Barbara wasn't happy about any of it. Hell, I wasn't happy. So I took this job and we moved out here. But by then it was too late." Stone paused. "She went back to school last year, moved out last fall. Now she has an MBA and more job offers than I could ever dream of."

The thin, strained quality to his voice reached out and grabbed me. "I'm sorry," I said, then stood up too and helped him toss the trash into the basket.

After Stone left, I listened to one of the bands for a while, glanced through an exhibition of serigraphs by my former art teacher and talked to Lisa Bloom, mother of Scotty, the boy who regularly pinched Anna and at least once a week kicked over the art-supply shelf at school. And out of the corner of my eye I continued to watch Stone, promising myself that tomorrow when I gave up sweets, I would also give up thinking about him. It was going to be clean, wholesome living from then on.

Finally Daria found me and we rounded up Jim, who seemed to have done his part to make up for those of us who weren't drinking. He listed slightly when he walked, and his eyes were glazed. I was glad when Daria offered to drive and Jim agreed to let her.

"Just remember," he warned her, "it doesn't handle like the BMW."

Daria patted his knee affectionately. "I'm well aware of that." Then she turned to me. "I can't believe the shop can't find a better loaner. This car is really something, isn't it?"

I had to agree. A blue fender, a red trunk, and rust dotted white everywhere else. "Very patriotic," I said.

"They promised us our car four days ago," Jim muttered, "but that was before they realized the part they needed was on back order." With that, he leaned back in the seat and began snoring softly.

"You all set for Monday?" Daria asked as we pulled up in front of my house.

"I'm looking forward to it, that is, unless you've changed your mind."

She laughed. "No way." And then she reached over and squeezed my hand. "I'm looking forward to it too."

I was halfway to the front steps when Mrs. Stevenson called to me, threading her way through the juniper bushes along the curb.

"Kate, I saw that car again."

I laughed. "Colorful, isn't it?"

"No, the other one. The one I told you about the other day."

I stared at her blankly.

"And you were right, it was a Cherokee. Dark blue."

Ah, *that* car! I'd forgotten all about it. "Did you get the license number?"

A frown crossed her face and she looked annoyed with herself. "I didn't even think about that, I was too busy watching."

"Watching what?"

"Mr. Livingston." She waited until she was sure she had my attention. "I was dusting the living-room blinds when I happened to look out at the street. There it was, parked right where it always is. I was shaking, I mean after our conversation and all. To see it there again, well, it just gave me the shivers."

I nodded.

"But I checked the name just like you said. I was thinking how clever you were to get from Apache to Cherokee, when I saw Mr. Livingston come out to the end of his driveway to check for the mail. Then he walked straight toward the car. For a moment there, I was in a panic. I thought the car might suddenly gun its engines and run him down. Or maybe an arm would reach through a crack in the window and shoot him." She punctuated her last sentence with a nervous laugh. "I guess I've been watching too much television, but with Mrs. Livingston's murder and all, my mind's been working like that lately."

Her imagination may have gotten the best of her, but she was clearly enjoying it. She looked over at the Livingstons' house, or what you could see of it from our front porch, and shook her head knowingly.

"Anyway Mr. Livingston walked over to the driver's side and leaned against the door like he was talking to someone through the open window. Then, a couple of minutes later, he came around to the passenger side and climbed in. About ten minutes after that, he got out and walked back to the house."

"When was all this?"

"This morning, about ten o'clock."

There were lots of explanations, I told myself, but I couldn't shake the feeling that the bad ones made more sense than the good ones. At best, it was odd.

"If you see the car again, try to get the license number. And call me right away. Okay?" She nodded, a flicker of disappointment crossing her face. Then I touched her hand. "You did a wonderful job Mrs. Stevenson. You're very observant."

She beamed.

Heather was lying on the floor, reading to Anna and Kimberly, when I let myself in. Fleetingly, I wondered how much her show of attention was an attempt to atone for past neglect.

"Mr. Livingston called to say he'd be a little late. Do you want me to stay until he comes?"

"That's all right," I told her, flipping through my

billfold and calculating how much I owed her. "I'll watch Kimberly until he gets back."

"Thanks." She took the money and stuffed it into a pocket. "Was the Wine Festival exciting?"

"I don't know whether exciting is the right word, but I had a nice time."

"That's good. I know Mrs. Livingston and Mrs. Wilkens and the other ladies spent an awful lot of time getting it all organized. Chris says his dad thinks the whole thing is silly, but of course he wouldn't dare breathe a word of that to Mrs. Wilkens." Here she giggled self-consciously, covering her mouth with one hand. "Sorry. I forgot she was a friend of yours."

Then, grabbing her purse and sweater, she waved to the girls and was gone.

After changing into a pair of gray sweats, I picked up around the house, which was not as cluttered as I expected. Heather hadn't actually put anything away, but she'd done a conscientious job of stacking toys, books and dishes. Although I felt too full to eat any dinner myself, I fed the girls and sat at the table with them, sipping a cup of coffee while they ate.

"Aren't you going to eat any dinner?" Anna asked.

"Not tonight. I ate too much chocolate this afternoon."

"Did you bring me any?"

"No, honey, these chocolates weren't for taking home." Anna always likes it when I bring her the mints from my occasional lunches or dinners out.

"I got to taste the fudge," Kimberly declared solemnly. "Mrs. Wilkens brought some over the other day and told Mommy she had to let me have some." Her eyes, which had been wide with the memory of fudge, filled suddenly with tears and her lower lip began to quiver, but instead of crying she took a big bite of a hot dog and chewed solemnly while staring hard at the plate in front of her.

Robert picked up Kimberly about an hour later, hastily thanking me as though I hadn't been the one to elbow my way into his sitting arrangements. "Claudia left this morning so I'm still a bit frazzled," he apologized. Then he swooped up Kimberly and carried her home before I had a chance to repeat my offer of assistance.

When at last I'd done the dishes and tucked Anna into bed, I lay down on the couch to read, but found myself crying instead. Real, wet, salty tears. Maybe it was the murder, finally getting to me. Or the look on Kimberly's face when she spoke of her mother. Or maybe it was the baby and Andy and the terrible indecision I felt. Or maybe it was Lieutenant Stone. Something about him made me ache in a way I hadn't for a long, long time. Whatever the cause, I felt shaky and terribly alone.

8

I knew I should tell Stone about the blue Cherokee, but since I had just yesterday sworn off even thinking about him, it was unsettling to be confronted with an honest-to-goodness reason to contact him. After breakfast, I shuffled around the kitchen, debating what to do. The whole business was probably nothing more than coincidence. Besides, Mrs. Stevenson wasn't the most reliable witness; there was a good chance her story was as much a product of an overactive imagination as some sinister plot. In any case, it could wait. Nothing was going to happen on a Sunday.

But then, as I was straightening the family room, I found one of Kimberly's hair ribbons on the couch where she and Anna had been playing the day before, and a quiet sorrow squeezed my heart so that I could barely breathe. A woman—a mother like myself—was dead. I couldn't not do my part to see that her killer was found.

Adopting a deliberately businesslike manner, I called the station and asked for Lieutenant Stone.

"He's not in at the moment, may I take a message?" The voice at the other end was female and soft, not at all the sort of voice I'd expected to hear manning calls for a tough, no-nonsense police force. Was she a fellow cop, I wondered, or merely a receptionist? And then I got angry with myself for wondering. What difference did it make anyway?

I left my name and number, and to prove to myself it was strictly business, explained that the matter was nothing urgent; Lieutenant Stone could return the call at his convenience. Then I hung up the phone carefully and sat for a long time, staring at the buttons.

Anna was in my bedroom absorbing her full dose of Sunday-morning cartoons, the house was clean—as clean as it gets—and the refrigerator was stocked with a week's worth of groceries, all wholesome and nutritious, and the day stretched ahead of me with nothing that demanded my attention. I couldn't understand why I felt so restless.

The painting I'd begun the other day in Pepper's garden still lay in the back room where I'd left it. What the heck, I didn't get time to myself very often. I found my brushes and paints, cleared a spot on the worktable and settled in.

Watercolor is a difficult medium for me, and the garden scene was going to be particularly challenging, but the effect, if I was successful, would be exactly what I wanted. First I polished up my sketch, and then I began dabbing paint on a practice pad, mixing colors and hues. It was proving especially difficult to find the right shading of light and dark for the pink blossoms, so I worked intensely, thankful for the lack of interruptions.

I'd always found it difficult to paint when Andy was around. He would come up behind me, silently peer over my shoulder and then, knowing my hands were otherwise engaged, wrap his arms around my middle or slide a hand into my jeans. "I'm just trying to have a little fun," he'd explain when I protested. "And I'm trying to work," I'd tell him. But he never understood.

Even when he was out of the house, I had trouble painting with any real passion, knowing he would come home at the end of the day and glance over my efforts in much the same way he sifted through the mail. "Nice," he would say with a little pat on my bottom. I never knew whether he was talking about my work or my body. So I'd taken to simply sketching, doing little things I could work in during odd hours of the day and then tuck away out of sight.

I hadn't minded really. My family—Andy and Anna—that was what was important.

Now the issues were different. I had told myself I wouldn't start brooding about the future until fall. After all, there's no sense coming up with a plan until you know where you want to go, or at least where you're starting from. But you can't close your mind to things like that, and quite unconsciously I found myself running through possible scenarios.

If Andy came back I would have money to live on, even if we got a divorce. I was pretty sure he would be fair, unlike some husbands who went for the throat even when the divorce had been their idea in the first place.

But it wasn't at all clear he would return, even for a divorce. Something had happened to him, a malaise of the soul, which was beyond my comprehension. It was possible he might just decide to keep wandering, living for the moment. He was the sort who would be able to do that quite successfully. He'd find an innkeeper who would give him a room in exchange for light labor, a ship's captain who would take him on, just for the pleasure of his company. Heck, he might even find a princess who would pack him along for a winter in the Alps. He was that kind of guy.

There was a third option, of course: Andy might

come sweeping home like a man returning from an extended business trip, head for the office and pick up right where he left off. But even then, I couldn't imagine that things would ever be the same.

Caught up in my painting and aimless rumination, I didn't realize how much time had passed until Anna showed up at my feet.

"I'm hungry."

"Can you wait a minute until I finish this corner of the sky?"

She peered at the picture and then lay down on floor, head propped in her hands. "Is that supposed to be a lady sitting on the bench?"

"That's right."

"You can't even tell where the head is."

"You're not supposed to. It's just the sense of the woman I want."

"I can draw a person with a face," Anna announced smugly. "I even know how to make curly hair."

Just then the doorbell rang and she raced to it, but was beat out by Max, who has the advantage of four legs and a permanent spot by the front window.

"It's for you, Mommy. A man."

I wiped my hands on a towel and followed her to the door.

Lieutenant Stone smiled. "I got your message."

I had thought he looked good before, but he looked even better now. Faded Levi's, a well worn tee shirt stretched at the neck and scruffy brown loafers. His arms were strong and tanned, and the hairs on them glistened golden in the sun.

My breath caught somewhere deep in my chest. "Lieutenant Stone."

"Can we stop with this 'Lieutenant' stuff," he asked, stepping through the door. "Especially since I'm off duty today."

"Mikey, then?"

He glared. "Michael would do quite nicely."

"Okay, Michael." The jeans were snug. So was the shirt, through the shoulders. And the body, well, the body was even better than I'd imagined. My hands still clutched the dish towel, and I was twisting it, weaving it through my fingers. "You didn't have to come all the way over, you could have called."

He looked me straight in the eyes, with just the hint of a smile, and nodded. "You're right, I could have." Then he started toward the kitchen and I followed, still coiling the towel around my fingers.

"Would you like some coffee?" I asked. "Or some lunch? I was just going to make something for Anna."

At the sound of her name, Anna, who seemed glued to my side, squeezed my leg tighter.

"Anna, this is Lieutenant Stone. He's a policeman." She eyed him suspiciously, and I realized that at that particular moment, he looked more like the kind of person I'd taught her to run from than to. "It's his day off," I explained.

"Do you have a gun?" she asked, her voice almost a whisper.

Stone surprised me then by lifting his shirt, exposing a small gun tucked into the waist of his jeans. I barely saw the gun, though; I was too taken by the flat, hard abdomen and a brief vision of other endowments.

Anna, however, was properly mesmerized by the gun. Only a real princess could detect a pea under a thousand featherdown mattresses; and only a real policeman would carry a gun.

"I thought it was your day off," I muttered. "Do you always take that thing with you?" Guns made me uncomfortable, even in the hands, or waists, of the law.

"Not always, but I'm here investigating a murder, don't forget."

"You think I'd leave a message for you to call *at your convenience* if the killer was at my door?"

Without bothering to answer, Stone took a seat at the table and stretched his long legs out in front of him. Then he reached over and began scratching the top of Max's head. I wondered if the metal of the gun was warm where it touched his skin.

"How about lunch?" I asked again. "Anna's having dinosaur-shaped pasta from a can, cold, but I could probably whip up a bologna sandwich for you, or peanut butter and jelly."

Stone leaned back in the chair and looked at me as if I'd suggested sautéed worms. "Coffee's fine, thanks."

"You sure?"

"Unless you have any more of those muffins."

"Sorry. A bag of cheese puffs is the closest I can come."

There was that look again. "Just coffee."

I put the kettle on the stove and opened Anna's can of dinosaurs. Sometimes I let her eat right out of the can, but today I poured the contents into a bowl. "Why don't you eat outside," I suggested, "with Marty and Clary." Marty and Clary were imaginary friends who bickered and fought with each other, but adored Anna. I wouldn't let them sit with us for meals, but when Anna ate alone they frequently joined her.

While I was busy getting Anna settled at the table on the patio, Stone wandered into the den off the kitchen.

"You paint this?" he asked when I handed him a cup of hot coffee.

"It's not finished yet."

He whistled softly. "It's really good."

"You sound surprised."

"I guess I am."

I wasn't sure if I'd been complimented or insulted.

"Do you ever sell your stuff?"

"I've just started again, really. I used to paint before Anna was born, but I've not done much lately."

"It would be nice to be able to earn a living doing something you really loved, wouldn't it?"

"You don't?" I'd always assumed detectives were fanatics of sorts, that the need to right the order of things was in their blood.

Stone shrugged. "I was a classics major—that makes it kind of hard to earn a living doing what you love."

I led the way to the living room where we sat, facing each other across the square, glass coffee table. No socks, I noticed. And the few hairs on the tops of his feet were as golden as the ones on his arms. I could almost see those bare feet running along the wet sand at the ocean's edge, or padding softly down for morning coffee after a hard, late night.

"Now, what was it you wanted to see me about?" he asked.

"I didn't necessarily want to *see* you. I told you, you could have called."

He grinned. "What did you want to *tell* me then?"

Taking a sip of coffee, and then a deep breath, I recounted for him what Mrs. Stevenson had told me— about the car which sometimes parked behind the oleander and then about seeing Robert talking to the driver.

"What do you think it means?" Now that I'd reported what I knew, it sounded silly. Nancy Drew, all grown up.

"Your guess is as good as mine. We could probably concoct a dozen stories based on sinister motives and another dozen with completely innocent explanations."

"Such as?"

"Well, it could have been a friend or a salesman or a delivery person from the local pharmacy. Mrs. Stevenson didn't actually see anyone sitting in the car those other times. Or maybe it's the local gossip columnist, trying to get the dirt on the Livingstons."

"And what about the not so innocuous explanations?"

Here Stone frowned. "Well, the most scandalous explanation, of course, would be that Robert hired someone to kill his wife. The killer staked out the house—that's when Mrs. Stevenson saw the car those other times—killed Pepper, and then came back for his payment."

"But wouldn't it be pretty stupid for Robert to meet that person in front of his house, right in the middle of the day like that?"

"You're right, it would."

"So forget that."

"Hey, you asked for some 'supposes.' If I had answers I'd be even happier about it than you."

He had been leaning back in his chair, and now he slouched down even further, studying his cup. His face was drawn, his eyes flat.

"More coffee?" I asked, feeling suddenly contrite. He continued to stare at his cup without even acknowledging me. "Would you like more coffee?" I repeated.

"What?" he said, looking up. "No, I don't think so."

I had stood up to get more coffee, but now I sat down again, tucking a foot under me. "I'm sorry." I wasn't quite sure what I was apologizing for, but his

mood had changed abruptly and I felt somehow responsible.

"It's not your fault, I'm just tired." He did look
tired, exhausted in fact. "I just can't get a handle on
this case. Usually things begin to take shape about
now. Not necessarily a clear picture, but at least some
of the pieces begin to coalesce. Here we just have a lot
of loose ends. It's like a room full of kindergartners.
You get one to sit down and two others pop up."

"What do you know of kindergartners?"

"Barbara was a teacher. Before she got her MBA."

"Oh."

He seemed ready to say something else, then
stopped and smiled at me instead. But it was a flat, mechanical smile.

"You don't seriously think Robert is involved in
this do you?"

"I don't know. Something about him bothers me,
but I can't put my finger on it. We've questioned him
twice and come up with zip, except that his alibi for the
night she was murdered stinks. There's absolutely
nothing to link him to the crime, and no motive that
we've been able to discover."

"What about Pepper's affair? Did he know she was
seeing someone else?"

"*If* she was." He crossed his legs and peered into his
cup. "So far we've come up with a big, fat zero in that
arena as well."

So much for my clever detective work.

"Still, we *have* grilled the guy about their marriage."

"And what does he say?"

"Just what you'd expect. They had a good, solid relationship, better than most. He loved her; she loved
him. Just your basic perfect couple."

"He's right, you know." Pepper didn't knock you
over with her Robert-is-such-a-prince routine the way

Daria did, but she never complained either, not even in the half-joking way a lot of us who'd considered ourselves happily married did. Pepper and Robert had seemed so . . . so balanced, almost synchronized. A perfect match, I'd often thought.

Stone shrugged. "Except if Pepper was sleeping around, then the marriage wasn't so good."

I knew women who would disagree with him. Women who found an afternoon of sex an interesting alternative to an afternoon of tennis. An innocuous diversion that had no bearing whatsoever on their feelings about their husbands. But I wasn't about to take that one on at the moment.

Setting his cup, now empty, on the table in front of him, Stone stood and went to the window. "The mayor is furious. He wants us to arrest someone soon, and he doesn't much care who it is. The chief feels the same. They don't like to have a blot like this by their names."

"That's what Pepper is now, a blot by their name?"

"This isn't Oakland, you know; murder's not an everyday occurrence in Walnut Hills. And the longer it takes us to come up with something, the more likely it is we never will."

Just then the phone rang and I went to answer it, leaving Stone hunched forward by the window, hands in his pockets.

"Kate, it's Robert."

For a minute I was struck with guilt. As though he'd caught me gossiping behind his back.

"I hate to ask you this again, but I have to go out for a couple of hours this afternoon. Do you think Kimberly could stay with you for a while. I'll buy you dinner some night as a token of my appreciation."

"She's welcome to stay here, there's no need for dinner."

"I'd like to, really. It would be a pleasure."

"You bring Kimberly over, we'll talk about the dinner part later."

I hung up the phone and turned to find Stone leaning against the door jamb, his long frame looking as though it had been arranged, a limb at a time, by the guy who shoots the Marlboro commercials. I waited for him to move so I could get through, but he didn't budge. Instead, he fixed his eyes on me and reached out, touching my shoulder. Then he ran his hand along to the back of my neck and pulled me toward him.

The first kiss was soft, tentative, like the caress of a gentle breeze on a warm summer day. But the second and third were more intense. I could feel the roughness of his skin against mine, the smooth warmth of his tongue against my lips.

"That was every bit as wonderful as I'd imagined it would be," he said.

Silently, I agreed—and then gave myself a mental kick in the butt. This was definitely not part of the new, orderly life I'd been envisioning.

I was leaning forward to kiss him again when I heard the back door slam; then Anna came into the kitchen humming softly to herself. With a quick step back, I ran my fingers through my hair, and probably adjusted my shirt as well, just for good measure. Stone remained draped against the door frame, watching, the hint of a smile crossing his face.

"I finished lunch," Anna announced as she set her bowl and spoon on the counter. "Can I have a Drumstick?"

Clever. She knew the Drumsticks in the freezer were for dessert only, but she also knew I was in the middle of something and wanted her out of the way. "Okay, but eat it outside."

"How about one for Clary, too?"

I shook my head. A second Drumstick was going too far.

Before she could fall into a funk and eat up ten minutes arguing with me, I took the Drumstick from the freezer, unwrapped it and handed her the cone. "Now, outside with you."

Then I walked to the sink and began rinsing dishes, keeping my back to Stone. "Would you like more coffee?"

"Kate, come here."

I turned to face him, but stayed rooted to the sink.

"Come on, I won't bite."

I shook my head. "I don't think I'm ready for this."

"Ready for what?"

"You know." Trouble was, in some ways I *was* ready. And that's what I found so frightening.

Stone walked toward me and touched my cheek lightly. "I wasn't expecting to carry you off to the bedroom."

I nodded, saying nothing. I would have gone. I would probably have locked the back door and done it on the kitchen floor if he'd suggested it.

"Not today anyway," he murmured.

"That was Robert," I said, trying to catch my breath, "on the phone."

"Hmm." Stone seemed uninterested.

"Are you going to ask him about the blue Cherokee?"

"Probably. But not right this moment."

He leaned forward to kiss me again, but I put my hands, damp and sticky with soap, against his chest and made a halfhearted effort to protest. It took remarkable effort to hold them there without kneading his shoulders or letting them fall to his belt. I flashed a bright, artificial smile. "If you don't arrest someone soon, will they force you to bring in another law-enforcement agency?"

With a resigned sigh, Stone moved away. "Let's talk about the other thing."

"What other thing?"

"Why you're afraid of me."

"I'm not afraid of you."

"Why you don't like me then."

"It's not that I don't like you." My voice sounded so calm and composed, I wondered for a moment what stranger was speaking.

"What is it then?"

"It's . . . it's not anything I want to discuss right now."

There was a moment of silence, broken only by the soft hum of the refrigerator. Stone was watching me intently, with an expression I couldn't read.

"You were saying," I continued brightly, "before the phone call, that the big shots want the case closed, sooner rather than later."

Another deep sigh, then he took a seat at the table and folded his hands. "Yes, they want the case closed."

"So," I said, with a touch more enthusiasm than was probably warranted, "what are the possibilities?"

"Endless." He looked bored.

"It's not that bad. You've got this blue Cherokee which parks suspiciously across from the Livingstons' house and is connected in some way to Robert."

"A friend, a workman, a messenger service perhaps."

Undaunted, I continued. "And then there's Tony, who shows up at his employer's memorial service . . ."

"Along with a hundred other people."

". . . and then mysteriously disappears."

"Or simply moves."

"Not to mention the likelihood that she was having an affair."

Stone moved his hand across the table as I yanked mine back into my lap. "Jeez, you're jumpy," he remarked.

"Maybe they're all connected. Maybe Tony was the person in the car, and he and Robert had some secret, illegal scheme—smuggling exotic plants into the country, for example—and Pepper was sleeping with the head of agricultural inspection. That's how she found out, and she went to Tony's apartment one day to try to convince him—"

"You've certainly got an imagination." He inched his chair closer to mine.

"It *could* be," I insisted, inching mine in the opposite direction. "Of course, if Robert was guilty he would have set up a better alibi, he's not stupid . . ."

"Kate?"

I looked up.

"Stick to your painting and leave the detective work to me. Okay?"

Then he leaned over and ran a hand down the length of my arm. Without meaning to, I trembled.

"Oh, and McGregory. I forgot about him."

"Who?" He sat up now, my arm forgotten.

"McGregory, the developer who wants to build a series of townhouses along the ridge line. Pepper headed the Save Our Hills coalition, which was trying to block that. He apparently threatened her after the last council meeting. Well, sort of threatened." I repeated what Lily had told me the day before.

Stone listened thoughtfully. "Any other potential suspects you've lined up and neglected to tell me about?"

"Not yet."

"Good, try to keep it that way." His tone was light, but there was an edge to it.

"So, what are you going to do next?"

A sly grin spread across his face. "See if I can find a way to sneak another kiss."

"I'm serious."

"So am I."

My look must have convinced him, because he stood up again and carried his empty cup to the sink. "I'm going to try to find out who has a key to the Livingstons' place. I'm going to keep talking to people, trying to dig up as much as I can about Pepper, to see if I can't come up with some motive. I'll continue to search for the blue Cherokee, the elusive Tony and the lucky guy who found a woman who didn't reject his advances." He headed for the door. "And I'll talk to McGregory."

The rest of the afternoon was clearly shot. How could I paint soft-hued scenes of pastoral tranquillity when inside I was churning like laundry in a tub?

As soon as Kimberly arrived, which mercifully was not long after Stone left, I packed up sand toys, juice in small cartons and a large bag of cheese puffs, then took the girls off to the playground in the center of town. While they swung from rings and slid down the big, twisty slide which the *San Francisco Chronicle* once listed as Walnut Hills' chief attraction, I concentrated on taking slow, rhythmic breaths and tried to shut out the images that rushed at me like so many wild harpies. There were some tough, certainly painful, decisions to be made, and I knew I wasn't up to tackling any of them just yet.

So instead, I nibbled cheese puffs and studied the play of light and shadow in the fluttering leaves, trying to think how I could capture the sense of that whispering breeze on canvas. The day was warm, but the temperature in the shade was quite pleasant, and the fresh scents of jasmine and newly mowed lawn hung in the air, soothing my nerves. Then, just when the craziness in my brain was beginning to ebb, a young mother sat down next to me, shooing her toddler off with an air-blown kiss before turning her attention to the stroller she'd parked to her left. And the little, blue bundle tucked inside.

Okay, just don't look, I told myself. There's plenty else to see in the park. But my eyes kept drifting back to the soft form to my right. So tiny, so perfect. Every so often his little mouth would quiver and twitch, sucking at some invisible source of comfort. I could practically feel the gentle weight of his body in my arms.

The mother caught me peeking, and smiled. "He's just one month old."

I nodded and tried to appear blasé, looking over the top of the carriage while I mumbled something appropriately appreciative.

Lovingly, the woman adjusted the blankets and then began gently rocking the stroller with her foot. "His name is William. His sister's thrilled at having a little brother." She laughed lightly. "My husband and I are kind of pleased as well."

It was too much. Standing abruptly, I made some hasty excuse about the time and walked over to the playhouse where Anna and Kimberly were busily working out the rules to some new game.

"How about a movie?" I asked.

"Can we have popcorn?"

"Sure."

"One carton for each of us?"

What the heck. I'd just devoured half a pack of cheese puffs all by myself. "A carton for each of you," I promised.

We were gathering up our things to leave when we spotted Zachary Fontaine and his Irish au pair, Tina, laden with rollerblades, remote control car and baseball bat. Anna called to Zachary who, by way of acknowledgment, made a running leap, jump-kicking in the air as he went. The girls looked at each other and giggled.

Tina, who was at least fifty pounds overweight, trudged up the path after him.

"Good afternoon, Mrs. Austen," she said when she caught her breath. "You've beaten us to a good afternoon I see."

Despite her weight, Tina was a pretty girl, with a soft, peaches and cream complexion. And a far more pleasant disposition than her predecessor, who had viewed herself as a guest of the Fontaine encampment at Camp Walnut Hills.

Each spring a new girl would arrive fresh from Ireland to clean, shop, cook and look after Zachary while his mother, Olivia, was at work. In exchange, the young woman got room and board, and a chance to experience a taste of America, or as much of America as one can taste from Walnut Hills. It seemed to me that Zachary's parents got the better deal, but there was never a shortage of applicants. The arrangement was not entirely legal, but that minor point never seemed to make a difference. Only once, Olivia told me, had they had trouble with the immigration officials, and that was right after Zachary was born, before she'd learned the ins and outs of the system.

Tina dropped her load of play gear into a pile on the grass, then plopped down on a bench in the shade while Zachary ran in circles uttering strange, gunlike noises. The girls continued to giggle.

"It's good to see Kimberly laughing," she said. "Even just for a moment."

I nodded.

"She's been coming over to the house Friday afternoons, you know. Until last week that is. She has gymnastics with Zachary, and I've been bringing them both home, then watching Kimberly for a couple of hours. I feel so terrible for her."

Nodding agreement, I took a seat on the bench as well. It was the kind of "what if" that worked its way into my mind in the wee, sleepless hours of the night, and for a moment the anguish washed over me anew. If I were to die suddenly . . . would Anna even remember me in the years to come? Would she ever know how much I loved her? Then, in a shameless fashion, I latched on to those Friday afternoons, and my thoughts jumped from the tragic to the mundane.

"Would you by any chance be interested in watching Anna a couple of afternoons a week?" I asked. "I'm starting a new job tomorrow. Though the hours are quite flexible, I'm going to need some extra help." The Fontaines lived down the street, across from the house which was being remodeled. The arrangement would certainly be convenient.

"Myself, I'd be happy to, but Mrs. Fontaine doesn't usually like me to take on extra jobs. The thing with Kimberly was really something she did as a favor to Mrs. Livingston. I'll ask her, though, if you'd like."

"That's all right. Don't bother." I knew already I was not the sort of socially prominent person for whom Olivia Fontaine would do a favor.

"The last time I saw Mrs. Livingston was when she came to pick up Kimberly that Friday . . . you know, before she was killed. Then, less than a week later, she was dead." Tina's voice wavered. She paused for a moment, fanning herself with an open hand. "I felt bad for her that day because she was obviously upset about something. She acted real flustered, and usually, you know, she was so composed." Tina's voice wavered again. "Something like this, it shakes you up a bit."

"It certainly does."

We sat in comfortable silence for several minutes, watching the children play. "It's funny," Tina said, raising an arm to shield her eyes from the glare. "That night Mrs. Livingston was killed, I . . . well, it was so hot I couldn't sleep. My room doesn't have air conditioning like the rest of the house." There was a moment of silence while she creased and recreased the cuff of her shorts. Then she looked over at me, squinting in the bright afternoon sun. "I got up to make sure the window was open, though in that kind of heat it doesn't make much difference. The moon was pretty bright that night, and while I was standing there, looking out, I—"

But before she could continue, a loud, unhappy howl had us both on our feet and running over to Zachary, who had tripped and skidded across the asphalt path. The wailing got worse when he looked down and saw blood on his palms and knees.

"It hurts, it hurts," he cried, working himself into near hysterics.

We washed his wounds, which were impressive but not serious, calmed him down some, and then I helped Tina carry her load of play equipment back to the car while Zachary sipped Hawaiian Punch from one of the juice cartons I'd brought. With profuse thanks for my assistance, Tina drove off with Zachary, and I took the girls to the movie. It managed to captivate them, but did nothing at all for my fit of restlessness.

Afterward, I suggested dinner at McDonald's. Anna was thrilled, Kimberly uncertain.

"My mommy says McDonald's isn't good for you."

"Sorry," I said irritably, "but I don't know where to find tofu burgers and carrot sticks." Then I immediately felt terrible. Even Anna looked at me in disbelief. Whatever my state of mind, there was no excuse for taking it out on an innocent child. I pulled Kimberly into my lap, half expecting her to resist. "Your mom was right, you shouldn't eat this way all the time. But it's okay once in a while, and I know she'd approve of bending the rules at a time like this."

As a concession to Pepper, I ordered milk for the girls instead of soda, but then spoiled it by taking them to Baskin Robbins afterward for ice cream cones. Kimberly had the good sense not to say anything.

As I turned onto our street I saw that Robert's car was in the driveway, so I stopped there to deliver Kimberly before heading home. Robert opened the door, blinked, and stared at us blankly for a moment before the pieces fell into place. "Kate, hello."

Bending over, he scooped up Kimberly, giving her an exaggerated hug before setting her down. "Would you like to come on in for a bit?" he asked me.

"I've got things to do . . ."

"Just for a little while. Please, I'd like the company."

I wasn't any too eager to be alone right then myself, so I relented. "Just for a little while."

"How about a drink?" he asked, ushering me into the hallway. Then, with a fleeting glance toward my midsection, he stopped. "I forgot. Calistoga okay, or would you prefer milk?" I looked for the mocking expression I was sure would be there in his eyes or in the twist of his mouth, but there was only a gentle reserve.

"Calistoga would be lovely, thanks."

After he'd freshened his own drink, a stiff scotch and water, we went into the living room, which was large and formal, with a vaulted ceiling and massive stone fireplace. At the Christmas party, with a roaring fire and a hundred happy voices, the room had seemed inviting, imbued with the kind of Martha Stewart elegance I'd always admired. But Pepper and I usually settled in the kitchen or out back, so I'd never simply sat in the room, and I realized now, even with the sub-dued lighting and Mozart concerto playing softly in the background, it was a room better suited for large parties than casual conversation.

As if reading my thoughts, Robert set his drink on the table in front of him and looked around. "Pepper never did like this room. Thought it was stiff and un-welcoming. But now it's the one room in the house where I can sit without being reminded of her." Then, with a wry, incongruous smile, he added softly, "I never imagined I'd miss her as much as I do."

"No one's ever prepared for something like this."

"I guess not. But being married to Pepper changed things in hundreds of subtle ways I hadn't really un-derstood." He had been gazing out at the garden, but now shifted his body so that he was facing me, spilling droplets of scotch on the leather upholstery in the pro-cess. "We met on board a cruise ship. Did she tell you that? The first night out. I came back to my cabin after spending the evening, a good part of the night actu-ally, in the bar, and found her sound asleep in my bed. She'd wandered into the wrong cabin, I thought, but I didn't have the heart to wake her. So I sat up the rest of the night watching her sleep. She was so beautiful, blond hair spilling over the pillow, her skin so smooth and soft. Finding her in my bed like that made me feel like a prince in some fairy tale, and with fairy tale–like logic, I fell in love with her before I even knew her name. I'd never been so captivated by a woman."

"What a wonderful, romantic story. She never told me that."

He laughed. "It wasn't until much later, after we were married, that she told me she'd known she was in my room all along. Pepper had a way of getting what she wanted."

I laughed too. "It's certainly a novel strategy."

"Then with Kimberly, well, we had a very good life. And now, suddenly, everything's come undone. I feel so helpless."

"That's understandable. You've experienced a tragic loss." My words sounded stilted, and I searched for something more comforting to add, but Robert appeared not to notice.

"The police seem to be getting nowhere," he continued, absently running a hand through his silver-streaked hair. "They found her jewelry, and now they think it wasn't a random break-in at all, but someone actually intending to kill Pepper." His voice trailed off so that the last few words were barely audible even though I was sitting only a few feet away.

An odd expression, perhaps a momentary stab of confusion and worry, passed quickly over his face, and then his features settled into an impassive heaviness. We sat in silence for a moment, studying the contents of our respective glasses; then Robert drew in a long, shuddery breath. "Forgive me," he said, standing and walking to the window. "It gets to me sometimes."

"Of course it does."

"The police are wrong, I'm sure. It has to have been some drug-crazed psychopath looking for a few bucks to support his habit. I can't believe anyone who knew Pepper would want to kill her."

I nodded, but said nothing. Robert's theory didn't explain the jewelry and wallet in the Dumpster, but he didn't appear to be in the mood for a lesson in logic.

"She was well liked, wasn't she, among the women in town?" he asked.

"Yes, she was." Not the entire truth maybe, but under the circumstances I felt any other answer would have been cruel.

"Good. She wanted to be accepted."

If you were beautiful and rich, I didn't see that you

had to worry much about being accepted, but then I'd never been either.

Robert turned so he was facing me and swallowed hard to clear his throat. "The police keep asking me the same questions over and over. And I have absolutely nothing new to tell them. They even asked me about drugs, if you can imagine. Hell, Pepper wouldn't even let us eat anything with preservatives."

"They said she'd taken a sleeping pill that night, though."

He laughed in a kind of breezy, offhand manner. "I know. I use the stuff sometimes, and I've been trying to convince her that taking a pill now and then isn't the end of the world. What with this Wine Festival and God knows what else on her mind, she'd had trouble sleeping the last few weeks. I guess she finally decided to take my advice."

Draining what was left in his glass, Robert went to the chest in the far corner and poured himself another, this time a straight scotch. "This morning someone from the police came by to ask me about the gardener of all people."

"They think the gardener might have had something to do with her death?" I asked this in a most astonished tone, more than a little relieved that my name had been kept out of it.

"Apparently he's left town." Robert began pacing around the room. "I just wish they would arrest someone and close the case."

"I'm sure it's certainly their highest priority at the moment." Suddenly, and a little guiltily, I remembered the car. My wild flights of inventiveness and sinister speculation earlier that afternoon with Stone now seemed laughable. "Do you by chance know anyone with a blue Jeep Cherokee?"

"No, why?"

"Mrs. Stevenson, the woman who lives diagonally across from you, has seen one parked in front of her house on a number of occasions."

"No, it's no one I know."

Of course Mrs. Stevenson had only said she *thought* it was Robert, and her powers of observation were none too acute. "She thought she saw you talking to the driver the other day."

"Which day was that?"

"Saturday."

He took a moment to think about it. "Oh, right. Tom. He works for me. Comes by to drop off things that need my immediate attention. I guess I never really thought about his car, but it is a Cherokee. A dark one, maybe blue."

Robert sat down on the other end of the couch and turned toward me, smiling so that his whole face relaxed. "I don't know why he parks down there, probably because it's easier to turn around or some such thing. I'll speak to him about it."

I found myself smiling back, feeling a fool for even mentioning the car to Stone. "That's okay. I don't think she minds, she just found it curious, that's all."

"When did she see it last? Before Saturday, that is."

"I don't know, maybe a couple of days before. Why?"

He shrugged. "Just wondering."

I looked at my watch and realized I'd stayed longer than I'd intended. Realized too, that if I hadn't had Anna to think about and a job to go to the next morning, I might have stayed even longer. In many ways visiting with Robert was easier and more pleasant than visiting with Pepper had been.

Just then a phone rang and Robert reached for it. It was one of those cordless things I hadn't even noticed resting there on the walnut table at the end of the couch. He listened in silence, then glanced at me.

"Can I call you back? I'm busy right now." Another pause. "No, a neighbor. One of Pepper's friends."

Without saying good-bye, he hung up and smiled at me. "Work, it never leaves me alone."

"I've got to be going anyway."

Standing, he called to the girls and then walked with me to the door. "I meant it about dinner. Maybe sometime this week? I promise to be better company than I've been so far."

"I'll have to let you know, but I'd like to."

"Thanks for watching Kimberly again. I shouldn't have to impose on you after this."

"It's no problem. Keeps Anna out of my hair when she has a friend to play with."

"And thanks for listening to me. I can see why Pepper was so fond of you." Briefly, he touched my hand, a friendly gesture that lasted just a trifle longer than necessary. "I'll call you about dinner."

10

Although the Courtyard Gallery doesn't open until eleven o'clock, I arrived the next morning a little after nine so that Daria would have ample time to brief me on my duties. But the whole time I was sitting there in one of her straight-back, ultramodern chairs listening to a detailed explanation of the inventory system, I was worrying about having made a fool of myself over the Cherokee the other morning with Michael Stone. And I thought that before he sent half the Walnut Hills police force out on a wild-goose chase, I owed him an update.

The problem was, I didn't want to talk to him. Well, in truth, I did want to, but a sleepless night of soul searching had convinced me it would be better if I didn't. Finally, just before eleven, when Daria went into the back room to check on something, I called the station and asked to leave a message for Lieutenant Stone.

"He's here right now. You can speak to him yourself." It was the same sultry voice as before, the kind that can make the word "hello" sound like an invitation. Unwittingly, I found myself wondering if the body matched the voice.

"Actually I don't really need to talk to him. It's a short message."

But my words were wasted; Stone was already on the line. "Lieutenant Stone here."

"It's Kate Austen," I said, trying hard to sound cool and businesslike.

His voice grew softer. "I was hoping it might be you."

A string of goose bumps rose along my neck and shoulders. So much for good intentions. "I just wanted to leave a message. About the Jeep Cherokee Mrs. Stevenson saw."

"Ah, a business call."

"Of course."

He laughed. "Too bad."

I explained that the car belonged to someone named Tom who worked for Robert.

"And just how did you find out all this?"

"I asked him."

"Asked who?"

"Robert."

Silence.

"I saw him last night, when I dropped off Kimberly."

"I thought I told you to leave the detective work to me," he said. "What if there had been something sinister involved?"

"He was hardly going to do me in with Anna and his own daughter standing there. Besides, he's not like that, he's nice."

Stone grunted. "It isn't likely he would admit to being buddies with a killer anyway."

Suddenly I felt deflated. "I just wanted to save you some trouble."

"Thanks, but I'd rather you let me do my job in my own fashion." He turned away from the phone and

mumbled to somebody nearby. "Sorry, there's another call. I gotta go." I was about ready to hang up,
kicking myself for even calling, when his tone grew
softer. "It's almost lunchtime," he said. "Why don't I
come over there in about half an hour and we'll explore the possibilities."

"You mean about Robert?"

"I mean *all* the possibilities." His tone left little
doubt what possibilities he was most interested in.

"I can't. I'm at work."

"I didn't know you worked."

"Today's my first day. I'm kind of a glorified gofer
at the Courtyard Gallery. A friend of mine owns it." I
looked around to make sure Daria was still out of the
room. "The one who reminds you of a hot oven."

He chuckled. "Then I won't even offer to stop by for
a visit. Thanks for the call."

A little before noon Daria announced that she was
taking me to lunch. Paul could tend the gallery himself.

"It's kind of a welcome-aboard present," she said.
"You won't get treated like this every day."

"I should hope not, I'd get fat."

"In fact," said Paul, looping his long blue-jeaned
legs around the rungs of the cashier's stool, "you'll be
lucky if you even get a lunch break from now on."

Paul's in his late twenties, angular of build, with a
long, thin face and hair the color of cornsilk. There's
something of the imp in him, particularly where
Daria's concerned. That was evident as he leaned his
elbows on the counter and smiled broadly in her direction. "Isn't that so?"

Daria glared at both of us and then picked up her
purse. "We'll be back in a couple of hours."

The restaurant was one of those trendy places serving Southwest cuisine, California style. Small portions and big prices. But it was one of my favorites, with an outdoor eating area and colorful shade umbrellas.

A waiter led us to our table, a slate and glass affair with a single yellow rose in the center. "Can I get you anything from the bar?" he asked.

After listening to the day's by-the-glass specials, Daria ordered a glass of Kendall-Jackson chardonnay, then looked at me expectantly.

"Just water, thank you."

"You're really crazy, Kate," she said when the young man left. "You won't drink, you won't get near a pollutant, and you take vitamin supplements. All to protect a baby you're not going to have anyway."

"What makes you so sure I won't be having it?"

"Because it doesn't make sense, that's why. More than that. You'd be really stupid to go ahead with it, especially if you have any hope of getting Andy back."

"That's a pretty barbaric choice, don't you think? My husband or my child. Sounds like something out of a Grimm fairy tale."

"Don't be so melodramatic," Daria said, taking a sip of wine and eying me over the top of the glass. "It's not a baby yet, and you know it. We've been through this before."

In the abstract, I totally agreed with her. But we weren't talking theory here. This was, or could be, my child. Anna's little brother or sister. And that changed things. Just how much was what I was still trying to decide.

Daria leaned back in her chair, looped a loose strand of hair behind her ear, and shrugged nonchalantly. "I guess it comes down to how much you value your marriage." Her silver earrings caught the sun, so that her words were punctuated with a flicker of light.

"You've got to look at the big picture. And I hate to sound like a nag, but you'd better do it soon or it will be too late."

I sighed deeply, feeling the full weight of her words in the pit of my stomach. "I know. It's just that every time I think I've made up my mind, I start thinking of all the reasons I should do just the opposite."

"Well, it's your life," she said, knitting her brows, "but I surely know what *I* would do in your place."

"But you always know what you want." Daria's world view was clear and crisp, and totally lacking in shades of gray.

"I understand it's not an easy decision Kate, but you've got to think realistically."

"Believe it or not, that's what I'm trying to do."

She reached out a smooth white arm and squeezed my hand affectionately. "I'll stand by you, whatever your decision," she said. "You know that, don't you?"

I nodded, and then swallowed hard to mask the lump in my throat.

When the food arrived, Daria lifted a forkful of grilled eggplant, then set it back on her plate and leaned across the table. "Guess what? Jim's taking me to Mexico in a couple of weeks. Just the two of us. White sand, blue water, lazy afternoons"—she grinned—"and *mucho* opportunity for frolicking."

"Frolicking?"

"Yes, you know." She smiled at her food while I stared at her blankly. "Making love," she said, mouthing the word almost silently. "Honestly, Kate, sometimes you're very difficult to talk to."

"Only when *you* speak in code."

"Anyway, I can hardly wait. We both need the rest."

"Jim did look pretty wrung out the other day."

She nodded. "Poor baby, he's been working *so*

hard. We haven't had any time to ourselves at all." She picked up the bite of eggplant again and this time it made it all the way to her mouth. She chewed dreamily. "He practically ordered me to go out and buy myself a new wardrobe of resort wear. Top to bottom."

"You're lucky. I'm beginning to think good marriages are an endangered species."

She stabbed the air with her fork. "That's why you shouldn't give up on Andy."

"What do you mean, give up? He's the one who left."

"Yes, but you didn't exactly beg him not to go."

"What was I suppose to do?" I asked, pulling myself up straight. "Deck myself out in Saran Wrap? Or maybe coat his body with whipped cream and lick it off, very slowly?"

"That might have done the trick. Really, Kate, sometimes you sound like you don't even care."

"I'm not sure I do anymore."

"You can't mean that?"

"I can, and I do." Although, until that moment I'd never actually put it in those terms. "Aren't you going to eat those corncakes?" I asked, pointing to the two thick fritters on her plate.

She shook her head. "They're loaded with oil."

I reached across the table and speared a corncake. "May I?"

"Be my guest." She moved her wine glass and pushed her plate in my direction. "What's so wrong with Andy? He's intelligent, good looking, considerate, fun."

"And the only person he gives a damn about is himself. He never really even saw me, Daria. It was as though I existed only as a reflection of his own wants and needs."

"Oh, for God's sake. Have you been reading some

feminist rubbish? You wouldn't be in Walnut Hills living the good life if it weren't for him. Nothing is perfect."

I thought of the men I might have married. Larry, my high-school sweetheart, had gained nearly a hundred pounds and lost most of his hair. Jonathan—who'd once told me I was the most exciting woman in the world; I thought, even then, that showed limited vision—was now a struggling playwright recently divorced from wife number four. And Bradley, with sorrowful puppy-dog eyes and a girlfriend in every city across the US, was dead of a drug overdose. All in all I could have done worse, and Daria was certainly right in saying that nothing is perfect. So why was I so increasingly unwilling to give Andy the benefit of the doubt?

"I'm not so sure Andy's going to be coming back home in any case," I told her, reaching for the remaining corncake.

"He'll be back, but he certainly won't stay long if that's your attitude." The waiter came to refill my water glass and Daria ordered a second glass of wine, then leaned across the table toward me. "You're not so young anymore. Being a divorced woman, especially one with children, is no piece of cake. Have you really stopped to consider what it would be like?" She brushed at an invisible speck in the air and shot me a meaningful glance. "Remember Jane Martin? I ran into her the other day and she looks awful. She's living in some rented tract house on the fringe of Walnut Creek, working two boring jobs just to afford that."

"Jane's experience is hardly typical," I reminded her. Until their divorce last year, the Martins had lived in a big, Spanish-style house, complete with pool and tennis courts. Jane had dressed like a model, thrown lavish parties and spent the better part of her week at the club spa being coiffed and manicured and massaged. But her husband was not only running around with his boss's wife, he was dipping into company profits as well. It finally all caught up with him. Jane had been lucky to walk away with her diamonds, which she promptly sold in order to buy food and clothing for her children. My situation wasn't exactly analogous. "Besides," I told her, "money isn't the issue here."

"Well, even if you don't end up in the poorhouse, you'll still be a divorced woman. A castoff. I hate to sound crass, but that's the truth." Daria scowled at the packets of sugar substitute she was busily rearranging. "You know those dreary groups of puffy-eyed women, the kind who spend half an hour with a calculator dividing up their restaurant tab, is that what you want?"

"Good God, listen to yourself. This is the nineties. Things have changed."

"Some things never change." Then she smiled broadly and patted my hand. "Just think it through carefully, Kate. I want you to be happy."

Daria declined dessert for both of us, without so much as a glance in my direction, paid the bill, and then spent ten minutes powdering her nose. And cheeks and eyelids as well.

"We need to stop by Mrs. Van Horn's on the way back," she announced gloomily. "She wants us to take a look at the decor before advising her on art purchases."

This, in itself, was not unusual. The gallery was more than a shop, it was a service, which was one of the factors accounting for its success. But it was clear from Daria's tone that she wasn't looking forward to this visit.

"Sounds like fun," I said, trying for the enthusiasm befitting a new employee.

"Wait until you meet Mrs. Van Horn."

Easing the car carefully out of a tight parking space, Daria headed for the Van Horns on the other side of town. She turned the radio on low and hummed along with a Strauss waltz for a few minutes before asking, "What's the latest on Pepper's murder? The papers have been useless."

"Probably because there's nothing to report."

She shook her head sadly. "I expect there's not much chance they'll ever find him. Some lowlife from Oakland scores a few hundred bucks and it costs Pepper her life."

"Actually, it might not have been a simple break-in. The police now think it might have been someone she knew."

"You're kidding?"

"They found her jewelry and wallet, so they're pretty sure it wasn't a burglary. And she wasn't raped or . . . mutilated, so they have pretty much discounted the thrill killer scenario."

"What d'ya know," Daria said, with a high-pitched laugh. "Being a snooty bitch is getting more dangerous by the day."

"She wasn't that bad."

"Maybe not to you." Daria paused and frowned. "She'd come waltzing into the gallery like it was her own private showroom, send me scurrying off looking for just the right little thing, then wrinkle up that plastic nose of hers and say, 'No, that's not really what I had in mind.' And then at the club, she'd look right through me as though she didn't have the foggiest idea who I was."

"Well, she had her faults, but she had her good points too."

Daria looked at me, then back at the road. We stopped at a red light and Daria clicked her nails on the wheel. "So," she said, after a minute, "who's on the suspect list?"

"Well, let's see. There's Connie." Daria looked at me like I was crazy. "Because she had a key. And then there's the gardener."

"What did Pepper do to him, load up on plastic daffodils?"

"And maybe Robert."

"Be serious."

"I know. But the husband is always a possible suspect." This last I said in my best television-cop monotone, which didn't elicit so much as a smirk from Daria.

"I've never been fond of the man myself," she confided, "too prissy for my taste. But I can't imagine him as a murderer either. Besides, he was probably at a client dinner or something that night. Airtight alibi and all."

"He was at work, but apparently no one saw him."

"Really?"

I nodded.

"Interesting." She pulled into the Van Horns' long, tree-studded drive. "You get all this information from that Detective . . . what's his name . . . ?"

"Stone."

I must have blushed because she raised a perfectly penciled brow.

"This isn't strictly a business relationship, I gather."

"I don't know what it is."

She gave me one of those chilling looks I've never mastered myself. "Just don't forget you're married."

"Married, sort of."

"Married enough." She parked the car. "You don't want to risk all you've got just for a quick fling with some hard, sweaty body, do you?"

I shrugged, but I thought I knew the answer.

11

“This is it?” I asked, when Daria pulled to a stop. I blinked and looked again. Before me stood a large, imposing castle. Or rather, a Disneyland replica of a castle, complete with turrets and arched doorways. Only instead of ancient stone and finely crafted embellishments, the exterior was a fresh, mauvish stucco embedded with flecks of shiny mica. And replacing the moat and drawbridge were a five-car garage and a flagstone walkway lined with juniper bushes.

“It’s one of McGregory’s creations. There’s another just like it up the road a bit.”

“He found *two* people willing to buy something like that?”

“Apparently so. And it wasn’t cheap either.”

That much I could believe. “What’s she looking for in the way of art,” I asked as we walked to the door, “a Rembrandt framed in Day-Glo acrylic?”

“Possibly.”

The inside was not much better. Floor-length balloon drapes of heavy velvet, brocade upholstery, crystal chandeliers. And on the wall adjacent to the fireplace, an ultramodern, wall-size home entertainment center of bleached oak.

"Eclectic," I whispered to Daria.

"Very."

Mrs. Van Horn patted her extremely blond and perfectly coiffed head. "Please call me Sondra," she said when we were seated around the asymmetric marble coffee table. "That's with an *o* not an *a.*" She smiled, revealing a set of even, bright white teeth. "Can I get you ladies anything? Coffee? Tea? Or some pear tart, I just bought it this morning."

"Thank you," Daria replied, again speaking for both of us, "but we've just had lunch."

Sondra Van Horn was probably in her late fifties, but, as the saying goes, well preserved. Or well repaired. Her skin had the tight look of a woman who has treated herself to one too many facelifts, and God knows what else. Her figure was trim, if not firm, and her wardrobe conspicuously up to date.

"You can see this is going to be quite a job," she said, lifting a heavily jeweled hand and gesturing broadly to the four walls. "There is so much empty space."

In fact, I thought there was not quite enough, but then our tastes obviously differed.

"And it's not just this room, you know," she continued. "There's the entry hall, the dining room, and the rooms at the back of the house." She laughed, a high, girlish laugh. "We'll leave the upstairs for a later date. Well, would you like the tour?"

For the next hour she clicked around the house in her backless high-heel pumps, pointing out blank walls and making sure we understood the mood she wished to create. Her taste ran to the traditional, she said, but she was willing to consider almost anything as long as it "worked"—a word she must have repeated at least a dozen times during the tour. Pieces that caught your eye and made a statement, that was what she was looking for.

"Good art can make or break a decor, don't you think?" she asked, stepping around a life-size porcelain hunting dog. "Of course, we'll have to consider the color scheme of each room. They're all different, as you've probably noticed."

Indeed it would have been difficult not to do so.

We ended the tour in the billiard room—family room to us everyday folk—and were just beginning to discuss Sondra's art budget when a door at the back of the house closed and two balls of white fluff with rhinestone collars—I assumed they were rhinestone, although they might well have been diamond—scurried into the room, yapping loudly.

"Rosa must be back. She's our maid." Sondra bent down to greet the new arrivals, clucking at them in a squeaky, singsong voice. "How's my babies? Was Auntie Rosa good to you on your little walkie?" She stood up then and introduced us to Duke and Duchess, who looked exactly alike except that Duchess had a yellow bow perched on the top of her head. Sondra's black silk pantsuit, trimmed in gold lamé, was now dusted with white hairs as well, but she seemed not to notice.

The dogs ignored Daria but sniffed at my feet and eyed me suspiciously. "They probably smell Max," I explained.

"Oh, you have a dog too?" Clearly, I had moved up a notch in Sondra's eyes. "Is he as cute as these two snookums?"

"He's . . . uh, different."

"You know, dear, you look awfully familiar. I think we've met before." Mouth pursed in thought, she studied me. "Ah, the Livingstons' Christmas party last year. Could that have been it?"

"Possibly, I was there."

"Kate lives next door to the Livingstons'," Daria offered, as if my presence at such an elite gathering demanded explanation.

"Terribly tragic, wasn't it, about dear Pepper?"

While Daria and I murmured our agreement, the dogs fell into a heap at the edge of the doorway.

"These times we live in . . ." Sondra shook her head sadly. "Of course, nothing like that could happen here at our place. We have a state-of-the-art alarm system."

"That's what's so strange," I said. "The Livingstons have one too."

Daria snorted. "Doesn't do much good if you forget to use it."

"Pepper was usually so careful about that, though."

"Oh, for goodness' sake, Kate, she wasn't infallible."

"You know," said Sondra thoughtfully, "she *was* acting kind of odd during the last couple of weeks. Kind of distracted and short tempered. We were both on the Sunshine House board," Sondra explained, "and then, of course, I used to run into her quite frequently at the club. Then she took that doozer of a spill, bruised her arm so badly she had to excuse herself from a board meeting to take some aspirin."

"Any idea what was going on?" I asked.

"No, none at all. I mentioned it to her once, very casually of course, just so she'd know she could come talk to me if she wanted. But she got all uppity and said she didn't think I should concern myself with her life."

"That's Pepper all right," Daria huffed. "And I doubt there was anything bothering her. She was probably just preoccupied with spending money and zipping around in that fancy car of hers."

Sondra appeared to miss the nasty tone in Daria's

voice. She laughed lightly, and said, "Well, she did like to do that. Though I'm hardly one to talk, am I?"

The phone rang and Sondra padded off to answer it, followed by Duke and Duchess. Daria and I measured rooms, took notes and then, mouthing a silent good-bye to Sondra, who was still on the phone, sneaked out the door before the dogs noticed us.

"Whatever are you going to show her?" I asked, thinking of the lovely works which filled Daria's gallery. None of them seemed the sort of thing Sondra had in mind.

"Nothing."

"Nothing?"

"I'm not going to show her anything, you are. This is your first assignment at Courtyard Galleries."

I looked over to see if she was joking, but apparently she was serious. "Thanks a lot."

"You'll manage. Somehow."

While Daria drove, I closed my eyes and tried to picture each of the rooms again, hoping for inspiration. Nothing.

"It was interesting," Daria said, slowing for a hairpin turn, "what Mrs.—what Sondra—had to say about Pepper, don't you think?"

I was still waiting for a revelation from the art god, and merely nodded.

"It made me remember, one day about three weeks ago when we were showering at the club, I noticed Pepper had two big bruises, one on her thigh, another on her shoulder. And a gash on her forehead."

I remembered the gash. She had slipped on one of Kimberly's toys and hit her head on the kitchen counter. "So?" The living room would be the hardest, I thought. It called out for big pieces, but the room was already so overdone I didn't want to add to the jumble.

"She said she fell down the stairs, but I don't think she was telling the truth. Something about the way she said it, kind of flip but agitated at the same time."

Pepper had clearly misled one of us, maybe both, but I wasn't sure what Daria was getting at. "She didn't die of internal injuries."

"That's not what I meant." Daria hesitated. "It's just an idea, probably a stupid one, but . . . but what if the bruises were . . . well, what if someone hit her, roughed her up a bit. And maybe that was just a prelude to killing her."

"Oh, come on, she'd have called the police if anyone hit her."

Daria shrugged dramatically. "Not necessarily. Especially if it was someone she knew. Someone she had an ongoing relationship with."

"Robert?" She had my full attention now.

"It certainly wasn't her hairdresser."

"But you said yourself you couldn't see him as a murderer."

"I couldn't, and I'm not sure I do even now, but that was before I realized the police think the killer is someone she knew." Daria braked abruptly, barely avoiding the car in front, which had stopped to make a U-turn in the middle of the road. "It makes sense, if you think about it. Robert has no alibi for the night she was killed, and they say a large percentage of crimes are committed by the spouse."

"That's hardly reason enough to accuse him."

"I wasn't accusing him. I'm just saying maybe he should be investigated." Daria tapped the wheel. "It would explain why the police didn't find any unusual fingerprints at the scene."

I nodded, but without conviction.

"And then there's that car her neighbor, Mrs. What's-her-name saw."

"Mrs. Stevenson, but it turns out the car belongs to someone who works for Robert."

Daria frowned, and then continued in a low, almost whispery voice. "Robert does have a temper, you know. Everyone thinks he's so polished and urbane, but he can be pretty nasty. Why, just a couple of weeks ago at the Patersons' party . . ." She hesitated, but without Mary Nell's embarrassment. "You weren't there, so I know you missed this. Well, there's this little alcove off the living room, and I was sitting in the corner catching my breath when Pepper and Robert stopped right at the entrance. They were arguing about something. Robert grabbed her wrist and twisted it. His eyes were like steel. The man was *angry*. Not that he didn't have his reasons, I'm sure."

"Even loving husbands and wives sometimes fight," I said. Although I wasn't sure the observation applied to Daria and Jim.

Flicking a strand of hair from her face, Daria turned to me, arched her brows and asked, "What does your little police friend think?"

"Quit needling me, will you?"

"Aha," she said with a wide smirk. "You wouldn't react that way if you weren't already feeling guilty."

I ignored the smirk, and the remark. "Why would Robert want to kill Pepper?"

"How should I know? Maybe he just got tired of her selfish attitude."

I twisted my mouth and rolled my eyes the way Anna does when she thinks I've been totally outlandish. "You never give up, do you?"

"Anyway, it wouldn't hurt to have the police keep an eye on Robert. You know what they say about these aloof, repressed types . . ." Daria let her voice trail off and finished the sentence with upraised hands.

Somehow I pictured Robert going for the jugular in

divorce court more readily than in the flesh, but then murder was hardly an exercise in rationality.

I spent the next hour updating the gallery mailing list and mulling over Daria's suspicions, which I had to admit, were not as outrageous as they at first appeared. If Pepper had been killed by someone she knew, especially by someone with access to the house, it limited the field quite a bit. How many people, even those who profess to loathe you, in the final analysis care enough to kill you?

Finally, I picked up the phone and called Sharon, whose husband George was an old school buddy of Robert's. Aside from our mutual involvement in the nursery school, we didn't know each other well—the unfortunate, but natural consequence of her having a son, and I, a daughter. But I'd always liked Sharon and felt reasonably sure she wouldn't be offended by my call. Sharon was rarely offended by anything.

"Can I talk to you sometime, about Pepper?" I asked when she had finally wrestled the phone from Kyle.

"Sure, you want to come over right now?"

"I'm at work."

"How about coming by for dinner then? George is out of town, and I'm always hungry for adult company when he's gone."

We agreed that I would pick up a pizza from Round Table and she would make a salad. Then, feeling quite pleased with myself, I finished the mailing list, flipped through a stack of paintings—two might "work" for Sondra—and picked Anna up at school, after assuring Mrs. Duval, the head teacher, that Anna did, in fact, know her left from her right, and would, I was confident, eventually learn to write her letters on the line.

"Guess what," I told her as we drove home. "We're

going to have dinner tonight with Kyle Covington and his mom.''

She gagged. "Yuk and double yuk."

"We're having pizza."

Silence.

"And I'll get some ice cream and chocolate sauce for dessert."

She didn't look exactly happy, but she wasn't on the verge of a tantrum either.

Promptly at six o'clock I rang Sharon's bell, balancing a hot pizza in one hand and a bag from Baskin Robbins in the other. Anna was unable to help me because her own arms were filled with Barbie dolls.

"I don't think Kyle likes to play Barbie," I'd cautioned as we left home.

"I know," she'd told me with a wide smile. "He hates them."

Kyle opened the door for us and gave Anna a glare which matched her own. He was a gangly, gap-toothed kid with a head of unruly reddish hair. He glared a moment longer, then turned abruptly and left, without a word. Anna's glare shifted to me as we followed him down the hallway.

While Anna and Kyle made faces at each other over cheese and pepperoni, Sharon and I talked about the tribulations of raising children in the nineties, compared notes on favorite authors, and delighted in finding that we had more in common that we'd known. Then she put a movie in the VCR and set the children down in front of it, with a strict warning that they'd better behave themselves if they wanted dessert. Handing me a cup of coffee, she led the way to the living room.

The Covington house was decorated in what could

only be called shabby chic. The upholstery was faded, the rugs worn, the wooden furniture amply nicked; and there were books and magazines stacked everywhere. Even the houseplants managed to look weary. But the total effect was one of relaxed elegance. Charm jumped out at you from every nook and cranny. Somehow the same imperfections that made my own house appear pitiful and a touch dingy even when it had just been cleaned, gave the Covingtons' home character, attesting to the fact that the folk who lived there had more important things to do than decorate.

Sharon settled herself into an overstuffed chair and tucked her bare feet up under her. She made a feeble effort to brush the hair out of her eyes, but it bounced right back. Her hair was dark, shortish, and so naturally curly that it tended to have a mind of its own. With her fair, freckled skin and gamine face, she wasn't what you'd call a beauty, but had looks that were appealing all the same. Sort of the Hollywood director's dream for the girl next door.

"Now," she said, twisting to look at me. "What was it you wanted to know about Pepper?"

"It's not about Pepper, actually, but Robert." I paused, feeling like something of a jerk, then forged ahead. "What's he like?"

If she thought the question odd, she gave no indication. "Cautious, deliberate, demanding, bright, a stickler for details, very proper. And not a heck of a lot of fun. He likes to be in control, and he likes to be right. But for all that, I like him. He's a true gentleman and knows how to turn on the charm." Holding her mug with both hands, she sipped her coffee thoughtfully, then shrugged. "He's really more George's friend than mine. Although we occasionally got together as couples, Pepper and I never really hit it off."

"But you've known him a long time?"

"George has. They went to boarding school together and then ended up at the same college. I met him once or twice way back when—and he was at our wedding—but until he and Pepper moved to Walnut Hills I never really talked to him." She laughed. "I still don't. He and George talk a lot about the tax code and rates of return. I generally don't pay much attention."

"So you didn't know Pepper before she married Robert?"

"Never met her until they moved out here. George was kind of miffed that we didn't even learn about the marriage until after it was all said and done. I gather it was kind of a spur of the moment thing. No real wedding at all."

I set my cup down on the table in front of me and thought how best to phrase my next question, but nothing seemed just right. "Did they get along okay?"

"As well as most couples, I think. They didn't argue or try to one-up each other in public, if that's what you mean. In fact, I remember noticing once the fond way Robert draped an arm over Pepper's shoulder as he was talking. It must have been one of those times when I'd had it up to here with George's sense of propriety." Sharon punched the pillow at the back of the chair and shifted her position before continuing. "They were certainly no Romeo and Juliet, but then who is after a few years of marriage?"

The next probe felt even more awkward, but I plunged ahead anyway. "I've heard rumors that Pepper might have been having an affair."

Sharon shrugged. "It wouldn't have surprised me."

Something must have shown on my face because she laughed.

"It's not uncommon you know." The laugh passed, but the gleam in her eye remained.

"You?"

"Don't sound so shocked."

I'm not sure I was shocked, exactly. More like amazed, and maybe a little awed. I was beginning to think I was the only woman in Walnut Hills leading a mundane, puritanical life. Except, of course, for Daria, who wasn't so much puritanical as blinded by love.

"Men like Robert and George," Sharon explained, "they're so sober and sedate. They make wonderful husbands, but lousy soul mates. And only passable lovers. Technically competent, but sadly lacking in passion."

I thought of Andy who had plenty of passion, all of it focused on himself. It wasn't even clear to me that he was technically competent, but I'd never thought of filling the void. Until recently that is.

"Why are you so interested in Robert? Are you planning to move in on him too?" she asked.

"Too?"

"Susie Sullivan. She was over here yesterday, pumping me with all kinds of questions." She leaned forward and patted me on the knee. "Kate, you can do better than Robert. He's worse than George, by a long shot."

A half-giggle rose up in my throat and I almost choked on a mouthful of coffee. "I have absolutely no romantic interest in Robert. He's definitely not my type." And besides, I wasn't the kind of woman who played around, was I?

Sharon studied me, trying to determine if I was telling the truth. "So why all the questions?"

"This sounds crazy I know, but I never knew him very well and . . ." I stopped and took a deep breath. "And it crossed my mind that he might have had something to do with Pepper's death."

She laughed loudly. "Robert? You've got to be kidding. If *he* were the one who had been killed, I might suspect Pepper, but never the other way around. It just isn't his style."

"That was my thinking too, but anything's possible. And he did have a temper I've heard."

She shrugged. "No worse than normal. Besides, *why* would he do it?"

"How would Robert take it if he found out Pepper was seeing another man?"

"I don't imagine he'd be too happy about it, but I can't see him *killing* her for God's sake. Besides, I don't know how he'd ever find out unless she told him. He has a fine eye for details which have a financial implication, but everything else seems to float by him. She'd have to practically bring her lover into bed with him before he'd notice."

"Several people have told me they saw bruises on Pepper's arms and legs."

She shook her head, but more in bewilderment than denial. "I don't know, it sounds pretty unbelievable. Still, I guess none of us can ever really know what goes on in another's head, can we?"

It was an idea I would have liked to explore further, but just then Anna and Kyle came in to announce that the movie was over and since they'd been *so* good, could they please have extra ice cream.

Our conversation turned to less weighty matters, and when the ice cream was gone Anna and I got ready to leave.

"By the way," Sharon told me at the door, "I've been meaning to tell you. My sister ran into an Andy Austen from Walnut Hills last week when she was in Switzerland, of all places, at this little out-of-the-way restaurant that had been written up in *Gourmet*. That's your husband, isn't it?"

I nodded. "It's a small world."

"He was with his cousin. Apparently she's a famous Italian fashion model. If she ever comes for a visit I'd love to meet her."

I promised I'd introduce them, though of course I never would. Couldn't, in fact. Andy had no female cousins.

12

Warm water pounded my back, easing the cricks and cramps resulting from a troubled night's sleep. You don't know anything for sure, I told myself. Maybe Andy really does have an Italian cousin, some distant relation he looked up on the spur of the moment. Maybe, I answered right back, but I doubt it. And some things you don't need to know *for sure*. High probability is enough.

Guiltily, I let the water run, even after I had soaped and rinsed my body and thoroughly washed my hair. California's water situation was going from bad to worse as one dry winter followed another, and our daily water allotment, already curtailed, was due to be cut even further now that summer was approaching. Just a minute longer, I promised myself—repeatedly, for a full ten minutes. Fortunately, Max's frantic barking saved me from a record-high utility bill, and maybe even a visit from the water police. A moment later, as I was stepping from the shower, Anna peered into the bathroom.

"There's a man at the door for you."

"Anna!" My voice was shrill and, I hoped, harsh. "I've told you time and again not to open the door to strangers." God only knew what wily con artist was, at that very moment, prowling around the front rooms of the house, trying to sniff out the Ming vases and silver tea sets we had so wisely put off buying.

"It's that same man."

Grabbing my terry robe, another of Andy's castoffs, I trudged down the hallway, hair dripping wet. In my haste, I didn't bother to think about Anna's words, using the precious seconds instead to formulate a suitably nasty threat about calling the police.

But they were already here.

Michael Stone slouched against the closed door, rubbing Max's ears. "Good morning, Kate. I wanted to catch you before you left for work."

Wiping away the rivulet of water which snaked down my cheek, I pulled the robe tighter around my middle and retied the sash. "Here I am."

"I guess you were in the shower."

"You're very observant."

"And you're very pretty, even dripping wet. Especially dripping wet in fact."

"Listen, I don't have a lot of time this morning."

"That's okay, neither do I. But I'll wait if you want to dry off first."

A little puddle was forming at the base of my feet, but I ignored it and tried my best to glower.

Michael waited, a lopsided grin creasing his face. "And if you keep tugging at that robe," he drawled, "it's going to rip right in two."

I knew when I was outgunned. "I'll just be a minute," I told him, trying for a hostess-in-control formality. "You can make yourself some coffee if you'd like. The filters are in the drawer next to the sink."

Ten minutes later, hair damp but no longer dripping, makeup artfully in place, and dressed, for a change, in something other than sweats, I waltzed into the kitchen. Stone eyed me for a moment, then, with an appreciative grin, handed me a cup of hot coffee.

"You're very pretty when you're not dripping wet too."

Ignoring him, I sat down at the table. "Now, what's all this about?"

He sat down across from me and sipped his coffee. "I wanted to see if you'd have dinner with me."

"Tonight?"

"Or tomorrow, if you can't make it tonight."

"Evenings are kind of hard for me. Baby sitters, you know."

There was that cocky grin again. "How about lunch then?"

"I work, remember?"

"Every day?"

"Except weekends and Wednesdays."

"Great, tomorrow then. I'll pick you up about eleven-thirty."

I watched his eyes crinkle with pleasure; then I set my cup on the table and laughed too. "Does this qualify as police harassment?"

"You haven't seen anything yet," Michael said with a wink. He leaned back in his chair. "Oh, there was another thing, too. There's no Tom working for Robert, and no one who drives a Jeep Cherokee, blue or otherwise." He waited, gauging my reaction. "Be careful Kate. If you play with fire you're bound to get burned."

I thought his warning applicable to numerous areas of my life right then, and Robert was the one that worried me least.

Several times that afternoon and the next morning I picked up the phone to cancel, but in between, I savored the giddiness of anticipation. And in an odd moment here and there, I found time to contemplate what I knew of Robert and what I did not. Why he might have lied to me about the car. All in all, it was a long twenty-four hours.

Promptly at eleven-thirty the next day, Stone arrived at my doorstep, whistling softly under his breath. We drove to Concord and pulled up in front of a newish-looking complex of garden apartments.

"What's this?" I asked.

"My apartment."

I looked at him blankly.

"A friend's actually, but I'm staying here while he's on assignment back East. Barbara has the house."

"What about lunch?"

He grinned. "Don't worry, I'm a wonderful cook." His grin grew wider. "Among other things."

"I'm not sure this is such a good idea."

"That's because you haven't tasted one of my omelettes yet. They're the best in the West, guaranteed."

Flipping his jacket over his shoulder, Michael began whistling again, a breezy, upbeat tune. He continued to whistle as we walked up the main path and turned left to his front door, but I noticed that his hand trembled as he put the key in the lock. It was that, I think, that finally did it. There was no longer a decision to be made.

Once inside, Michael kissed me lightly, just barely brushing my lips with his, and then, when I didn't protest, he pulled me tight against him and kissed me again, a longer, more serious kiss that seemed to go on almost forever.

And thus it was that I found myself at high noon in the middle of the week, when I should have been pulling weeds or folding laundry, recklessly tossing my carefully selected wardrobe onto the floor.

Michael, who had helped with the tossing, pulled me onto the bed next to him and kissed first one eye, then the other. As he was working his way toward my mouth, I suddenly giggled, and he looked stricken.

"It's not you," I hastened to explain. "It's the bed. I've never slept on a waterbed, much less made love on one. It feels as though I'm about ready to bounce off onto the floor."

"It does take some getting used to."

I bit my lip. "It's that—and the fact that I'm nervous as hell."

With soft, cool fingers, he brushed the hair from my face. "You don't have to be nervous, Kate."

"But I am."

Michael moved to the left and gently tucked the pillow around my head. Then propped himself on an elbow next to me and began stroking my body with a slow, soft touch. "You tell me when you stop feeling nervous, okay?"

In the end, I didn't have to tell him, it was obvious. But Michael didn't rush anything, even then.

"I want you to enjoy this," he murmured, his breath warm on my neck.

"I am," I murmured back, and later, curled beside him, my head nestled in the hollow of his shoulder, I told him again. "I don't remember when I've felt this good."

"I wasn't a complete incompetent then?"

"Hardly." I ran a hand over his chest and down to the inside of his thigh, feeling the hard curves of his body beneath my fingers. "In fact, you were terrific."

"So were you, Kate. I can't begin to tell you how terrific."

"Yes you can—go ahead and try."

But he just grinned. "You hungry?"

"You mean food?"

"I invited you for lunch, didn't I?"

"It wasn't just a ploy to get me into bed?"

"That too, but I did get stuff for lunch. In case you said no."

I sighed contentedly. "Maybe later. I don't think I'm ready to move just yet."

"Good, neither am I."

We nestled in comfortable silence, soaking up the pleasure of intimacy. After a time Michael leaned across and kissed me on the chin.

"Kate?"

"Hmm."

"I know it's a little late to be asking, but are you on the pill or anything?"

I shook my head. "But it doesn't matter, I'm already pregnant."

There was a moment of absolute stillness, like the ringing silence that follows the crash of good crystal. Then he rolled onto his back, hands behind his head, and stared at the ceiling.

"Jesus, Kate, you might have said something earlier."

"The timing never seemed quite right."

"Well, you certainly waited for an opportune moment."

"Does it bother you?"

"Of course it does. I guess. I mean, it *should*, shouldn't it?"

In truth, it had barely crossed my mind. And that was a frightening realization. During all those moments when I'd entertained erotic fantasies of Michael Stone, I'd never once thought about what came next. A bright, blinding flash of passion—and then a Hollywood fadeout. But in real life there is no fadeout.

"I'm sorry." I longed to reach out and touch him, but I was afraid he would pull away.

"When *were* you going to tell me?"

When I knew you better, I thought. But that was a heck of a thing to say to a man who's lying naked in bed with you.

"Or maybe this is just a quick roll in the hay for you," he said coolly. "No need to get personal. Just have your fun and be gone. Is that what you're thinking? Because that's certainly not the way I see it."

"And that's not the way it is."

Michael continued to stare at the ceiling, his jaw tensed.

"Really, I am sorry," I said again, this time braving a quick kiss. "It's just that it's kind of an awkward thing to bring up, in these particular circumstances I mean."

He grunted and then, with a shy smile that reached all the way to his eyes, rolled back to face me. "Actually," he said, "it wouldn't have made any difference. I've been thinking about this since that first morning I met you. And lately, I've thought of little else. You could have told me you were from another planet and I wouldn't have cared." His eyes skimmed the length of my body. "You don't look pregnant though."

To my eye, I did, but he had no way of knowing that the rounded belly and full breasts before him were not the real me. "Not quite two months," I told him. And then, without meaning to, I also told him about Andy and how mixed up everything was. My eyes began to smart, and then suddenly, unexpectedly, my cheeks were wet with genuine tears.

"Geez, Kate, I'm sorry. I didn't mean to make things harder for you."

"You haven't," I managed to burble between shallow, uneven breaths. "You've made me very happy."

Michael leaned over and kissed me again, on the

forehead. "I can make you even happier," he said. "Want me to show you?"

We did, finally, get lunch. And Michael was absolutely right about his omelettes. They were superb. We sat on the little deck off the kitchen, balancing our plates on our knees, stealing kisses between bites.

"What are you thinking?" he asked, spearing a piece of mushroom with his fork.

I shrugged. "Nothing much."

"Then why are you frowning?"

"Was I? I'm sorry. It's not the company, I assure you."

Setting his plate on the bench next to him, Michael reached for my free hand and held it between his own. I could feel him looking at me even though my head was turned. "You're the first woman I've been with since Barbara left," he said slowly. "The first woman I've wanted to be with."

I nodded and smiled weakly, not trusting myself to speak.

"I don't want to rush you, Kate. I know how hard it is. And I don't want you to feel uncomfortable." His voice was soft and low, like a gentle summer rain. "But I can tell when something's right."

"Please, let's not talk about it now."

"We're going to have to talk about it sometime."

I nodded. "But not right now, okay?"

With a quick squeeze, he released my hand and leaned back, stretching his long frame. "Okay. What shall we talk about then?"

"Tell me what's new with the investigation," I said, taking a bite of lettuce.

"Good grief. Here I am feeling like a million bucks,

and you have to bring up that." But he laughed and resumed eating.

"Well?"

"Let's see. I told you yesterday about there being no one in Robert's office who drives a Jeep Cherokee." I nodded. "Then there's Mrs. Aldridge, over on Chestnut Street, who says when she was at Pepper's one afternoon, a man selling driveway cleaner came to the door and turned belligerent when Pepper declined a demonstration. Mrs. Curtis, who lives a couple of houses to the east of you, reports a 'suspicious-looking Mexican boy' delivering fliers to the houses on the street. We still haven't been able to locate Tony Sheris, but we've run a check on him and he comes out clean." Michael gazed at the cloudless sky for a moment. "Oh, and we've questioned a lot of Pepper's friends. No one has any idea who she might have been seeing. Exciting stuff, no?"

"So Tony's not a suspect and Robert is?" I asked, cutting to the core of the matter.

"We're not ruling out anyone just yet."

I took a deep breath, and then, somewhat reluctantly, told him about Daria's conjecturing. It all sounded pretty farfetched, but Robert *had* lied to me about the car, and it was becoming pretty clear that something had been troubling Pepper.

Michael rocked back in his chair and listened, grinning goofily. When I finished, he leaned forward so that his face was only inches from mine. "You have the most amazing green eyes," he whispered. "They're soft and deep, like the first grass of spring."

"And you," I told him sternly, "have the most amazing way of changing the subject." But I fluttered my lashes and turned my "amazing green eyes" to meet his gaze. "I take it you don't think much of Daria's scenario."

Michael shrugged. "Anything's possible."

We sat in silence for several minutes. Michael continued to look steadily in my direction, the hint of a smile playing at the corners of his mouth, while I searched my mind for a safe topic of conversation.

"Tony's behavior still strikes me as suspicious," I said finally. "Why would he just pick up and leave like that if he wasn't involved in Pepper's death?"

"Who knows."

"Surely there must be someone he was friendly with, someone who knows where he's gone."

"No one we've been able to locate." Michael sat up straight and took a long gulp of beer. "You'd really rather talk about all this stuff, than us?"

"At the moment anyway. Murder's a lot less scary."

A smile tugged at the corners of his mouth. "Okay, we'll do it your way." He stood and walked to the railing. "Tony moved to this area about eight months ago from Minnesota. He graduated from high school last year with mediocre grades, but he was never a troublemaker. His mother was killed when he was ten, and his dad's an alcoholic who works odd jobs only long enough to buy another bottle. Somehow Tony seems to have come through it all in one piece. People from his home town have only nice things to say about him, although no one seems to have known him all that well."

"What about the apartment in Berkeley?"

"The manager says he was an ideal tenant. Kept the place clean and never caused any trouble. Doesn't know where he's moved to though."

I thought of the fresh, young face at the back of the church. The high cheekbones, the sun-bleached hair, the timid manner. He certainly didn't *look* like a killer, but why else would he just disappear like that? "Have you tried asking at nurseries or garden centers?" I asked. "He must have worked for someone besides Pepper."

Michael shook his head. "Not that we've been able to discover, although he did take on some cleanup work for the city and he helped on a small landscape job for one of the spec houses Burt McGregory is building."

"McGregory!" I sat up and cleared my throat. "That's the man who threatened Pepper, you know, because of her involvement with the Save Our Hills Committee."

Michael's eyes narrowed, and he cocked his head to the side. "I know," he said evenly.

I slouched back down. "Sorry."

He studied his bottle for a moment, picking at the label with his fingernail. "Tell me once more, how long had you known Pepper?"

"Two years. Roughly."

"Did she talk much about her past?"

"I'm sure she must have, but I don't remember anything in particular. Why?"

Michael appeared to be weighing something. "Same rules as before. This is strictly confidential, okay?"

"You think just because I slept with you, I can't be trusted? Maybe it was all a ploy to get the inside scoop on Pepper's murder for the *Walnut Hills Sun?*"

A gentle smile crossed his face. "No, that's not what I think."

"Good. So tell me what this is all about."

"Pepper Livingston wasn't who she pretended to be."

"Who is?"

He looked mildly annoyed. "Her real name was Rosalie Simms, and she was raised in Ohio, not on Long Island. She ran away from home when she was sixteen, was arrested once for petty theft and twice for prostitution. Along the way she also made a couple of porno films, strictly low-grade stuff."

"There's any other kind?"

He patted my knee. "There certainly is." Then he removed his hand from my knee and rubbed his chin. "In nineteen-seventy-five she was peripherally involved in an armed robbery in which two men were killed. By cooperating with the DA, she got off with parole, but her testimony put her boyfriend behind bars."

"You're joking."

"You think I'd joke about something like this?" He was clearly offended.

"No, I guess not." But I didn't see how it could be true either. The woman he described was nothing like Pepper. "There must be some mistake. Maybe somebody who looked like her or had the same name. I never believed Pepper was her given name anyway."

"No mistake. We'd have had all this sooner except for some glitch with the central computer." He fell silent a minute, then added, "That's not all. The boyfriend, Jake Turbino, has just been released on parole. He arrived in San Francisco two weeks ago."

"Oh, my God, poor Pepper." As stunned as I was by Michael's revelations, what I felt most was a new found sympathy for this woman, the friend I had never really known. "You've questioned him? This Jake Turbino?"

Michael glared at me, but there was a twinkle in his eye. "Of course we've questioned him."

"And?"

"Says he didn't even know Pepper, Rosalie that is, was living in California."

"Certainly you're not going to—"

Hand raised in protest, Michael interrupted. "No, we're not going to let it go at that. Jake was apparently a model prisoner, though. Took Jesus Christ as his savior and all. Swears he bears no grudge for the years he spent in prison. But he can't, or won't, tell us what he was doing the night she was killed."

Michael went inside for a moment and came back with a manila folder from which he extracted two photographs.

"This is the guy. Have you seen him before?"

Taking the photos, I turned so that my body blocked the glare of the sun, and studied them. They were obviously prison shots. Head only, one full face, the other a side view. Jake had dark eyes, hair dusted with gray, and surprisingly delicate features despite his heavy frame. Definitely not a mobster face. Something about the mouth caught my attention, but the longer I looked the more certain I was that I had never seen the man before.

"No, I don't recognize him."

Michael retrieved the pictures and stuck them back in his folder. "We'll be asking other neighbors and friends of Pepper. Hopefully we'll be able to find someone who does recognize him." He looked pleased, like a cat with his eye on an unsuspecting canary. "This just may be the big break we've been waiting for."

We carried the dishes into the kitchen, where Michael insisted we leave them for him to wash later. Wrapping my arms around his waist, I pressed my head against his chest. The scent of beer and sex and aftershave mingled in my head and filled me with a curious sense of peace.

"Thanks," I said, faltering somewhat with even so simple a statement.

"It's nothing. I do dishes all the time."

"That's not what I meant."

"Oh?"

"It was the nicest lunch I ever had."

He kissed my forehead, and then the tip of my nose. "Likewise," he said softly.

Then he drove me home.

"When's your next day off?" Michael asked as he turned the car onto my street.

"Saturday. But Anna's home then."

"Send her to a friend's."

"It's not that easy."

He looked skeptical.

"She has her own, very strong, opinions about how she does and does not want to spend her days."

"So be persuasive," he said.

I leaned over and kissed him quickly, then got out. "I'll try."

The phone was ringing as I let myself in. Guiltily I raced for it, worried suddenly that something had happened to Anna. What if the hospital had been trying to reach me all afternoon? Calling repeatedly, frantically, the whole time I was giving way to unbridled lust.

But it was only Susie Sullivan calling to invite me to a dinner party for Robert. "Nothing elaborate," she said. "But I do think the poor man needs our support. I was over there the other day to take him a lasagna, and he just seemed so . . . so lonely. Oh, wait a minute, there's a call on my other line." The phone clicked and I was left holding a silent receiver until she returned. "Sorry, wrong number. Anyway, I thought I'd call a few of his friends, though of course I don't want all couples—that would be just too uncomfortable for him. And, well, I thought you'd be the *perfect* person to ask."

Perfect, I thought, because I was only momentarily single and clearly not perceived as competition. I wrote down the date, told her I'd have to let her know. Then, picking up the mail from the counter where I'd dumped it in my rush to reach the phone, I sat down at the table. Among the bills and advertisements was a card from Andy, who was indeed in Switzerland. As usual, he'd written to Anna, describing for her a bicycle trip he'd taken through back-road farm country. Vertically up the side of the card, he'd scribbled a P.S.—Give Mommy a hug for me. I miss you both.

I stared at the blue ink until it grew blurry in front of my eyes. Grabbing the orange juice glass I'd left on the table earlier that morning, I threw it with as much force as I could muster, so that it shattered loudly against the kitchen wall. And then I burst into tears.

13

"Yes, of course, we'll come take a look," Daria chirped, holding the receiver away from her ear and grimacing in my direction. "That's correct, no charge for the visit. Yes, this afternoon will be fine."

She hung up and returned to the stack of bills in front of her, proffering only a cursory greeting. "Morning, Kate, did you enjoy your day off?"

"Very much."

Absently, she nodded and began punching at the calculator with the tip of her pencil, missing entirely the self-satisfied smirk I was unable to suppress.

"That was Art somebody," she said without looking up, "the new owner of Zoey's Café in Berkeley. He's changing the motif from Middle Eastern to chrome and glitz, and wants some 'stuff for the walls.' "

"What kind of 'stuff'?"

"That's what we're supposed to tell him. But nothing costing 'big bucks.' I told him you'd drop by this afternoon."

I groaned. "You're all heart."

"Which reminds me, Sondra Van Horn will be here in about an hour. She wanted to start looking through our stock right away. I tried to convince her to wait a few days to give you a chance to pull some things, but she insisted. Don't fret about it, though. Just show her *something.*"

"Actually, I've already pulled a couple of pieces and I have a few more in mind."

Daria raised her head and looked at me over the top of her reading glasses. "My, haven't we been efficient."

"It's just a beginning." The sarcasm in her voice stung, though I knew I shouldn't let it.

"Whatever," she mumbled, returning to her numbers. "I'm just thankful I don't have to deal with that woman."

"Oh, come on," said Paul, who had entered a moment earlier, balancing a cup of coffee and a stack of the Pepperidge Farm cookies we set out for customers, "you could deal with Attila the Hun and have him eating out of your hand in no time."

Daria grunted without raising her eyes. Paul winked at me and began leafing through phone messages, spreading a patina of cookie crumbs across the ledge. "When are you going to bring in more of that fantastic fudge of yours? For a while there it was nearly every day."

"If you'd bought a ticket to the Wine Festival, you could have eaten your fill."

"Thirty dollars a pop is a little stiff for my budget," he said, and then turned to me. "You should have been around this place a couple of weeks ago, Kate. Daria was trying to perfect her recipe, using us as guinea pigs. We had something new every day. All of it, I might add, first rate."

I laughed. "Daria has quite a culinary following. Kimberly Livingston said the same thing, and she's only five years old."

Daria looked up. "Kimberly told you about my fudge?" I nodded, and Daria pursed her lips. "What did she say?"

"That it was yummy. I think she was somewhat awed by the fact that you managed to talk Pepper into letting her have some."

Paul chuckled. "See, I told you, you could take on anyone."

Daria smiled blandly and returned to her work, but I could tell Paul's remark struck a chord.

By the time Sondra arrived, sashaying into the gallery in a pair of tight pink leggings and a black halter top, I had ten pictures set out in our private viewing room, along with coffee and a plate of cookies.

"I thought I'd show you a few things I picked out, just to get your reaction," I explained. "Then, once I have a better idea of the sort of thing you like, we can look through the files together."

The Courtyard Gallery, like most galleries, was able to display only a small fraction of the work it carried. In two back rooms lined with vertical cubicles, the bulk of the pieces were stored, and it simplified things enormously if we knew the type of work the client wanted. No need to spend hours sifting through boldly colored geometric abstracts if you knew you were looking for an impressionistic landscape heavy on greens.

Sondra took the coffee I offered, waving away the cookies as though they offended her. She crossed her legs at the knees and wiggled her ankle impatiently, like some 1950s film star. The clear plastic, open-backed shoes slapped against her heel.

"Okay," she said, "shoot."

Surprisingly, Sondra's taste in art was nothing like her taste, or lack of it, in other things. She liked all of the pieces I thought she would dismiss as too bland, and was politely noncommittal about the one awful piece I'd stuck in there just to gauge how different our artistic preferences really were.

In the end, she selected two pieces—a black ink drawing of a nude figure, and a lithograph, which actually depicted the countryside near Florence but reminded me of the California foothills. These she bought on the spot, assuring me that she had no need to think it over. There were two others she was quite fond of, but neither of us was sure they would be right in her house. I would bring them out the next day, I told her, and we would see if they "worked."

The minute Sondra left, Daria grabbed the check and waved it through the air with a nod in my direction. "See, I told you you'd do fine. Hell, better than fine." She smiled broadly. "Kate, you're a wonder."

I was feeling pretty pleased myself, but I wasn't thinking dollar signs. It was just plain old reassuring to discover I was capable of something besides baking cupcakes and scrubbing floors. And molding myself to Andy's needs. If I'd been alone I would probably have kicked my heels in the air and hollered, but since that sort of behavior was clearly not befitting my new image, I smiled demurely instead and began replacing the paintings Sondra was no longer considering.

A few minutes later the phone rang and Paul handed it to me.

"Hi, it's Michael."

"I'm at work," I told him, hoping the blush I felt creeping up my neck wasn't visible to others.

"I know you are, but I wanted to hear your voice."

I mumbled something unintelligible.

"What I really want to do is undress you—very slowly. But I guess that's out of the question, huh?"

"For right now," I replied, turning to face the back wall.

"You're not having second thoughts, are you?"

Daria cleared her throat, loudly and rather pointedly.

"I've got to go," I told him.

"Tell me you'll see me **Satur**day."

"Okay, Saturday." Somewhat guiltily I thought of Anna, but only for a moment.

"And Kate . . ."

"Hmm?"

"Yesterday was just a beginning."

Zoey's Café, located on Shattuck Street, in the heart—or bowels—of downtown Berkeley, was one of those restaurants which changed ownership at least annually. The last time I'd been there it had still been a taqueria but, stepping inside, I could see remnants of the intervening Middle Eastern phase. For the most part, though, the layout and decor hadn't changed all that much over the last few years, a sure sign that the succession of owners had been operating on shoestring budgets.

The young waiter greeted me with an artful smile, which faded the moment he learned I was not a paying customer. Art was on the phone, he informed me and then ushered me to an empty table in the back, by the kitchen. While I waited, my stomach grumbling with the aroma of frying onions and garlic, I tried to get a feel for the place.

Only it wasn't easy. The walls were an uneven magenta, the carpeting a black and gold Persian, and the chairs contemporary bleached ash with rattan seats. A string of red chili peppers hung from the archway which led to the kitchen. I could only hope that Art Whatever-his-last-name-was had spent the bulk of his money on a first-rate chef.

"Ms. Wilkens?" A short, round, balding man stood in front of me and offered his hand.

"Kate Austen. I work for Ms. Wilkens."

"Art Shapiro," he said, hoisting his pants with his free hand. I thought he might be offended that Daria had sent an underling in her place, but if he was, he had the good sense to hide his disappointment.

"So, what do you think?" He extended his arms, like a actor before his final bow, and then pivoted a hundred and eighty degrees to make sure my gaze took in every corner and crevice. "You shoulda seen this place before. Heavy drapes, table cloths, knickknacks everywhere. Real dark and closed in. Who wants to eat in place like that?"

I nodded agreement.

"What we're striving for is something more fluid. The kind of place you want to come to because it's *fun.* 'Course money's kinda tight right now, so we haven't been able to do as much as we'd like. But after the place takes off, well, maybe then."

I nodded again, searching for the right words.

"I wasn't gonna do anything at all with the walls—I mean, who notices?—but my wife thinks we need some art work. Something to give the place a little class. Can't cost too much, though; there just isn't room in the old budget. She met Ms. Wilkens at some function a couple of months ago and has been pestering me ever since. Finally I agreed to at least see what you gals thought."

What I thought was that the place needed more help than I could give it, but I couldn't say that. "You're absolutely right," I told him. "Nobody is going to come to your restaurant for the art. But I agree with your wife that the walls are a bit stark. Posters might be nice. They're not terribly expensive, and you'd have the leeway to inject a little humor, if you wanted. We've got a few at the gallery, but we've also got catalogues from all the major museums, and properly framed—"

"Hell, I can get posters at Payless."

I agreed, and silently urged him to do so. But, anticipating Daria's tight-lipped disapproval should I make such a suggestion out loud, I carefully explained that museum quality posters were a different thing altogether. Warming to my sales pitch, I pointed to a blank wall near the front, which was the first thing you saw upon entering. "You could hang a large abstract piece there, something in several sections. A white background to provide contrast and catch your eye, a touch of magenta to pick up the color of the wall, and some softer complimentary shades. Maybe something . . ."

My words trailed off midsentence as my mind came to a complete standstill. There, at a table near the window, deep in discussion with a companion, was Tony Sheris. At least I was reasonably sure it was Tony. I squinted against the glare of sunlight from outside and waited for him to raise his head so I could get a better look.

"Maybe something what?" Art was still staring at the wall, sharing with me what I suppose he thought was a moment of artistic creativity.

"Uh, something . . . uh, that would set the tone of the place. Light, trendy, but just a touch unusual." I jabbered on without really focusing on what I was saying; my attention was still riveted on the young man I was now sure was Tony. Then suddenly his friend, a heavyset older man, stood and began weaving through the tables toward the rest rooms. That was when my mouth stopped working altogether. The man with Tony was Jake Turbino.

"Is something wrong?" Art asked me.

"I . . . I, uh, think I see someone who looks familiar."

Art nodded. "You'd be surprised how often that

happens in restaurants." Again tugging at the waistband of his pants, he began quizzing me on prices, shipping times and so forth. It was with tremendous effort that I forced myself to listen and feign attentiveness.

When Jake returned to the table, Tony stood also, and the two men left the restaurant. I mumbled something about dropping off some poster catalogues and then raced for the door. Jake was nowhere in sight, but I spotted Tony about half a block to the north. By the time I caught up with him, I was panting. Hardly a testimonial to the conditioning benefits of jogging.

"Excuse me," I said, falling into step beside him. "I'm—"

"Sorry, no money today." He was obviously accustomed to the panhandlers who lined the city streets.

"I'm not asking for a handout. I'm Kate Austen."

Tony turned and stared at me blankly.

"I live next door to the Livingstons. You work for them, don't you? Gardening."

His blank stare gave way to shock. "What of it?"

What indeed? I had run after him without any thought about what it was I wanted.

"I've been thinking of hiring someone myself." This was the story I'd planned that day I drove to his apartment. It seemed silly now, but it would have to do. "You do such a nice job at their place, and Pepper spoke so highly of you . . ."

I observed him carefully, both for his reaction at the mention of Pepper's name and for a knife. It was the middle of the day and the streets were crowded, but it *was* Berkeley after all; things could get pretty weird before anyone noticed, much less made an effort to intervene. Live and let live, that was the unofficial city motto, and it was a good one I supposed, except that in my case it might become die and let die.

But there was no knife, only a slight tremor in his jaw when I said Pepper's name.

"I'm not looking for any new jobs," Tony said, and started walking again.

I followed.

"Ours isn't a big job, you could do it in an hour when you've finished at the Livingstons."

"I don't work there anymore. Not since, since—"

"Since Pepper died," I finished for him. Up close, I realized how young Tony was. His skin still had the soft, dewy sheen of adolescence, and his eyes, which were an unusually bright blue, fixed themselves on me with a directness I found disconcerting. "Did Robert fire you?" I asked, feigning ignorance and trying, at the same time, to come up with a plan.

"Robert?"

"Her husband."

Tony shook his head, then continued down the street at a quickened pace. I scurried to keep up, but his long legs gave him an advantage so that I ended up half trotting beside him like some obedient dog. "Listen," he said, stopping abruptly, "I've got to go."

"Why don't you give me your number, just in case?"

His eyes fixed on the pavement. "Sorry, I'm really not interested." And then he turned into the Bart station, taking the stairs two at a time.

Damn, he was going to get away from me, vanish once again into thin air. "The police were asking about you," I shouted after him.

Stopping in the middle of the stairway, he turned and faced me. "The police?" He actually sounded surprised.

"They think you might know something about Pepper's death."

It was hard to read the expression on his face. Something between outrage and terror—the look of someone who isn't sure himself what he feels, or ought to feel. He ran a hand through his thick blond hair, started to say something, then turned and continued down the stairs. I followed, but by the time I reached the platform he was already out of sight.

Cursing my luck, and my stupidity, I looked for a phone, aware that among the jumble of emotions I felt, was a trace of . . . not compassion exactly, but something akin it. Something that touched me the way the plaintive meow of a hungry kitten would. Yet he might be a killer, I reminded myself.

Finally, I spotted a phone at the other end of the platform, and ran for it, only to discover that the cord connecting the receiver had been cut and the words "Fight Bureaucracy" spray-painted across the front. The phone next to it was intact, but also in use. By the time I found a phone that was in working order and free, a good ten minutes had elapsed. Not that it mattered, I told myself. Gone was gone, and I didn't even know in which direction.

Michael greeted me warmly. "Change your mind about today? I think I can still find the time."

"Oh, for God's sake, this is serious. I just saw Tony Sheris having coffee with Jake Turbino, at least I'm pretty sure it was Jake."

"Is this your idea of a joke?"

"Of course not," I barked.

"Where are you?"

"In Berkeley. They were at Zoey's Café and then Tony went into the Shattuck Avenue Bart station, and I lost him."

"You were following him?"

"Sort of. Michael, what does this all mean?" My voice came out wobbly and I realized for the first time that I was shaking.

"I don't know." He asked me a few more questions, and then with hasty, mechanical thanks, he was gone.

By time I reached the car my teeth had stopped chattering and my shaking was pretty well under control, so I couldn't understand the high-pitched whir which vibrated in my ears as I backed out of the parking space. But it wasn't my nerves; it was my engine—the Datsun's engine that is. And it grew considerably louder during the trip home.

14

The car continued to whine and groan until I pulled onto my street, where suddenly and inexplicably the noise stopped. I uttered a silent prayer of thanks, and for good measure added a P.S.—Please don't let it happen again. That morning I'd balanced my checkbook and been shocked to discover how little was left; the last thing I needed now was a major, unforeseen expense. And given the age of my Datsun, anything that needed repairing was going to cost plenty.

Anna was spending the afternoon with Kimberly in the care of her new sitter, Mrs. Marsh, who told me the one time I'd met her, and foolishly offered my assistance, that she'd raised eight of her own and didn't see why she would need any help from me, but thank you all the same. She was a heavyset woman—more accurately, downright fat—with loose skin, thinning gray wisps of hair, and a monstrous bosom which rested on her stomach. As far as I could tell, she spent the better part of the day watching television and smoking Winston Lights, although she did obligingly step outside to partake of the latter activity, turning the set volume up high so that she could hear it easily from the back deck. But she was apparently reliable, and somehow managed to prepare meals and deliver Robert's shirts to the cleaners.

She greeted me at the door with a thin-lipped frown. "They was just getting ready for a party. I baked up cupcakes special."

"How nice of you," I said, genuinely appreciative. "I hope having Anna here wasn't a problem."

The expression on her face, a disdainful kind of scowl, made it clear that Mrs. Marsh was not the sort of woman who often encountered problems, and certainly none that were beyond her capabilities. "One more don't make much difference."

I followed her into the kitchen where Anna, who was busily arranging Kimberly's doll collection in a half-circle at the end of the table, shot me a stony glare. "You're early," she huffed. "I'm not ready to go yet."

"I'll wait."

"You can stay for the party," Kimberly offered magnanimously, "but you only get one cupcake."

Mrs. Marsh waddled over to the counter for the chocolate milk and set it on the table while the girls raced upstairs to retrieve Bethany, who had somehow failed to make it downstairs with the other dolls. "You want some coffee?" she asked, with a flap of her broad arms. "Won't take but a minute to reheat it."

"No, thanks."

On the television a young blond with fashionably disheveled curls was quoting the latest homicide figures, county by county.

"Terrible isn't it," said Mrs. Marsh. "Nobody's safe anymore. I'll tell you, just working here gives me the shivers." She set a plate of cupcakes on the table and then reached for a stack of napkins. "Mr. Livingston, though, seems he don't let it get to him."

"He's a man of great reserve."

She gave a throaty chuckle. "Lordy, you got that right."

When the girls returned, Mrs. Marsh eyed me critically. "You staying for the party?"

I nodded.

"In that case, think I'll take me a little fresh air. Just let me know when you're fixing to leave." With that, she grabbed several cupcakes and a pack of cigarettes, turned the TV up even louder than it was already and removed herself to the back patio, where she plopped down on the chaise longue just outside the door. Beside her were several big pots of yellow calendula, now limp and faded. Nobody had thought to water them since Pepper's death.

The queasiness I'd felt on my way home from Berkeley returned. "Do you remember the man who took care of your garden?" I asked Kimberly, who looked up from the job of placing candles in cupcakes long enough to shrug. "Did you ever talk to him?"

"Sometimes."

"What did you talk about?"

"Nothing."

What did I expect, that they had had a detailed discussion about where her mother kept her jewels? "Do you remember anything about him in particular?"

"He liked roses." She thought a moment. "And marmalade on his scones."

"He told you that?"

"I saw him. Mommy ate them plain, but he globbed marmalade on them."

"Your mother and . . . the gardener sat down for scones together?"

"Sometimes."

I must have looked puzzled because Kimberly drew herself up and, in her most proper, Pepper-like voice, explained, "He was the best gardener we ever had, and a very kind soul too."

"I'm sure he was." I sat down woodenly at the far end of the table, away from the dolls. "Was there anyone else your mother liked to visit with? Besides her friends that is."

Kimberly acted as if she hadn't heard me, but I saw her mouth begin to quiver. Nice going, I told myself. The poor kid manages to forget her troubles for a few minutes, and you have to jump in and ruin it. I felt truly penitent, but that didn't stop my from trying once more. "Maybe an older, heavyset man with grayish hair?"

She shook her head, but just barely, and I could see tears threatening. Guilt got the better of me and I gave up.

When the box of candles was empty, Kimberly nodded to me. "You can light them now." Then, after a pause, she added, "Please."

I found a matchbook and struck the one remaining match, which sputtered and then went out. With a disdainful glance in my direction, Kimberly ran to get a new book. When the candles were finally lit, we sang happy birthday to Crystal Dawn, the redheaded doll with a figure I would kill for.

Absently, I picked up the matchbook and began to fiddle with it while my mind reviewed the events of the day. Jake and Tony and Pepper. Surely it wasn't all coincidence? But for the life of me, I couldn't come up with an explanation that was even remotely plausible.

That was when the matchbook cover caught my eye—the Royal Arms Motel, in Danville.

"Where did you get these?" I asked Kimberly.

"They were in Mommy's purse. The one you gave me the other day."

Once a quaint little town about twenty miles east of

Walnut Hills, Danville was now consummate suburbia. Not the sort of place you would vacation and too far away for putting up out-of-town relatives. Besides, Walnut Hills was now home to Park Manor, a brand-new, tres chic motel that made me long to be a visiting out-of-town relative myself.

"Where did your mom get them?" I asked.

Kimberly gave me one of the blank stares she'd mastered so well.

Okay, I told myself, enough. As I stuck the matches in my pocket I thought how negligent I'd been to hand the purse to Kimberly without checking it first. In the hands of a less wary child the results might have been tragic.

When the plate of cupcakes was gone, I thanked Mrs. Marsh, who grunted some response I couldn't quite make out, and took Anna home. Connie was at my front door wedging a note into the crack by the knob. She's about my age, a slender woman with a strong, athletic build and dark, deep-set eyes. Her hair is dark too, and short, except for the long blond tail which hangs down her back.

She looked up as we approached. "Oh good, you're home. Do you have a minute?"

I felt a moment of panic. Connie couldn't quit on me. Not now. One morning a week, wasn't much, but her four hours of uninterrupted scrubbing and tidying up was the only thing that kept household chaos at bay.

Without waiting for an invitation, she followed me into the house. "I'd like to talk to you, about Pepper."

I heaved a heartfelt sigh of relief and nodded. The dirt and grime wouldn't get the upper hand after all. "I was just going to fix some pasta for dinner, you want to stay?"

"Thanks, but I'm meeting a friend." Trailing me

into the kitchen, she pulled up a chair and, with one efficient swipe, swept the bread crumbs off the table and tossed them into the garbage. "I was over at the Livingstons' today, cleaning."

"So you've met Mrs. Marsh?"

She rolled her eyes in exaggerated fashion. "Twice. Where did Mr. Livingston find her anyway?"

"Some agency. She's supposed to be one of their best."

Connie reached into her handbag, a scruffy-looking brown sack large enough to hold her entire wardrobe, and pulled out a manilla envelope, then handed me a newspaper clipping from inside it. "I was cleaning Mr. Livingston's study when I found this, tucked into his datebook." She paused a moment while I examined the piece of paper. "That's Pepper, isn't it?"

In the center of the clipping was a picture of a young blond woman in a short skirt and handcuffs. Above it, the headline—SIMMS TO TESTIFY.

Before I could answer Connie handed me a typed note, explaining, "This was with it."

> *You've come a long way, Rosalie. I bet a lot of people would be interested to know just how far. Back off and we'll keep it our little secret.*

"I would have recognized her even without the note," Connie said.

I nodded. The woman in the clipping was younger and, surprisingly, less attractive, but it was clearly Pepper. Even in handcuffs, without benefit of makeup, there was a regal haughtiness to her I recognized.

Connie leaned forward and started to explain. "As far as I can tell from reading the story, Pepper was involved in some burglary ring—"

I interrupted. "I know."

"You knew about this?"

"Not from Pepper, but from . . . other sources. I just found out a few days ago." My mind was reeling, trying to absorb what it all meant. It must have come from McGregory, I thought. That sort of thing was just his style, but how had he found out? "Have you told the police yet?"

She laughed harshly. "Are you kidding? They sent some moron out the other day to question me. He practically started drooling when he learned I have a house key *and* I know the alarm code. Big fat guy—his shirt didn't even button all the way across his paunch—with bad breath and greasy hair. But he thought he was one cool dude."

"They need to know about this, though," I told her.

"Then you tell them. You're better at that sort of thing than I am. You're even married to a man, or at least you were at one time."

Her logic escaped me, but I let it go. I did, after all, have an inside contact at the police department.

"I remember when it came," Connie continued, "at least I think it was the same envelope. A couple of days before she was killed. I brought in the mail, took Mr. Livingston's stuff to his study, and set the rest on the counter the way I always do. While I was scrubbing out the kitchen sink, Pepper began sorting through the stack, muttering about bills, and then suddenly she was quiet. But it wasn't simply that she stopped talking, there was a kind of resounding stillness that made me look over at her. She was white as a sheet." Connie stopped and considered for a moment. "I remember thinking 'that must be one hell of a MasterCard bill.' Pretty snide of me, wasn't it?"

"What happened next?"

"Pepper left the kitchen, and I went back to my cleaning. But as I was leaving that afternoon, she

asked me to bring her *all* the mail from now on, Mr.
Livingston's as well as her own." Connie looked at her
watch, then tapped her fingers on the table. "You'll
take care of telling the police?"

I nodded. "But they'll probably still want to talk to
you since you found the envelope and everything."

She groaned. "Tell them I'll write it all out and save
them the trouble." As we walked to the door Connie
stopped to pick up a leaf that had been tracked into
the house. "Pepper sure had me fooled," she said,
handing me the leaf. "Turns out she was pretty cool
after all."

After Connie left, I tried to reach Michael, both at
work and at home, but decided against leaving a message. I certainly didn't want him to think I was the coy,
flirtatious type. I tried again several times on Friday,
and finally, in the early afternoon, relented and left a
message. Never let it be said that I impeded the course
of justice.

Only I wasn't sure that I was doing anything but
muddying the already murky waters. None of it made
sense. What possible connection could there be between Tony and Jake? But if Tony wasn't involved,
why had he disappeared after Pepper's death and then
run from me the other afternoon? And where did
McGregory fit in? Then finally, of course, there was
Robert and the mysterious blue Cherokee. Not to
mention what was probably a long list of other possible suspects I wasn't even aware of.

My head was swimming and I longed to talk to
Daria, who seemed able to make sense out of almost
anything. But she was in and out all day, barking or-
ders continuously.

About two o'clock I remembered Susie Sullivan's
invitation and called, praying somewhat guiltily that
I'd reach her machine instead of the woman herself. It

hadn't been so long ago that I'd stood on principle and refused to talk to anything that couldn't respond in kind, but now I often timed my calls just so I could leave a short message and be done with it. Luck was with me. At the sound of the beep I left a message thanking Susie for her kind invitation and explaining that I was, regrettably, otherwise occupied that evening.

"What was that all about?" Daria asked as she breezed past, her arms loaded with boxes.

"Susie Sullivan is giving a small dinner party for Robert. Sort of a genteel hand holding."

"And she asked *you?*"

"Thanks, you really know how to make a girl feel good."

Daria balanced her boxes against one hip and laughed apologetically. "I didn't mean it the way it sounded. It's just that I didn't think you and Susie were chummy."

"We're not." I explained my theory about the invitation, and Daria laughed again.

"God, I'm glad I don't have to hassle the singles' scene," she said, stepping into the storeroom.

About three o'clock I took a break and went across the street for an apple, but ended up buying a candy bar instead. A large Hershey's with almonds, which I devoured in four bites. When I returned, there was a pink message slip for me on the counter. "Michael Stone returned your call. He'll pick you up tomorrow at eleven." The handwriting was Paul's, and with luck Daria had been too preoccupied to notice it sitting there. I grabbed the message slip and tucked it into my pocket. Path of justice be damned; Michael would have to wait until tomorrow to hear about Connie's discovery.

That evening I took Anna out for pizza, and as we

were rounding the corner onto our street, a blue Jeep Cherokee sped by in the opposite direction. By the time it sank in, the car was long gone, and I hadn't noticed either the driver or the license number.

Wearily I parked the car, taking note of Susie's silver Porsche parked in the Livingstons' driveway, directly in front of the house. It was still there when I went to bed at ten o'clock that evening.

15

At ten minutes to eleven the next morning, Michael arrived at my doorstep, right on the heels of Heather, who had agreed to watch Anna for the afternoon so long as I was home by four-thirty. Not the best arrangement, but better than the other alternatives available. Besides, I figured five hours of wanton pleasure were about all anyone could take and still function.

Michael greeted me with a chaste peck on the cheek. "Guess I'm early," he said, managing to sound sheepish while not looking it. In fact, he looked something like a young man who had just been handed the keys to the family car. "It's only my great endowment of willpower that's kept me away this long."

I pecked back, not quite so chastely. "It's your other endowments I find most interesting," I whispered, and left him to fend for himself while I finished getting ready.

I got Anna settled, left a list of instructions and phone numbers for Heather, and then took one last look in the mirror. For a woman who expected to spend most of the afternoon naked, I'd spent an amazing amount of time getting dressed, discarding one selection after another, until half my closet lay spread across the bed.

Although I could never be accused of being fashionable, I had a fair idea of what was considered proper attire for most occasions. But I'd forgotten completely, if I'd ever known, what one wore for an afternoon of sin. I'd finally decided on a soft jersey dress which invariably brought forth compliments and, perhaps more importantly, was easy to get off and on.

"Ready," I said finally, rescuing Michael from Anna's garbled narrative about the recent adventures of her imaginary friends.

When we were in the car Michael turned and gazed silently in my direction for a moment before grinning. "So, what'll it be. You want to try the Powerhouse Special again?"

I choked. "Is that what you call it?"

His grin widened. "The omelette. My college roommate named it."

"Oh."

"But we can try the other thing too." When I laughed—and also blushed, I'm sure—he reached for my hand and squeezed it. "Did you think about me at all?"

"Some."

"I thought about you," he said, switching on the ignition. "Lots."

We smiled at one another, and then I told him, "I actually tried to reach you all yesterday morning. And the night before."

"You did?"

I nodded. "I have some information about Pepper."

His face fell. "So it wasn't my irresistible charm."

"Not entirely, anyway." I pulled the envelope from my purse and started explaining what Connie had told me. He took his eyes from the road long enough to glance at the newspaper clipping while I read the note aloud. "That sheds a whole new light on this thing, doesn't it?" I asked when I had finished.

"It's interesting."

"Interesting? It's more than that. McGregory threatened Pepper after a city council meeting, joked about her death, and now this. We knew he had a motive and now you've got evidence to prove it. Everything fits."

"Except that McGregory was at dinner with friends the night Pepper was killed."

"How do you know that?" I snapped.

He raised an eyebrow and regarded me with amusement. "I checked on it, that's how. I'm a cop, remember? In fact, you were the one who alerted me to McGregory in the first place, after your conversation with some lady friend at the Wine Festival."

And here I thought he'd merely been humoring me. "You mean you actually listened to me?"

"Of course."

I savored a moment of private pleasure, then frowned. "I wonder how he found out about Pepper's past?"

Michael shrugged. "It wouldn't be too hard. She wasn't part of a witness-protection program or anything. Whatever story she created for herself, it was strictly informal."

We turned off the freeway and drove east along Willow Pass Road. Uneasily, I started to stuff the note and newspaper clipping back into my purse. It had seemed such an important piece of the puzzle, I couldn't believe Michael was going to dismiss it so easily. "Maybe McGregory didn't actually kill Pepper himself, but that doesn't mean he isn't involved."

"True."

"Tony has got to be the connection here," I persisted. "He knows Jake somehow, he worked for McGregory, and then suddenly McGregory knows all about Pepper's past."

"It does look suspicious, I'll grant you that. But what would McGregory gain by killing Pepper? As influential and headstrong as she may have been, she was still just the head of a broad-based committee. Getting rid of Pepper wasn't going to get rid of community opposition. And while McGregory may not qualify for the good citizenship award, he's smart. I can't see that he'd risk murder without good cause."

"Why would he send her that note then?"

"We don't know for sure that he did, although he's an obvious candidate." The car in front, a big gray Lincoln, flashed its left-turn signal and then pulled abruptly to the right. Michael jammed on the brakes, cursing under his breath.

"Where are the cops when you need them?" I sighed.

My flippant remark brought only a bleak, fleeting, smirk from Michael, who turned back to the road and drove on in silence, seeming to forget that we were in the middle of a conversation.

"You were saying . . . about McGregory and the note? Why would he send it? If he did, I mean."

"Maybe he was hoping to intimidate her. Having Pepper off his back would certainly make things easier for him, even if it didn't alter the final outcome."

It made sense, although I would have preferred to have Michael praising my investigative efforts instead of logically explaining them away.

"We'll follow up on it just the same," he said, observing me out of the corner of his eye. "In this business you go with your hunches, but you learn never to discount anything either. Can I keep your folder for a few days?"

"Sure. Maybe you can trace the typewriter or something."

"Maybe, but I wouldn't count on it." Michael pulled into his own driveway and parked the car. "We talked to Jake last night."

"You did?"

"Says he doesn't know the kid. Just met him that afternoon at some Preserve the Rain Forest gathering."

"Surely you don't believe that!"

If looks could kill, I would have been dead instantly. "No, I don't," he said smoothly. "And that's why we're tailing him. We'll find Tony, sooner or later, and I think we may then be onto something." He opened the car door and led me up the walkway. "Now, let's forget about all this murder stuff, okay?"

The sensation of his palm against my waist was all it took. Pepper's death, and the mystery surrounding it, seemed terribly unimportant.

As soon as we were inside the apartment, Michael pulled me to him and kissed me squarely on the mouth, not with passion exactly, but with a great deal of fervor. While he whispered my name, his hands stroked my cheek and neck, and then my back, sliding slowly down the smooth jersey. My own hands were just as busy, exploring the wondrous mystery of hard muscle and warm flesh. But just as I began fiddling with the buttons of his shirt, he adjusted his position, resting his arms on my shoulders, and kissed my nose in brotherly fashion.

"Maybe we should just talk instead."

"Talk," I croaked. "About what?"

"You know, who we are, what's important in life." He brushed the hair from my forehead. "There's a lot about you I don't know—where you grew up, what your favorite food is, where you stand politically, how

long you were, uh . . . how long you've been married
. . ." The last words sort of caught in his throat,
though he did a fine job pretending they didn't.

"I grew up in a small town north of Sacramento; I
like too many foods to pick a favorite; although I'm
growing more conservative every day I still consider
myself a liberal; and I've been married six years. But
none of that's what I'd call important." I unbuckled
his belt and began working on the zipper. "Anything
else?"

He grinned. "Nothing that can't wait." Then, lifting
my hair, he nuzzled the nape of my neck and nibbled
at my ear. I could feel his breath, warm and moist
against my skin, and I sank into the inviting firmness
of his body.

But only for a moment. Abruptly, the lazy, timeless
drift of seduction was shattered by a shrill beeping.

"Oh, shit. I've got to call in."

"Right now?" I asked hoarsely. "We could finish up
pretty quickly."

Michael wasn't listening, though. He'd already
tucked in his shirt and rebuckled his belt, as though he
were going to greet a guest at the door rather than
make a phone call. Hastily he punched in the number,
grunted into the receiver, then grabbed a pencil and
scribbled something in his notebook. "Okay," he said
finally, "I'm leaving right now." When he returned to
the alcove by the door, his face was taut, his eyes som-
ber. "They've located Tony. I'm sorry, but I've got to
go."

"Can I get a rain check?"

"A double," he said softly. "At the first opportunity."

Grudgingly, I refastened rows of buttons and
hooks.

"You might as well come along," Michael announced after a moment. "There isn't time to drive you home anyway. Do you mind?"

I thought it probably wouldn't have mattered if I did, though of course I didn't. "Where are we going?"

"Somewhere near San Pablo Avenue in Oakland. One of the men followed Jake there this morning. He and Tony went out for coffee, then Jake dropped Tony off. And now we've got him."

Like an animal caught in a snare, I thought, remembering the frightened eyes and the quick, sharp motions of the young man fleeing down the steps at the Bart station. "Are you going to arrest him?"

"Not at the moment. We just want to ask him some questions."

While Michael drove, quickly and silently, his face devoid of all expression, I slouched on my side of the car, fighting the urge to reach over and stroke his cheek. The steely control of a policeman was apparently beyond my grasp.

We headed west into the depths of Oakland and pulled up, finally, in front of a vacant storefront. The buildings on both sides were vacant as well. A faded For Sale sign was propped against one grimy window. Although the space above appeared to be inhabited, it didn't look any brighter or cleaner.

Michael switched off the ignition, then turned to face me. "Keep the doors locked. I shouldn't be too long."

"No way," I protested. "I'm coming with you."

He started to say something more, but I was already out of the car with my door firmly shut, so I didn't hear him. "At least stay out of the way once we're inside," he muttered over his shoulder.

As we approached the narrow doorway, a young, lean black man stepped into our path from the shop entrance next door. "Lieutenant Stone? Rick Myer,

Oakland Police Department. You got here quick."
Myer looked briefly in my direction, but when Michael
said nothing, he dropped his gaze, secretly wondering,
I imagine, what sort of dingbat cop, even undercover,
would wear a clinging, narrow-skirted dress and high
heels to question a murder suspect. But then he was
Oakland and we were Walnut Hills, and I'm sure he
thought we were an odd breed to begin with. "Sheris
went inside about forty minutes ago and hasn't come
out since."

"Is there a back entrance?"

"Your man Lawton is there now."

As if he'd been waiting for the right moment to
make an entrance, a short, redheaded man joined us.
"Michael," he said, looking directly at me, "you got
my message."

Lawton went first, then Michael and then me.
Through the door and up a decrepit, narrow staircase.
The light, if there was one, was burned out and I was
glad. The discolored stains and dried puddles were disgusting enough in dimness; I couldn't imagine what
full illumination would have revealed.

"Watch it," Lawton warned, "the banister is loose. I
wouldn't count on it for any support."

I wouldn't have touched it for anything in the
world.

At the landing there were four doors, none with
numbers. "You stay here until I tell you otherwise,"
Michael snapped, and this time I didn't protest. It
looked exactly like the kind of shabby, lowlife place
I'd seen in movies. The kind of place where gangsters
leap out from nowhere and shoot at you. Or worse.

Lawton pointed to the third door, then pulled out
his revolver. Michael knocked and the door opened,
but just barely.

"Tony Sheris?"

"Yes." The voice was wary.

"I'm Lieutenant Stone with the Walnut Hills police. I'd like to talk to you for a minute." The door opened wider, I could tell by the shaft of light on the tattered hallway carpet. "Inside, if you don't mind."

Michael motioned to me and I stepped forward, followed by Lawton, who, I was happy to see, had returned his gun to its holster.

Tony looked at me in surprise. "You again! You're a cop."

"No, I'm just . . ." But it hit me suddenly that this wasn't a social call, so I shut my mouth. "No, I'm not," I said finally, and let it go at that.

The room was sparsely furnished with a metal-frame bed, a bureau and a chipped, green table. A sink, tiny refrigerator and hot plate were in the far corner next to the bathroom, such as it was. The door was missing and I could see the yellowed toilet, propped up with bricks. I was beginning to wish I'd stayed in the car after all, where I might have been bored, but would at least have been spared the worry about germs and fleas. And rats.

Tony shuffled apologetically. "I'm not used to entertaining." His hesitant smile was met by Michael's cold silence. Tony sat on a stool and pointed to the bed. "Go ahead. It's the most comfortable spot in the room." Lawton and I seated ourselves at opposite ends. I could feel the springs poking through the mattress into my hips and thighs. Michael, wisely, remained standing.

"We're investigating the death of Pepper Livingston," he said.

Tony sighed. There was that tentative, oddly touching smile again. "I figured as much."

"So, what can you tell us?"

"Not a lot, I'm afraid. I did some work for the Livingstons, took care of their garden, did some odd cleanup and maintenance jobs. That's about it."

"You were generally there a couple of times a week, weren't you?"

"It varied."

Michael rubbed his cheek thoughtfully. "But you haven't been back since Mrs. Livingston's death. Even once."

Tony hunched forward, resting his elbows on his knees and rubbing his palms together. "No, I didn't think there was any urgent need."

"Do you have a key to their place?"

He nodded. "Mrs. Livingston gave me one a couple of months ago when I was washing windows for her."

"And you still have it?"

"She said I should keep it, for getting gardening supplies out of the garage and stuff."

Shifting his body so that he was perched on the very edge of the bed, Lawton cleared his throat and spoke for the first time since entering the room. "Why'd you leave your apartment in Berkeley?" He looked around pointedly and smirked. "Moving into better quarters?"

Tony shrugged.

"I'd like an answer. Why did you pull out a day or two after Mrs. Livingston's death, without even a forwarding address?"

"I don't know, I wanted a change maybe. Is moving a crime?"

"You'd paid rent through the end of the month."

Another shrug.

"But maybe you're so rich a month's rent here or there doesn't matter." The snide tone of Lawton's voice made me uncomfortable, but Tony seemed able to ignore it. He rested his arms on his knees and stared hard at the floor.

Lawton stood and approached Tony. "Where were you on the night of May fifth?"

"Home, probably. That's where I am most nights."

"Alone?"

"Yeah."

"Doing what?"

"I don't know, reading."

"Not much of an alibi, is it?"

"Why should I need an alibi?" Then it hit him, you could see it in his face. "You think *I* killed Pepper?" His voice broke, but it was hard to tell if the unevenness was a laugh or sob.

"Did you?" Michael's words were sharp, but his tone was tinged with an odd gentleness.

"No."

"Do you know who did?"

There was a pause, brief but telling. "No."

Even I could see that Tony knew more than he was letting on, and I was struck by his use of Pepper's first name. Then, from out of nowhere, Kimberly's comment popped into my mind. "You and Pepper were pretty friendly, weren't you?"

Three heads turned and stared at me. "You sometimes had tea, and she once visited you at your apartment, isn't that so?"

Tony looked pale, Lawton looked confused—and annoyed—and Michael simply looked, regarding me impassively with clear, gray eyes.

"She came by once, to bring me a check."

Lawton snickered. "Such service." He turned and started to amble around the room, peering into shelves and closed drawers.

"That's kind of unusual," Michael commented absently.

"She was an unusual woman."

Lawton took a book from the shelf above the sink.

"Tolstoy. Pretty highbrow tastes—for a *gardener.*" He leafed through the book, and without looking up asked, "You know a Jake Turbino?"

This time the pause was so pronounced even Tony seemed to feel it. Finally he nodded, then dropped his head into his hands.

The smirk on Lawton's face annoyed me, though I couldn't see why my sympathies lay with a possible killer rather than the law. Maybe it was my own discomfort which gave me pause. Greed, anger, betrayal—whatever raw emotions had paved the way to Pepper's murder, whatever intrigue or mystery lay hidden just beneath the surface, it was all going to come out in the next few minutes. I braced myself, caught between fascination and revulsion.

"What's your relationship with Jake Turbino?" Michael asked evenly.

"Is he a suspect too?"

"Just answer the question."

Tony took a deep breath and let it out slowly. "He's my father."

"Your father!" Michael's official, dispassionate calm deserted him.

"And Pepper," I said, as things began to fall into place, "she was . . ."

He nodded. "My mother."

Lawton, who had not reacted at all except to rein in his smirk, stepped forward, shaking his head skeptically. "Wait a minute; we had information that your parents live in Illinois."

"My adoptive parents." Tony lifted his head, but stared at the wall in front of him. "They adopted me when I was a baby. A couple of years ago I found the note my real mother wrote when she gave me up. She seemed warm and gentle, like a storybook mother. When I turned eighteen I began trying to locate her.

Last fall I finally made contact with Pepper; she told me about Jake. I wrote to him, and when he was paroled, he came to California." With a deep, ragged sigh, Tony looked directly at Michael. "She was a very special person. A mother I could have loved. A mother who would have loved me in return." He paused. "And now she's dead."

"Why didn't you tell us this in the beginning?"

"I didn't . . . It didn't seem important."

"And why the move?" Lawton asked, his tone still steely. "You tried to disappear in fact."

Tony chewed on his lower lip. "I don't know why, really. Everything just sort of fell apart with her gone. I couldn't go back and keep on working for her husband as if nothing had happened. And I didn't want to see . . . anyone. At first I was going to move away altogether, just pretend the last six months hadn't happened, but I couldn't, not just yet anyway."

"And there was Jake. Your father."

Tony ran his tongue along his bottom lip and nodded.

"Is he a very special person too?" The snide overtones had returned to Lawton's voice.

"I don't know him that well, we've only met twice. Once before Pepper's death and again yesterday."

"And this morning."

"Right. I'd forgotten about that." Tony was silent for a moment, studying his fingernails. Finally he asked, "Did Jake tell you where to find me?"

"No," Michael replied. "In fact, he said he didn't know you."

A smile crossed Tony's face briefly, then faded, and I thought once again how young he was. And vulnerable. I wanted to comfort him as I did Anna, shielding him from hurt and disappointment. But of course I couldn't; no one could. No one ever had.

Lawton had been watching this last exchange through half-closed eyes. Now he sprang to life, stepping in front of Tony and leaning over him. "This story, *if* it is true, and you can be sure we will check it out, still doesn't let you off the hook. In fact, I'd say it raises more questions than it answers. And you don't seem any too willing to help with the missing pieces, if you get my drift."

There was a sour taste in my mouth, and I stood up abruptly, unceremoniously. "I'll wait outside," I said.

The sadness of it all came washing over me like a bad dream. I darted for the door and raced down the stairs, not even noticing the filth or the stench on my way out.

16

"You okay?" Michael asked, when at last we were in his car headed home.

"How do you do this, day after day, year after year?"

"It beats sitting at a desk your whole life. Besides, sometimes you convince yourself you're doing some good."

An icy shiver worked its way down my spine and then settled in the pit of my stomach. The entire episode left me feeling queasy and dispirited.

"It's funny," I said finally, "I want to believe Tony, but something in his manner makes me think he knows more than he's telling. It's almost as though he was trying to protect someone."

"He was," Michael said. "His father."

"Jake killed Pepper?"

"I don't think so, but Tony was afraid he might have. That's a big part of why he started to run, I think. And why he was reluctant to tell us the whole story up front. But it's also the reason he stuck around; he had to know whether Jake was involved."

I shivered again. "How awful. The poor kid suffers through a lousy childhood, finally locates his real parents, and then not only does he find his mother murdered, he has to confront the fact that his father may be her murderer."

Michael nodded glumly. "And I suspect Jake was afraid Tony might have been involved."

"But neither was?"

"Jake has a pretty solid alibi—he spent the night in San Francisco with his minister."

I turned and looked at Michael. "I thought he wouldn't tell you where he was the night Pepper was killed."

"He wouldn't at first, but after he found out we considered him a prime suspect, he was a bit more cooperative."

"Still, why hedge the question at all?"

Michael's eyes crinkled into a smile. "Because the minister is a woman. And someone else's wife."

"I take it they weren't holding a prayer meeting."

"Not in the conventional sense anyway."

"And what about Tony?"

"Tony . . . I don't know. He still says he was home alone that night, but what would he have had to gain by killing Pepper? She seems to have welcomed him, gone out of her way to help him, in fact. He admits she paid him much more than she needed to."

"Maybe he resented being abandoned by her," I said, swallowing hard. "Here Pepper was, sitting pretty in a fancy big house, bestowing on Kimberly all the advantages he'd never had. And, don't forget, Tony was friendly with McGregory. Somebody tipped McGregory off about her past." These were not thoughts I entertained with any enthusiasm. Rather, I wanted my doubts about Tony laid to rest once and for all.

Michael frowned deeply and rubbed his jaw. When he finally spoke his voice was weary. "If Tony felt resentment, he certainly did a good job of hiding it. And

I asked him about McGregory. Claims he didn't know anything about the development battle, and he quit the landscaping job as soon as he learned McGregory and Pepper were adversaries. He thinks McGregory hired him only because he worked for Pepper. Seems the man tried to hire her house cleaner too. A new form of harassment I guess."

The notion of Connie being approached by a man like McGregory provided me with a private moment of amusement. I was certain she wouldn't have declined the offer politely. *If* it was true. "Do you believe Tony?" I asked.

"Unfortunately," Michael sighed, "I do." Suddenly he looked tired, beat in fact. His face was drawn, his eyes flat, his skin pale and etched with shadows.

"What's wrong?" I asked, giving his knee a gentle pat. "You look as though you've become a prime suspect yourself."

"I was so sure this thing with Jake and Tony would turn out to be an important lead. Tie off a few loose ends and we could wrap up the case. Now it looks like we're back at the beginning, with nothing. Less than nothing, in fact. Our list of potential suspects gets shorter by the day."

I tried to be encouraging. "Something may turn up," I said, so brightly that it sounded hollow even to my own ears.

"Yeah, and scientists may discover the moon is made of green cheese."

My hand slid from his knee to gently run up his thigh, but Michael only smiled wanly. "I've got to go into headquarters and make a report."

"That's okay, Heather will be happy to get off early." I pulled my hand back to my lap and stared at it for several moments. "You could come by a little later. I've got stuff for dinner and a whole case of beer in the basement."

"Thanks, but I don't think I'd be very good company tonight."

"Well, if you change your mind . . ."

His right hand touched my cheek. "I'm sorry, Kate. This isn't the afternoon I wanted."

"Nor I," I whispered, kissing his fingertips. Then I got out of the car and quickly went inside, where I found a card from Andy, addressed, for a change, to me as well as Anna. The message was brief: Thinking of you both, Love, Andy.

When I'd paid Heather and straightened the mess in the kitchen, dropping the card unceremoniously into the trash, I contemplated the ways I could spend what was left of the afternoon. I could do something loving and motherly with Anna. I could do the laundry or mow the lawn. I could even sit in the yard and read a book.

Instead, I settled Anna in front of a *My Little Pony* tape, pulled my slinky, easy-to-get-off dress over my head and climbed into bed. A brief nap first, then I'd tackle the question of what to do next.

Closing my eyes, I cuddled up to the image of Michael and the pleasant afternoon we'd planned. But Andy kept intruding. From the murky realm of unconsciousness, memories forced their way to the surface and clicked through my mind like a progression of unwelcome commercials.

There was the crisp November afternoon we went sailing on the bay with Jim and Daria. I could see Andy, blond head thrown back, laughing into the wind and cold ocean spray while the rest of us trembled and held on for dear life.

There was the time, before Anna was born, when we rented a small cabin outside Yosemite and were snowed in for three days. We lived on Oreo cookies, dried salami and a case of champagne—and danced endlessly to the only album we could find, a scratchy recording of The Grateful Dead.

And the night of the big earthquake when I was alone in our San Francisco apartment, without power or phone service. I'd stood at the window watching the orange sky and wept with the fear that Andy had been killed.

Snippets of conversation, the scent of his aftershave, the pleasant roughness of his hands against my skin. These visions came and went with a life of their own. Finally they blurred into one misty dream, and I slept, drawn into the pleasurable tide of muted memory.

I dreamed that Andy and I were making love, the way we did in the beginning before tension and doubt edged out the joy. He was caressing me, my whole body, with long, slow strokes which turned eventually to kisses. His mouth and tongue were everywhere, and I could feel the pleasure mounting. It grew deeper and hotter, until it began to sear. Then I saw that he wasn't licking at all, but wrapping a red-hot wire around my belly, tighter and tighter. Pleasure turned to pain, and the pain grew sharper. Finally Andy laughed and left me lying in a pool of tepid water.

I awoke in a sweat, but the pain did not subside. If anything it was stronger. Then I felt the warm stickiness between my legs and knew, without looking, that it was blood.

I lay there for a minute, muted as much by sorrow as pain, thinking that if I closed my eyes again it might all go away. But I was gripped suddenly by a fiery spasm so strong it brought tears to my eyes and took away my breath.

I did the only thing I could think to do. I rolled over and phoned Daria.

17

"Is the pain gone?" Daria asked, brushing a cool hand against my forehead. She was sitting by the side of my bed on a white plastic, hospital-issue chair. She'd been by my side ever since we'd arrived at the hospital earlier that afternoon, except of course for the hour or so I'd been in surgery. Even then, I suspect, she'd hovered about by the nurses' station, awaiting word that she would be allowed into recovery.

"It's much better anyway," I told her. I was still feeling a little groggy, and what pain there was, felt far away.

"I'm so sorry it turned out this way, Kate." It was probably the tenth time she'd told me that, but her effusiveness was tempered by the fact that she'd never once said it was all for the best, or that this way, at least, the decision was out of my hands. She leaned forward and offered a wan smile. "Can I do anything for you?"

"You've done so much already."

"Nonsense."

"I'm fine, honestly. It's only because Dr. Lewis is such a fussbudget that I have to stay overnight anyway. You go on home, there's no need for you to stay any longer."

"I won't stay forever. I've got to rescue Anna from Jim before he lets her eat a gallon of ice cream. He thinks that's how you charm children."

"Tell him I appreciate this. And everything else." I reached for the glass of ice water by my bed, but Daria beat me to it, adding fresh water from the pitcher before handing it to me. "He's been so kind to me since Andy left," I told her. "Both of you have."

She gave me one of those oh-nonsense looks she's so good at, but it was tinged with genuine affection. "I talked to him about twenty minutes ago," she said. "He and Anna were playing hide-and-seek."

"I hope you reminded Anna not to climb on the furniture." Daria's house was always picture perfect. Nothing worn or mussed or out of place. Even the flowers she habitually bunched in vases seemed to dip and fall with artistic grace. It was the sort of place Anna could destroy in short order.

"We'll get along just fine. Don't worry." Daria took my half-empty glass and placed it on the bedside table.

I took her hand and held it between my own. "I'm so lucky to have a friend like you. I can't begin to tell you how much it means."

"Don't be silly. That's what friends do, they help one another."

When Daria left I closed my eyes again, but didn't sleep. In a little while the nurse came in, took my temperature and blood pressure, then leaned over the bed and peered at the pad between my legs, like a mechanic doing a quick oil check. "You're coming along just fine," she observed, scratching something on my chart before turning to an older woman in the next bed who had been snoring and moaning in her sleep since I'd arrived. When she'd poked and muttered around there for a bit, she left.

Fifteen minutes later the nurse returned with two

trays which she placed next to our beds. "Enjoy," she announced brightly as she swooped out of the room.

The older woman sat up in bed. "You got anything serious?"

I shook my head. "I had a miscarriage."

She removed the lid from her tray and inspected the meal. "Well, you're young, plenty of chance to have another. Least you can go home tomorrow. Me, I'm here for a while."

"Oh." Then, thinking my response probably sounded rude, I added, "I hope it isn't bad."

"Just the usual female complaints." With that, she switched on the television and fixed her attention on the screen.

My mind sorted through possibilities, trying to determine what, exactly, the usual female complaints were. Finally I gave up, pushed away my tray, rolled over and pressed a pillow to my ears to block the sound of the television.

But I didn't sleep. I didn't cry either, at least not outwardly, but warm tears stung my eyes and tightened my throat. It wasn't the sharp, all-consuming grief you'd feel for the loss of a child or other loved one, but there was a sadness all the same. A quiet sadness deep inside.

If Andy had been there with me, would he have been sad? Would he have felt any sort of loss at all? Part of me was glad I was alone, so that I wouldn't have to know.

When Daria arrived at ten the next morning, I was already fully dressed, discharge papers in hand.

"You don't have to prove how tough you are, Kate, especially to me."

"I'm not."

"Yes you are. Up and dressed before I arrive, refusing to come stay with me for a couple of days, talking about work already. Just as though nothing had happened." Without looking at her, I started gathering my things, but Daria placed a hand lightly on my arm, momentarily halting my frenetic activity. "You would have had the baby, wouldn't you?" she asked softly. "Even though it would have made things more difficult with Andy."

"Things are already about as difficult as they can get."

Then her arms were around me, gently rocking, quieting the raw, uneven breaths that caught in my chest. "It's okay to feel sad, Kate. This isn't something you can just ignore."

Wiping a wayward tear, I hugged her in return. "It's not just that. I'm beginning to feel like I'm mired in quicksand. Every step sends me deeper. You've got a family, a husband who adores you, a job you're good at . . . a sense of purpose. Me, I'm floundering."

"Just take it one step at a time; it's the only way."

I thought it an odd comment from a woman who had her 1995 Daytimer half filled by July of '94. Never one to leave things to chance, Daria orchestrated her life with a precision I was sure the CIA would find admirable. But the advice was sound, particularly for someone like myself, who couldn't think far enough ahead to manage a whole week's grocery shopping at once.

Following hospital regulations, I left in a wheelchair and Daria picked me up at the front door. She drove slowly and carefully all the way home.

"I'm not ill," I told her.

She smiled. "Are you sure you won't come to my house for the afternoon? Chris and Heather took

Anna to the park, so you'd have quiet if that's what
you want."

"I'm sure, but thanks."

"How about an early dinner then? Jim's got a poker
game."

"Can I let you know later?"

"Of course. Give me a call this afternoon."

In the end I went to Daria's, sooner rather than
later. My own house was empty and cold, like my
body. The lone message on the machine was from Michael. Although the sound of his voice was instantly
soothing, I couldn't bring myself to call him. Not yet
anyway.

Jim was leaving just as I arrived, but he got out of
the car to give me an affectionate bear hug. "You managing to hang in there?"

"Absolutely."

"It's been a rough couple of months for you—what
with Andy, Pepper . . . and now this."

I'd never thought about it in that way, but he was
right. There'd certainly been a lot of loss to deal with.
"You and Daria have been a big help to me," I told
him.

He tweaked my chin. "It's good to see you feeling so
chipper." Then he trotted back to the car and drove off
with a wave.

Daria was in the kitchen, making salad. Although it
was only four o'clock in the afternoon, she was already sipping a glass of wine. "Pull up a chair and
pour yourself some. I'll be finished in a minute."

While Daria was accustomed to midday imbibing, I
was not. But the idea sounded suddenly appealing. I
grabbed a glass from the cupboard and poured with

theatrical flourish. "I guess this is the silver lining. I can drink again."

I caught Daria about to utter one of her infamous caustic remarks, but she stopped short and handed me an avocado instead. "Why don't you cut this while I finish up with the dip?"

"Dip no less. I might have known you couldn't keep a simple meal simple." Daria was given to excess, and before I knew her well enough to understand that she didn't expect people to reciprocate in kind, I had been intimidated by her lavish spreads. Now I simply enjoyed them.

"Dips are hardly complicated."

To my mind, anything that didn't move directly from freezer to microwave to table was complicated. "How did you make out with the little terror last night?"

"If you're talking about your daughter, we made out splendidly." She began chopping tomatoes. "You act like I'm some frail old thing."

"It *has* been a number of years since you've had a five-year-old around full-time."

"I'm only a year older than Pepper, and *she* seemed to manage just fine." Her voice had a clipped, almost arrogant tone to it, a tone I'd noticed before when she spoke of Pepper. Envy was an uncomfortable companion, I thought. "By the way," she chided, "I understand you spent yesterday morning with that detective friend of yours, the one who's investigating Pepper's death."

Her remark caught me by surprise, and I looked up.

"Anna mentioned it," she explained.

I watched as she scooped the tomatoes into a bowl, biting her lip to avoid the question she didn't want to ask. "It's okay," I assured her, "nothing happened. We spent the day questioning a potential suspect."

"Oh? Who?" She leaned across the counter eagerly, her curiosity apparently topping her relief in having my virtue confirmed.

I explained about Tony as best I could without mentioning Jake. I wasn't sure what information was classified, but I didn't see how clearing Tony could hurt anything. "So now they're back to looking for leads," I told her.

"What about Robert? I thought he was on their list."

"I guess he is, but there's nothing that ties him to the murder."

"Still, he doesn't have an alibi for the night she was killed."

I agreed, he didn't.

"And then there's the stuff with that car. What did the police decide about that?"

With a groan, I explained they hadn't decided anything. "They questioned Mrs. Stevenson, and now she's not so sure what she saw, and they talked to Robert who says the Tom he told me about was a client, not an employee; I just got it mixed up."

"The way women are apt to do."

"Right, only I don't think he said that in so many words. It turns out the man's car isn't a Cherokee anyway, but some other kind of similar car, and now Robert thinks I've been meddling."

"And your detective, what does he think?"

Unfortunately, I'd been too preoccupied with the kisses and caresses to find out. "He's keeping an open mind," I told her, figuring it was probably the truth. Heck, even I didn't know if I was remembering things correctly.

Forehead creased in thought, Daria dumped a bag of blue corn chips into a basket. "I don't like to gossip," she said after a moment. Like hell she doesn't, I thought. "But in times like these we have to be objective. Robert does drink heavily and you know what that does to people with a temper."

"We've been over this before. Besides, he seems to have adored Pepper."

Daria scowled. "Maybe. But she could be a real bitch. And for a man of his disposition, not to mention his prominence in the community, well, having a wife like Pepper must have been quite a challenge. Then this thing with Tony. I mean a grown son popping up like that out of nowhere. Imagine if Robert found out. Maybe he never planned to kill her, but something set him off and he just . . . just snapped." She punctuated her last words with a click of her fingers.

"I don't know, I can't imagine Robert snapping. I'm not sure he even knows the meaning of the word." I drained the last of my wine and refilled my glass. "This is all so sordid. Let's talk about something more cheerful."

"I just hope the police are keeping their eyes on Robert, that's all," Daria said. Then she smiled, a perfect dental-ad smile, handed me the chips and salsa, grabbed the bottle of wine and motioned to the back deck. "Let's sit outside. You can give me some ideas for Jim's birthday next week. I got him a book, some golf stuff and a new leather briefcase, but none of it is really special."

Daria liked things to be special. Anniversaries, birthdays, Father's Day, Valentine's Day. She had even discovered holidays most of us had never heard of. And she orchestrated them all to the hilt.

"Since we're going to Mexico the following week, I didn't want to plan a big trip for his birthday, but I can't just treat it like an ordinary day either. What do you think? Maybe a simple breakfast of croissants and fresh fruit, and then a drive through the Napa Valley.

I've already set things up with his receptionist so that he has the day off, but of course he doesn't know that."

"It will be a wonderful surprise," I told her. Knowing Daria, I was certain the house, and maybe the car too, would be decked out with balloons and streamers and cutesy little heart decals. She'd wish him happy birthday at least a dozen times, then ask if there wasn't really something he would rather be doing that day than whatever she had planned. And she would meet his reassurances with grateful kisses and tender little love pats.

We poured ourselves a third glass of wine and settled down to the serious business of nibbling and catching up. I leaned back in the warm sunshine and stretched, feeling, in spite of everything, remarkably lighthearted.

The amazing powers of wine and friendship.

18

The doorbell rang the next morning just as I was sitting down to coffee and blueberry muffins spread with real butter, an indulgence I did not usually allow myself. Daria had insisted I take the day off, and although I'd argued with her at the time, now I was glad. Not because I was feeling ill—except for some mild cramps and a gray, shadowy sorrow, I felt pretty good—but because there is something wonderful, almost magical, about playing hooky, kind of like the extra hour when we turn the clocks back at the end of October. A stretch of time outside of time.

But not, apparently, outside the mundane trappings of everyday living. Anna, Max and I arrived at the door simultaneously. One of us barked, one of us pressed her nose against the glass, and one of us adjusted her robe, then opened the door warily.

"What a reception," Michael said, and kissed me on the forehead.

I'd finally returned his call when I stumbled home from Daria's the night before, but seeing him sent an unexpected spark of pleasure through my body. "Is that the best you can do?" I chided, lifting my face to his.

He grinned, then kissed me again, on the mouth this

time and not as hastily, but it was still a sweet kiss rather than a seductive one. "These are for you," he said, handing me a bouquet of yellow roses tied with a shiny white ribbon. "It's kind of sappy, but I didn't know what else to do."

"They're lovely," I said, touched as much by his gentle shyness as the gift itself. "And flowers are never sappy." I lifted the bouquet from Max's prying nose. "Can you stay for coffee?"

"A mind reader as well."

Anna and Max followed us into the kitchen, setting themselves down, one on each side of Michael. With equally large eyes, they watched him, Anna somewhat suspiciously, Max with studied anticipation.

"Can policemen do whatever they want?" Anna asked after a moment.

"They have to obey the laws, just like everyone else."

"But if you did something bad, who'd catch you?"

Michael leaned back in his chair and launched into an explanation, but I interrupted, shooing Anna away. "This is grownup time," I told her. "Go watch television." I could see her weighing the options. That I'd actually encouraged her to watch television meant I really wanted her out of the way, and those were precisely the times she found my activities most interesting. "Go on," I prodded, "you can take a muffin with you."

Reluctantly, she grabbed a muffin and ambled off. While Michael gazed out the window, his eyes dark and unreadable, I set a plate of muffins on the table and handed him a cup of coffee. Then, standing behind him, I draped my arms around his neck and kissed top of his head. "You're awfully quiet."

"Sorry."

"No need to be." I sat down next to him in the chair

Anna had vacated, and smiled. "How was your weekend?"

"Lousy. I spent most of it working and the rest of it arguing with Barbara."

"About?"

He shrugged. "Money mostly, I guess. At least that's what we started on."

I took a long, slow, sip of coffee and then studied the rim of the cup. "Did you fight a lot during your marriage?"

"Not really." Michael's fingers picked at the nicked edge of the table. "Do you and Andy fight?"

"No, hardly ever."

There was a long silence during which we looked at one another uncertainly. Finally Michael spoke. "Kate, maybe this isn't the right time, but we need to talk about things."

I nodded. "But not just yet."

"When?"

"Soon."

A weak smile flickered across his face. "You do care for me though, don't you?"

"A great deal," I said softly, running my hand along the bare skin above his wrist. Then I took a muffin from the plate and handed it to him. "Now, about the work part of your weekend. Tell me what's happening with the case."

He frowned. "I only wish there were something to tell."

"You followed up on Tony's story?"

Michael nodded glumly. "It appears he's telling the truth."

"Which means?"

"Which means we're back at the beginning, with virtually nothing. Yesterday I sat down and went over things once more, but I came up empty-handed." He paused for a moment, pressing his lips together tightly. "We know Pepper was strangled. We know there was a brief struggle first, during which she was hit on the head with some kind of heavy, sharp object. But we haven't been able to locate it or come up with any leads based on physical evidence. The only thing we have is that swatch of silk fabric that got caught in the bedpost."

"The tie she was strangled with."

"At this point that's just a theory." Michael shifted his weight, leaning forward with both elbows on the table, and continued his analysis. "We're pretty certain it wasn't some psychopath, killing just for the fun of it. Somebody was out to get Pepper, but we're having a devil of a time coming up with a list of possible suspects. And every time we think we're on to something, it turns out to be a dead end."

I got up and poured him a second cup of coffee, which he accepted with a distracted nod of his head.

"It's crazy," he said, "there's more we *don't* know about this case than we do know. Hell, we can't even pinpoint the means of entry, although I'm betting the killer was someone with a key, and possibly the alarm code."

"That limits it, doesn't it?"

"You'd think so." His words were weighted with defeat, and I felt his frustration. Like women throughout time, I wanted to make things right.

"What about Robert?" I asked. "Isn't he a possibility?"

Michael picked at his muffin, which he'd barely touched. "The guy's peculiar, no getting around that, but there's not one shred of evidence which suggests he killed her. And you can't arrest a guy just because something about him strikes you as odd. Not in this country anyway."

"But he's still a suspect?"

"Yeah, most definitely."

During the last few days I'd done my best to avoid Robert, but try as I might, I hadn't been able to avoid thinking about him. How could a man I knew, a man I was truly fond of, be a murderer? Sometimes the absurdity of the notion made me laugh. But deep down in my heart, I wasn't convinced he was innocent.

"Right now," Michael continued, "he's the only name we've got."

"Besides McGregory."

"Right, and we'll know more about that when we finish analyzing the note Connie found."

"Well," I said philosophically, "something's bound to turn up sooner or later."

He shook his head. "Not necessarily. And the longer it takes, the worse the odds." Pushing back his chair, Michael stood and stretched. "One thing's for certain, we're never going to make any progress if I sit here feeling sorry for myself."

"I wish you didn't have to go just yet," I said, standing also and moving close.

"Me too." His eyes fixed on mine and lingered there while he brushed my cheek with his fingertips. "You sure you're okay about . . . about what happened?"

Most of our conversation the previous evening had focused on my miscarriage, and I'd been acutely aware of both the concern in Michael's voice and the guilt, though I'd done my best to allay both.

"I'm fine," I assured him. "So stop worrying."

He leaned over, kissed me gently, and then, arms entwined, we walked to the door.

Sharon was wandering up the walkway just as Michael was leaving. Her eyes followed him to his car and she waited until he'd started the engine before speaking. "I thought I'd drop off that price list for playground equipment. Give you a chance to look it over before the next board meeting."

Replacing the old swing set and slide was the board's final project for the year, and I *had* agreed to study the issue, but Sharon's timing was bad nonetheless. It was quite a picture—me in a bathrobe waving good-bye to a strange man at nine in morning. That was enough to cause even Sharon to raise an eyebrow.

"Well, well," she said after Michael had driven off, "I see the benefits of having a husband who's gone. Myself, I'm always stuck with those dreary motels."

"It's not the way it looks," I told her firmly.

She laughed and handed me a thick manila folder. "Too bad. It looks kind of nice."

A little after five that afternoon Mrs. Marsh called to ask if I would watch her pie while she took Kimberly to some magic show at the club. Since she offered to take Anna too, I could hardly refuse. Besides, I could sit and stare mindlessly out a window from the Livingstons' house as easily as I could from my own.

"I don't know what I was thinking of, waiting so long to make that pie," Mrs. Marsh said, as she ushered me into the kitchen. "Some days my mind's like that. You sure this isn't a bother?"

"Not at all. And Anna is excited about going to the show. It's kind of you to take her."

After the three of them had gone, I sat down on the couch and began leafing through the stack of magazines on the coffee table, but they failed to hold my interest. Finally I gave up and went to check the pie. On the counter by the oven, next to a basket of pens and paper clips, I found a recent newspaper article about Robert and his amazing investment acumen. The article had run several weeks earlier; I remembered saving my copy for Pepper to send to Claudia. Some other friend had obviously clipped this one and just now sent it on.

The article was flattering, but the accompanying picture was not. Although Robert was smiling, his face was unnaturally tight and his eyes stared out blankly from the page. When I'd first seen it, I'd made some cynical remark about newspaper photographers training at the DMV. You almost had to go out of your way to take an attractive, polished, deliberately postured guy like Robert and fail to capture any of that on film.

Now, as I studied the photo again, I was struck by something about his expression. Maybe it was the aftermath of Daria's repeated hints about Robert's temper. Or maybe it was simply the oddness of the picture, or the fact that I was alone in the house where Pepper had been murdered. Maybe the timing, all these things coming together at once. For whatever reason, I was no longer able to brush aside the doubt that had been hovering, like an elusive gnat, at the edges of my mind.

Robert could be charming, for sure, and I'd been touched by his helplessness in the wake of Pepper's death. Yet there was something about him, not dishonest exactly, but . . . well, something almost Machiavellian. Michael had noticed it, although he'd put it a little differently, and with all honesty, I'd noticed it, despite my reluctance to admit the fact, even to myself.

And then there was the thing with the Cherokee. There may have been a perfectly innocent explanation, but if that was the case, why had Robert lied to me? And I was sure he had. Besides, he'd been decidedly cool to me since the police had talked to him. If the car didn't mean anything, why was he acting like a man who had something to hide?

Reluctantly, I began to sort through the details of

Pepper's death. Robert certainly *could* have killed her. There was no one to verify his whereabouts the night she was killed. It would explain how the killer gained entry to the house and why there were no unusual fingerprints or other bits of physical evidence in the room. I remembered, too, that Robert hadn't thought the open downstairs window odd in the least, even when I'd asked him about it specifically. In fact, he'd been careful to point out that the window wasn't connected to the alarm system. As though he *wanted* the police to believe the killer gained entry in that way.

But why? While I was pondering the reasons a successful, reasonably happy man might kill his beautiful, reasonably nice wife, the oven buzzer sounded. Grabbing a potholder, I opened the oven door and turned the pie, then adjusted the temperature, just as Mrs. Marsh had instructed. Pepper might have been a bit self-centered, bitchy even, to use Daria's words, but that was hardly grounds for murder. Besides, he'd married her in the first place, and it was unlikely her personality had made a complete flip-flop following their wedding.

Then I remembered the letter from McGregory. It was addressed to Pepper, but Connie had found it tucked into *Robert's* datebook. Had he somehow stumbled across the letter and so learned the sordid details of her past? What would he feel, a meticulous, proper man like Robert, a man who put great store in "keeping up appearances," when he discovered that his wife had deceived him, maybe even used him for her own purposes?

It was only a theory, but it *was* plausible.

I checked the clock above the oven. The pie had another thirty minutes. It wouldn't hurt to look around, I told myself. Michael had asked me to do that very thing not so long ago, and Claudia had readily as-sented. The feeble voice of my conscience tried to convince me that this wasn't quite the same, but I wasn't persuaded. This is murder, I argued back. You do what you have to do.

Robert's den was at the back of the house and I went there first. The room, like the man himself, was neat and orderly. His papers were stacked efficiently on one corner of the desk; his books, dull gray and green volumes on taxation and investment strategy, lined the shelves with militarylike precision. There were no pictures or personal mementos of any kind. Boldly, I checked his drawers and files, then leafed through his datebook, which was filled with meetings and appointments. But nothing struck me as unusual. Of course, he was hardly going to write "kill Pepper," under his list of things to do for the day. I had hoped there might be *something* out of the ordinary, though, some small, telltale scribble or scrap of paper. There wasn't a thing.

Carefully, I backed out of the room and shut the door, which clicked loudly in the heavy, afternoon stillness.

Upstairs, I headed straight for the bedroom, where I stood for a moment, taking it all in, waiting for a revelation. When none appeared, I began methodically opening drawers. Robert's were filled with neatly folded socks, sweaters, underwear; Pepper's, newly empty. Equally unenlightening was the large walk-in closet, where at least fifteen suits hung neatly along one wall.

What was I expecting to find anyway? A yellow and black silk tie, complete with revealing tear at the edge? Or maybe the heavy, sharp object used to bash Pepper's skull? If Robert was a killer, he certainly wouldn't be the sort to leave evidence lying about in open view. And besides, the police had been through everything already.

Feeling both foolish and guilty, I was turning to go when my foot kicked against a wadded-up shirt lying on the closet floor. Only there was something solid at the center of the wad. Out of curiosity, I picked up the shirt and unfolded it. Inside was a heavy, bronze rabbit, its peaked left ear coated with dried blood.

My first inclination was to drop the thing as quickly as I could and run. Then I thought perhaps I should carefully rewrap it, tuck it back in the corner, and simply forget I'd ever seen it. Instead, I stood motionless, staring at the bloodied creature and listening to the heavy pounding of my heart against my ribs.

So it *was* Robert, after all. This man I'd sat and talked with—Kimberly's father, my friend's husband—was a murderer. Behind that cool, reserved veneer lurked a monster, a crazed maniac with so little emotional depth that he could kill his wife in cold blood and then feign innocence. So lost was I in these thoughts that I didn't hear the approaching footsteps until they were right behind me. When I turned, I was standing face to face with Robert, who glared at me the way the school bully glares at the teacher's pet.

"What's going on here?" His voice was low, tighter than usual.

"I, uh . . ."

Then, as simple astonishment gave way to outrage, Robert stepped closer. "What in the hell do you think you're doing snooping around in my closet?"

Again I opened my mouth and closed it, without uttering a word. His face, darkened and tense, pressed closer, and I could smell the alcohol on his breath. There was none of Robert's customary reserve or gentlemanly good humor in the face before me.

"Well?"

They say that in moments like this you get a rush of adrenaline which empowers you in ways that stretch the imagination. A frail man is able to lift the weight of a car single-handedly; a bedridden invalid is somehow able to crawl through a darkened house to safety; a young child sees suddenly and clearly what must be done to save her younger brother.

But it didn't work that way for me. My mind went utterly blank and my body froze. I wasn't sure I even remembered *how* to speak, had I had anything to say. Somewhere from deep within, a little voice urged me to *think*—there had to be some reasonable excuse that would explain my presence and allow me to escape. But my brain refused to cooperate. Like a frightened animal, I cowered in the threatening silence while Robert watched and waited.

Then he saw the bundle in my hands and his mouth began to twitch. "You bitch," he hissed. "You sneaky, underhanded bitch." He stepped into the doorway, blocking the closet entrance—and my only way out. "What are you doing with that?"

"Look," I squeaked, lifting the rabbit to the light, "Pepper's blood is still there."

"You don't really think I'm going to let you get away with this, do you?"

Robert made a grab for the figurine, but I turned and he gripped my arm instead. His fingers pressed into my flesh, their strength surprising me. I remembered Pepper's bruises and Michael's description of her lifeless body. Suddenly my mind started working again. Twisting free of his grip, I shoved him hard against the back of the closet and took a step closer to the doorway.

"Lieutenant Stone knows everything," I said, wishing I spoke the truth. "And he knows I'm here right now. If anything happens to me it will only make matters worse."

"Lieutenant Stone knows what you're doing here? Surely you don't expect me to believe *that*."

"Oh, but he does," I insisted, amazed at my bravado.

Robert's grip on my arm tightened and without thinking I twisted toward him, bringing the bronze rabbit down hard on his knuckles. Cursing, he released my arm. I darted for the bedroom door, but again Robert blocked my path. His steely blue eyes glared at me, and my own eyes, which I feared were not nearly as steely, glared right back.

"It took a while to figure out," I told him, "but all the pieces fit. The arguments with Pepper, the lies you told about the Cherokee, the note from McGregory which Connie found in *your* datebook." Keeping my distance, I circled around to the far side of the room by the open window. If he tried anything I could scream. From that position at least, there was a chance someone might hear me. "Is the note what did it?" I continued, unable to hide my disgust. "Was it discovering that your beautiful, remarkable wife wasn't quite the princess you thought she was?"

Robert stepped closer, his breathing thick and throaty.

And then another idea sprang into my mind. "Or was it her unfaithfulness? Is that what finally got to you? Your fragile male ego couldn't take that, could it?" Once I got started, I couldn't stop. Fear, and my shock at finally confronting the truth, were too great. "It must have been so easy. You had a key, you knew the alarm code, and you knew the back windows weren't wired. So you took Pepper's wallet and some of her less valuable jewelry, opened a window and made it look like a burglary." I laughed nastily, forcing myself to look him straight in the eye. "No wonder the killer didn't tear up the house or take anything of real value."

Robert stopped his advance and stared at me. "You actually think *I* killed Pepper?"

"I know you did, the police do too. And now that I've found the object you hit her with—"

"Found?"

"In your closet." He shifted his eyes momentarily, and I readied myself. I was a runner after all, I just needed a break, a few seconds when his attention was diverted. "It's a pretty stupid place to hide it, practically out in the open."

Robert stepped toward me again. "You've made a big mistake, Kate."

Watchful and ready, I waited for him to pounce, to grab for me, but he instead shook his head bleakly and walked past me, over to the bed. With a deep, throaty groan, he dropped down, head in his hands. And when he finally spoke, his voice was a faint monotone. "I knew it would all come out eventually. Some things you just can't hide."

Still gripping the bronze rabbit, I inched over to the door. It was a trick, I felt certain. I couldn't believe the man was going to give up so easily. "You're right," I said sharply. "And murder is one of them. It was pretty gutsy to think you could get away with it in the first place."

Robert looked up, fixing his eyes on mine. Except for the soft hum of the electric clock by the bed, the room was perfectly quiet. "Kate, I didn't kill Pepper. You've got to believe me. I loved her. She and Kimberly were . . . were my salvation, my life." He clasped his hands together, pressing thumb against thumb. "It's probably not the kind of relationship you'd understand, but it was real, based on love and trust."

I was at the door now, my safe retreat assured. This sense of security, and the almost imperceptible quiver in his voice, prompted a moment of kindness. "Disappointment, hurt, anger—emotions like that can be overwhelming," I told him. "Can make people do things they ordinarily wouldn't." I paused, imagining for a moment the fiery tides that had driven Robert to kill his wife. "It must have come as quite a shock," I said, "to learn about Pepper's past."

Robert rubbed his cheek wearily. "I knew all about her background, even before we were married. It didn't matter in the least."

"You knew about her brushes with the law? And Jake?"

He nodded.

"What about Tony?"

"I knew she'd had a child, but I didn't put the pieces together until the police came by asking about him. Then I remembered some of the things she'd said. A few discreet inquiries and I had the answer."

Robert hadn't moved from the bed, had hardly stirred at all, in fact; but I wasn't taking any chances. I remained by the bedroom door, poised to run at a moment's notice. "You think anyone is going to believe you? If your marriage was so full of love and trust, why didn't she tell you when Tony showed up?"

"I don't know the answer to your second question, I can only speculate. But as to the first, no one has to take my word for it. The night she was murdered I was with friends. I didn't get home until almost two A.M."

I gave him an icy glare. "You told the police you were at work, alone."

He nodded, pressing the knuckles of one hand against the palm of the other. "I spent the evening at a sex club in San Francisco." He looked at me and smiled wanly. "You know what that is?"

I did. Or at least I thought I did. But it didn't make sense. The city's sex clubs, hangouts for prurient, no-holds-barred homosexual activity, had made the news frequently since the advent of AIDS. I'd read the articles with almost painstaking thoroughness and then tittered with my friends at the bewildering exploits alluded to.

Robert watched me closely. "I'm gay, Kate, bisexual actually. There's a man I've been seeing quite a bit of, and I was with him all evening, although there are others who can vouch for me as well."

I took my free hand from the doorknob and shoved it into my pocket, but I didn't step from my post by the door.

"It's something I tried for years to change," Robert continued. "It doesn't work like that, though, so finally I've come to accept myself for what I am. But I have a reputation to protect, and the rest of the world, particularly the business and financial world, isn't exactly broad-minded when it comes to things like this." He let out a deep sigh. "I didn't want to tell the police where I was that night unless I had to."

"What about the Cherokee?"

"It belongs to Bill, the man I've been seeing. He's very young—impetuous and possessive. I've asked him to stay away, but he won't. He doesn't understand my need to walk a fine line between two worlds."

His words pitched and rolled about inside my head, like a ship on stormy seas. It made sense, yet it didn't. Cool, reserved, proper Robert . . . with a young, male lover? "You told me you loved Pepper," I said skeptically, "that your marriage was for real."

"Pepper knew about my . . . proclivities from the start. Not that she was particularly happy about them, of course. She had thought once we were married I might change. And I did try. For her sake, I tried very hard, but . . ." He smiled apologetically, then blinked and looked at his hands. "In fact, we had words about it just the week before she died. Bill followed us to a party at the Patersons' and Pepper threatened to invite him in—you know, introduce him just to embarrass me." Robert paused and then sighed, an uneven, trembly sound that made me look away. "Pepper had been on edge about something all week, and I guess seeing Bill was sort of the last straw."

I said nothing, not so much because I disapproved, but because I could think of nothing to say. Robert must have read my silence as an expression of doubt, however, because he stood and faced me.

"Pepper and I had an understanding—respectability and acceptance we couldn't have had singly—but we also loved each other. Maybe not in the romantic, Hollywood way, but in the old-fashioned sense of caring deeply for another human being."

I don't know what it was exactly, the tone of his voice, the pain in his eyes, or maybe just the fact that his story was outlandish enough to have come from the heart. But I believed him.

"I'm so sorry," I told him softly. "For everything."

There was a moment of silence while we regarded each other uneasily; then he moved to the window and gazed out at the garden below. "Was she really seeing someone?"

"I don't know for sure," I said, embarrassed now at my excesses. "For a while I thought she might have been, but I really don't know. You didn't suspect anything?"

"No, but it wouldn't surprise me. As I said before, ours was not the sort of marriage I'd expect you to understand."

There was really nothing more to be said. I turned to leave, then realized I still clutched the bronze rabbit tightly to my side. Warily I stepped back to face him once again and held out my hand. "If you didn't kill her, how did *this* end up in your closet?"

"I haven't the faintest idea," he said, looking genuinely perplexed. "In fact, I thought *you* were placing it there in order to frame me."

"**H**is story checks out," Michael said, reaching for a piece of the cucumber I was slicing. "In addition to Bill, there are three others who will vouch for the fact that Robert was at that . . . club until after one A.M. And Bill drives a blue Cherokee with tinted windows, although he maintains Robert never tried to dissuade him from visits to Walnut Hills."

I scowled at the cucumber and kept right on slicing. "I feel like such a jerk," I muttered. "I can't imagine what came over me, snooping around his house like that, accusing him of killing Pepper. How in the world will I ever be able to face him again?"

"Tell him it was some female thing—hormonal," Michael suggested. "He'll understand."

Glaring, I picked up the wet sponge and threw it, hitting him squarely on the cheek. It was just the sort of nasty comment Andy would have made.

"Hey, it was only a joke."

"Well, it wasn't funny."

"Okay, you're a natural-born, bona fide fool with no rational explanation at all for your embarrassing conduct. You like that better?"

Drying his face with a dishtowel, Michael grinned at me, a wonderfully good-natured, I-admit-I'm-a-dope grin that was impossible to ignore. That was clearly *not* the way Andy would have reacted, and my irritation faded. But I wasn't about to let him off the hook that easily, so I poked him sharply in the ribs—which is not a wise thing to do to a policeman trained in self-defense. Before I knew what had happened, he'd turned me around and pinned both arms behind my back.

"My remark was crass. I acted like a crude, sexist pig, and I apologize. Am I forgiven?"

"Just don't let it happen again."

He released my wrists and turned me around so that I was facing him. "It *was* a pretty stupid thing you did, though. If Robert *had* been the killer, you'd be dead by now."

"At least you'd have a fresh lead."

"That's not the kind of lead I want."

I slipped my arms around his waist. "Besides, I *did* find that bronze rabbit. Was the blood Pepper's?"

He nodded.

"How'd it get in Robert's closet anyway?"

"I imagine the killer left it there."

I saw a cloud pass over his face. "But you searched the whole house right after the murder."

"Not well enough obviously." His tone was flat; his mouth set in a thin-lipped scowl. He looked about as grim as I'd ever seen him. "We talked to McGregory again too. Tony had nothing to do with passing on the information about Pepper. McGregory uncovered it all himself, though that wasn't what he was after. Apparently, he started checking out Pepper and a couple of the other vocal leaders of the Save Our Hills Committee. He was sure the organization was fronting for a group that wanted the ridge lands for a private park. And he didn't send that note to Pepper; it was his wife."

"Lynette?"

"You know her?"

"I know who she is," I said, reaching for the salad bowl. "Why would *she* send the note?"

Michael grunted, then explained. "Apparently she resented Pepper. They'd had a disagreement over something that had nothing at all to do with her husband's construction business."

Vaguely, I was able to recall the incident. Something about chairmanship of the Guild fashion show. I'd heard some of the other mothers talking about it, but I hadn't paid much attention since the social comings and goings of the Guild are about as pertinent to my life as those of the English royal family.

"Anyway," Michael continued, "she used the information her husband dug up out of spite, just to annoy Pepper."

"Maybe Lynette is the killer."

Michael grinned at me and tweaked my chin. "I already thought of that, but she was in New York at the time." Then, leaning against the door frame, he watched as I pulled plastic bags from the refrigerator and dumped them unceremoniously on the counter next to the sink. "Hey, watch how you treat the lettuce. It bruises."

I ignored him and hacked off the end of the romaine.

"And it's better to do a leaf at a time."

I turned and glared. "You want to make the salad?"

He smiled. "I thought you'd never ask."

While Michael rinsed lettuce leaves, one at a time, then drained and gently patted them dry, I checked on the pizza in the oven, which looked just as it had when I'd taken it from the freezer half an hour earlier—like a dish of plastic dog food. "The cheese hasn't even begun to melt," I grumbled.

Michael, who regarded my culinary endeavors with more than a touch of disdain, had the good grace to simply smile.

"I make an excellent enchilada casserole," I told him defensively. "It's just that I was at work all day today."

"Hey, don't worry. Generic cardboard with shredded imitation cheese topping is a special favorite of mine." Then, before I had a chance to bean him again, he ran a cool, damp finger across my lips and kissed my nose. "The company's what matters, not the food."

I kissed him back. "How do you do it?"

"Do what?"

"Make me want you so much."

"Do I do that?"

"You most definitely do."

We stood with our arms entwined, smiling contentedly like a pair of matched buddhas.

"Why don't you open the champagne," I suggested after a moment, my voice so throaty I hardly recognized it as my own. "I'll get the glasses."

Michael had brought a bottle to celebrate the sale of my first painting, which I supposed was an occasion to be celebrated even if the exhilaration was tinged with regret.

I'd stopped by Sondra's house the previous morning to pick up a swatch of fabric I needed in order to match blue tones in a print we were matting for her. My watercolor was in the back of the car on its way to be framed. "Don't tell me it's already sold," she shrieked. "I love it."

I couldn't imagine the picture hanging in any room in Sondra's house, and I told her so. Besides it wasn't for sale; I'd painted it for myself.

"But artists always sell their work," she protested. "Name a price."

I thought of the check she'd written to Daria the previous week, and my fondness for the painting faltered. "One thousand dollars," I told her, knowing full well the price was ridiculous.

"I'll take it."

"Unframed."

She nodded. "Will you take a check?"

That Sondra's taste in art was less hideous than her taste in other matters did little to comfort me. And much as I welcomed the money, it was an odd sensation to think a part of me, a part born of private, impassioned sentiment, would be displayed so publicly.

Michael opened the champagne, poured two glasses, then handed one to me. "To your continued artistic success."

We touched glasses lightly while I tried to think of some pithy rejoinder. Finally I gave up and smiled instead. The champagne was very good, not the six-dollar-a-bottle stuff I bought for birthdays and anniversaries. It went down smoothly and sent a silver tingle through my veins. I felt lightheaded after one sip.

"What's Barbara like?" I asked, running my tongue around the rim of the glass.

"Who?"

"Your wife."

He shrugged, very noncommittal.

"Please, I want to know."

Frowning, Michael set his glass on the counter and steadied it with both hands. "Bright, competent."

"Pretty," I added, almost without thinking.

He ignored me. "Extremely self-centered and demanding. As the only child of wealthy parents she's been indulged her whole life."

I watched the play of emotions on his face, quick and ephemeral, like firelight.

"I was husband number two. I lasted longer than number one, but that's only because he was a cad—whereas I was merely boring." Michael was quiet a moment; then he took a long swallow of champagne. "I can't wait to see who number three will be, probably some stockbroker or investment banker—that's the phase she's going through at the moment. Barbara tends to collect people the way a child collects playthings."

I was unable to detect even a trace of bitterness in his voice. Weariness, yes. Even bewilderment, as though he spoke the words while still pondering their meaning.

"She wants us to remain friends," he continued, his mouth curving into a half-smile. "In fact, she's already invited me to the graduation party she's throwing for herself next month. She told me to bring a date."

"What?"

"It is weird, isn't it? I sometimes lose track of what's truly normal and what's normal for Barbara."

That was a problem I was having myself lately. Not about Barbara, of course, but about life in general. Nothing was as I thought it was, but I couldn't tell if the problem was in me or everyone else.

Michael opened the oven door and peered in. "Pizza's done," he announced.

I got a bottle of Kraft Italian Dressing from the cupboard and began shaking it.

"You're not going to use *that* are you?"

"What's wrong with it?"

His gaze shifted from the bottle to my face. He grabbed the olive oil, a lemon, some garlic and a few assorted spices, then began mincing and whisking and shaking. A pinch of this, a dab of that and he presented me with a fully dressed salad. Then we called Anna and settled down to serious eating. The salad was delicious, the pizza pretty terrible. Michael made a real effort, but I noticed that he fed his second piece to Max, who liked it just fine.

After dinner Michael cleaned up the kitchen while I read to Anna and tucked her into bed. He was standing in the family room when I returned, holding a picture of Andy and Anna taken in the fall.

"Is this your husband?"

Peering over his shoulder, I nodded. Blond, blue-eyed, and athletic. Movie star good-looking, even in the harsh white light of early November. I was used to the impression Andy made on women, but I'd never tried seeing him through a man's eyes, and I was suddenly self-conscious. "It was taken at Tilden Park," I said, not because the information was important, but because I needed to say something.

Michael set the picture back on the shelf. "When's he coming back?"

"I don't know. I'm not even sure that he is."

"And if he does?"

I took a deep breath. "I don't know."

A grim tautness rippled across Michael's face and settled in his jaw. "Jesus, I wish I could figure out where you're coming from."

There was a moment of silence while I studied my nails, which were short and unglamorous. Artist's hands. A mother's hands. Certainly not the hands of a hot-blooded adulteress. "Michael, I . . ."

"Do you still love him?"

Did I love Andy? I wasn't sure. Certainly not in the way I once had. Not even in the way I had before he left. But there was history between us, and more than that, a daughter. There were things I couldn't turn my back on easily.

"He's Anna's father," I said.

"You didn't answer my question."

I slouched against the fireplace. "Let's not get in to all this right now."

"What do you mean 'all this'? It's what's important here. At least it is to me. You can't dismiss things simply because they make you uncomfortable."

"It's just that everything's so confusing." I could see that Michael was watching me closely, and I shifted my position self-consciously. "Can't we sort of do what we've been doing for a little while longer?"

A curious, drawn expression settled over his face and he looked suddenly very vulnerable. "I don't know that I can take being someone's plaything once again."

"You're not that," I told him, and pressed my head to his chest, feeling the soft, warm *swoosh* of his heart against my cheek. "Most definitely not that."

Slowly, Michael began to stroke my hair, pulling me closer.

"We can't," I whispered. "The doctor said a couple of weeks."

"I just want to hold you, Kate. You're so warm and soft, and you smell sweet, like apple blossoms."

I tilted my head and kissed him lightly. "That's funny, you smell like generic cardboard with imitation cheese topping."

He led me to the couch, where we kissed and cuddled. And then cuddled some more. In fact, we ended up cuddling all night, warm and snug and content under the covers of my king-size bed. I woke once during the night and watched Michael's sleeping face in the silver moonlight. It was a moment I wanted to capture and hold forever. And when he left the next morning, early, before Anna could wake up and come into bed, I felt as though some part of me had been wrenched away.

Daria was in no mood for a soul-searching conversation. "I'm really rushed at the moment," she said briskly when I sat down in the chair next to her desk. "Is it something that can wait?"

"Sure." In truth, I didn't know what I wanted to say anyway. But I felt the need to talk to someone. It was the only way I could think to ease the icy tightness in my chest.

"How about tomorrow after work?" Daria asked, skimming through a sheaf of papers as she spoke. "You want to go out for a drink? We can catch up then."

"It's not important anyway." I pushed back the chair and stood. "Is there anything I can do to help?"

This time she looked up. "As a matter of fact there is. I hate to ask this, you should probably still be taking it easy, but there's so much to be done before I leave for Mexico next week."

"I feel fine. What is it you want me to do?"

"There's a lawyer by the name of Gatskill out in Pleasanton. He's in the process of setting up his own office and asked for help in selecting some art work. I told him I'd be out there today, but it's such a long drive and I have so many things to take care of here . . . Would you mind terribly?"

By the tone of her voice, you'd think she was asking me to scrub the floors. "No problem," I told her brightly. "It's a lovely day for a drive. Besides, I work for you, remember? It's not as if you're asking a favor."

She hesitated. "No, but you're my friend too. My friend, first and foremost. You sure you don't mind?"

"Positive."

Daria stood and went to the file cabinet. "Get blueprints if you can," she said as she handed me the file, "otherwise sketch the floor plan and take measurements. It would be helpful if you could get paint and fabric samples as well."

"I'll take care of it all."

"Thanks, Kate," she mumbled, her head already bent over the papers on her desk.

Charles C. Gatskill, Esq. was a shortish man, with a substantial, rounded bottom and thinning hair. The gold chain around his neck and the diamond pinky ring on his left hand did little to improve his image. He was on the phone when I arrived, but managed to introduce himself anyway, cupping the receiver with his shoulder as he shook hands. He had a grin that flashed at unexpected intervals like a bulb with a loose connection. "Call me Charlie," he said. He, in turn, called me "hon."

"Look, hon," he said, finally dropping the receiver into its cradle, "I don't know about art for beans. I'm a hard-nosed divorce lawyer with a golden track record. Betrayal, deception, greed—these things I know. But line and beauty . . . Hell, a judgment in my favor and a big check, that's what I call beauty." He sat on the edge of his desk directly across from my chair, his crotch at eye level, and grinned. "But the office has to look nice, you know, to instill confidence. So basically you do it, hon, I don't give a shit what goes up there." He flung an arm out toward a blank, green wall.

He gave me a quick tour, during which time he took three telephone calls, waving his arms and mouthing words to me while listening to the person on the other end. "Haven't found a secretary yet. You don't happen to know any gals interested in office work, do you?"

Sorry, I told him, I didn't.

I got the blueprints, but no color samples, although I did get the name of his decorator. "What was your name again?" he asked as I was getting ready to leave.

"Kate Austen." I wrote it down on the back of Daria's business card and handed it to him. "Call me if you have any questions."

He studied the card. "Austen. You any relation to Andy Austen?"

"He's my husband."

Charlie slapped his thigh. "No kidding? What a small world. We were fraternity brothers together at San Jose State, way back when. How long you two been married?"

"Nearly seven years." My voice had a prim, almost defensive quality to it I didn't like.

"What-a-ya know." Charlie chuckled. "Watch out for that seven-year itch. It's what brings in half my business." He chuckled again. "Any kids?"

"A daughter. She's five."

"God almighty, Andy a father. Who would have thought? Guess he's settled down after all, the old rogue."

I left Charles Gatskill chuckling over some private memory and headed for my car. Between the blueprints, the file, my notes and handbag, I had trouble finding my keys. I began searching my pockets, where instead of keys I found a matchbook from the Royal Arms Motel. For a moment I couldn't remember where I'd picked it up; then I recalled that Kimberly had found it in Pepper's purse the day of the dolls' party. Tossing the matches onto the seat beside me, I searched some more, finally locating the keys at the bottom of my purse, and started home.

I tried to think about Gatskill's office and what was needed, but found myself instead pondering the intricacies of the seven-year itch. Was that Andy's problem? Was it my own? Had we somehow been tripped up by the colorless routine of familiarity, or did the rift strike much deeper? And did it matter, ultimately? At some point didn't you just accept things for what they were?

Of course some women, like Sharon, simply filled the void with rumpled sheets and sweet, sticky passion. In some ways it was the easiest solution. Then I thought of Michael curled around me in bed last night, the sleepy early morning kiss that woke me, and wondered if I would ever be satisfied with a steamy afternoon in some drab hotel with the shades drawn.

And that was when I understood, suddenly, what Pepper had been doing at the Royal Arms Motel. It was so obvious I couldn't believe I hadn't thought of it before. Uneasily, I glanced at the matchbook on the seat next to me. El Camino Way, Danville. The freeway passed right by there; I could get off and back on in an instant. And be back at the gallery in plenty of time to go over the Gatskill file with Daria.

I found the motel easily. It was one of those indistinguishable, L-shaped things you find in every city. This one was pink stucco, with a neon sign announcing showers and cable TV in every room. Clean and neat, but hardly elegant. As I parked the car, my mind hastily sorted through possible strategies, tossing out one after another.

Mentioning the word "murder" was an iffy proposition. It might bring out the public servant in some people, but would be just as likely to make others clam right up. I could, of course, rely on the tired old ruse of pretending to be a private investigator tracking down the beneficiary of a large inheritance. But if anyone asked to see my ID, I'd be in trouble. Finally, I concocted an elaborate story about my sister who was suffering from amnesia and had been missing for several months. Fortuitously, someone resembling her had been spotted in this very area. The family was, of course, anxious to learn all we could.

As it turned out, the young man behind the desk was very accommodating and not at all interested in my story. He was simply happy to have someone to talk to.

I described Pepper, realizing as I spoke, that the qualities which made her so stunning in the flesh were actually pretty commonplace when reduced to mere words. "About my height but thinner, blond hair, green eyes." The young man shook his head sadly. He would really like to help, but the description didn't ring a bell. Then I remembered the picture Mary Nell had given me last week. Like everything else that goes into my purse, it was still there. I only hoped the man at the desk didn't connect the picture with the recent front-page murder story.

"Yeah," the young man said eagerly when I handed him the snapshot. "I remember her." His eyes left the picture long enough to inspect me, head to toe. "You two are *sisters?*"

"Stepsisters, actually."

"Oh, that explains it."

I did my best to smile graciously. "Did she stay here long?"

"She didn't stay here exactly." His face grew red. Serves you right, I thought. "Mostly she came Friday afternoons, pretty regular. With a guy. I don't think they ever stayed the night."

I nodded to show I wasn't shocked.

"She hasn't been here for a couple of weeks, though."

"I see." Then, remembering my story, I added excitedly, "Mama will be so happy to know we're getting close to finding her. Would you by any chance have a name or number?"

"The records are locked up, I'd have to ask my boss. You want me to do that?" He reached for a paper and pencil and shoved them at me with puppylike eagerness. "Tell me where we can reach you, and I'll ask him tonight."

"Maybe you could just describe the man she was with. She used to have a boyfriend who lived around here. If it's the same guy, we might be able to locate her that way."

"Let's see." The young man scratched his chin thoughtfully. "He was big, at least six feet, curly red hair. With a mustache."

The shock must have shown on my face.

"Is that him?"

"It might be." Keep cool, I told myself. Jim isn't the only six-foot redhead in the area, even with a mustache. But I felt a sharp chill at the center of my brain, nonetheless.

"You know where to reach him?" the young man asked. I stared at him blankly. "There's a chance you can track him down through that car he was driving last time they were here. It was the craziest thing you ever saw. A Volvo with one blue fender and a red trunk. He said it was a loaner or something."

If my face was white, it went even whiter. Poor Daria, I thought. It wasn't fair. The most trusting woman in Walnut Hills, one of the few who still believed in faithfulness and the sanctity of marriage. And probably the only woman who still loved her husband with the same devotion and fervor as the day she married him. I thanked the young man behind the desk, who seemed puzzled by my sudden lack of enthusiasm, and left quickly.

Back on the freeway, I drove as slowly as I dared, dreading my return to Walnut Hills. I'd have to call Daria and make some excuse for not going back to work that afternoon. Facing her would be too difficult right then; I needed time to prepare myself.

As it turned out, an excuse found me. Out of the blue, my car ground to a complete stop just as I approached the interchange. I managed to pull to the side of the road and flag down a policeman, who called the towing company for me. He offered to call a friend too, but I declined and, just to be safe, waited until I'd been towed to our local repair shop before calling Daria. Busy as she was, that wouldn't have prevented her from dropping everything and rushing out to rescue me, whether I wanted her to or not.

20

The mechanic, a skinny little man with tobacco breath, broke the news gently, handing me a cup of lukewarm coffee before sitting himself down in the pink plastic chair next to mine.

"Looks like the engine's blown," he said, with a doleful twist of his mouth. "You musta' had an oil leak you didn't catch."

I nodded numbly, picking at the Styrofoam cup with my fingernail. "How expensive will it be?"

"Probably around a thousand dollars. Can't say for sure till we get the thing apart."

I didn't know whether to laugh or cry. I'd sold my watercolor, a piece of my heart and soul, for a rebuilt engine!

"Just be glad it happened close to home," the man said reassuringly. "You wouldn't believe some of the awful things that can happen to people."

Oh, yes I would, I thought. And most of them have nothing to do with automobiles. "How long will it take to get the car running again?"

"A couple of days at the minimum, maybe a week. We've got a loaner you can have for twenty bucks a day. Doesn't look like much but it runs real well."

I nodded bleakly and followed the man to the back

of the shop. I had a terrible feeling, even before I saw which car the loaner was.

"Looks like a crazy quilt, I know, one blue fender, a red back end, but the car's in good shape mechanically so you don't have to worry." With a chuckle, he handed me the keys. "Least ways it's easy to pick out in the grocery parking lot."

Gingerly, I slipped into driver's seat, taking shallow little breaths and holding my body erect, as if I could squeeze myself clear of the deception and betrayal that hovered in the hot, stale interior.

The car did run smoothly, the man had been right about that, and I was able to get to school in time to pick up Anna, who took one look at our new vehicle and wrinkled her nose. "What a dorky car," she said, without the least bit of humor. I explained about the blown engine and told her the story of Joseph and his coat of many colors, but she remained unimpressed. So unimpressed, in fact, that she crouched in the seat and ducked her head below window level so that none of her friends would recognize her on the way home.

When I'd parked the car—in the garage rather than on the street, much to Anna's relief—I let myself into the house, ready to kick off my shoes and collapse. But the phone rang before I'd even put away the keys.

It was Andy, calling collect. "Where are you?" I asked.

"London."

"What's wrong?" He didn't sound sick, but I couldn't think why else he would be calling.

"Nothing's wrong. Do I need an excuse to call home?"

"It's just that it's been a while."

"Yeah, I guess it has." His voice wavered, and he

paused a moment before asking, "Have you and Anna been getting my cards?"

Anna's been getting them, I thought. And I've gotten a couple of hastily scribbled postscripts you managed to add for my benefit. But I told him, "Yes, they've been getting here."

Another pause.

"How is Anna?"

"Fine."

"And you?"

"Fine."

"You sure? You sound kind of funny."

"It must be the connection."

Silence hung in the air for a moment; then there was a loud crash on the other end and a muffled "Shit."

"Sorry," Andy explained when he got back on the line, "I knocked over a bottle of beer. It's a real mess. So, what's new?"

Well, let's see . . . I've been screwing a man who knocks me off my feet, I've got a job, I sold a painting, I've had a miscarriage and I've made a fool of myself by accusing Robert of murder. Then I remembered he didn't even know about Pepper. "Pepper Livingston, our neighbor to the left, was killed a couple of weeks ago, murdered actually, in her own house."

"Jesus, is that for real?"

"Even *I* would not be stupid enough to make up something like that."

"I didn't mean that, it's just such a shock. How did it happen?"

I told him about the murder and then summarized the investigation by saying the police appeared to have no suspects and no leads.

"Holy shit," he said when I finished.

I could see that six weeks of European culture had not done a lot to smooth Andy's rough edges, but something in his tone brought back to me, very vividly, an image of the Andy I had fallen in love with. "See what happens when you run off," I teased. "You miss all the excitement of living in Walnut Hills."

"That's not all I missed," he said softly.

"Oh?"

Then he laughed. "Right, 'Oh.' "

"There's more," I said, reverting to safe ground. "Turns out she was having an affair. I found out just today the man she was seeing was Jim."

"Hmm." Andy coughed lightly, the laughter gone.

"You knew?"

"Kind of."

"Kind of?"

"Well, yes."

I was incredulous. "You knew Jim was cheating on his wife, my best friend, and yet we'd all get together for dinner and kid around as if nothing had happened? You even sympathized with Daria about Jim's hectic schedule."

"Listen, Kate, everybody has their own style. And Jim is my friend. You don't judge friends." His voice had a clipped, condescending edge to it. "Nothing was going to come of it anyway."

"You mean Jim's conscience was catching up with him?"

"No, Pepper wouldn't divorce Robert, if you can believe that. A guy like Jim has the hots for her— wants to marry her—and she opts for money, a pampered life and marriage to Robert."

"Maybe she loved him."

"Don't make me laugh. She wanted a sugar daddy, and there was no way Jim could compete there. Anyway, she finally put a halt to it, said Jim was putting too much pressure on her. He told me a couple of weeks ago, right after she broke off with him. God, the guy was hurt. And humiliated. I mean here he is, head over heels in love with her, and it turns out she's just out for a good time."

"A couple of weeks ago?"

"Yeah. Must have been about a week before she was killed, now that I think of it."

"He *told* you this?"

There was a long moment of silence; then Andy cleared his throat. "I called him, wanted to sort of touch base with things at home."

"You called Jim a couple of weeks ago, but not me? You didn't even write *me* a letter."

"Hey, you know I needed to work some things out."

I felt a prickly sensation at the back of my neck. "And have you?"

"I'm not sure." His voice sounded hollow. "But I'm coming back. I should be there in about a week. There are a few loose ends around here I need to wind up first."

I wondered if one of those loose ends was an Italian model posing as a cousin. "Why come home if you're not sure?"

"I've missed you and Anna." He paused, waiting for me to respond, and when I didn't, he took a deep breath. "I don't know if I can be what you want me to be," he said finally, "but I'm willing to give it another shot."

"Give it another shot? You make it sound like you're trying to unstop the kitchen drain." All the hurt I'd tucked away, trying to pretend it didn't exist, suddenly dropped like a heavy metal ball to the pit of my stomach. "Nothing's going to be any different unless you really want it to be. Unless you care enough to work hard to make it happen."

"Don't start in on me already, Kate. We'll talk when I get there."

"I had a miscarriage," I said, blurting out the words before the thought had fully formed in my mind.

Andy was quiet a moment. "Well," he said at last, "that's one thing we won't have to deal with."

"That's it?" My voice sort of squeaked, but I don't think Andy noticed.

"Look, Kate, I know you want another baby, but this isn't the right time. That's gotta be pretty obvious."

Nothing had changed. That was pretty obvious.

Anna danced around the room when I announced that Andy would be coming home. "But it might only be for a visit," I warned. "He might not stay."

"But why not?"

I pulled her onto my lap. "It has nothing to do with you, honey. Daddy loves you very much, and he misses you." Tucking a wisp of hair behind her ear, I took a deep breath and tried to explain something I was having trouble understanding myself—how the wonderful, loving feelings that brought people together initially could sometimes wither to indifference. "It's sad," I told her, "but wishing it weren't so doesn't change a thing; wishing just isn't enough."

Anna raised her head and scowled. "Still," she insisted, abruptly jumping from my lap and continuing her twirling about the room, "it will be nice to have Daddy back home, won't it?"

For the rest of the afternoon she busied herself making cards and pictures to welcome Andy back. "If he knows how much we missed him," she said, looking at me with wide, serious eyes, "maybe he won't leave again."

My chest grew tight watching her.

When Michael called later that evening, asking to

drop by, I begged off. "I'm not up to company right now."

"I'm hardly company," he chided. "Just for an hour or so."

"I'm tired."

"I'll rub your back then. You don't even have to talk. Ever since this morning, when I woke up next to that warm, sweet, beautiful body of yours, I've been walking around with a silly grin on my face. I just want to make sure I wasn't imagining it all."

"Back off, will you?" I snapped. "I said I was tired."

There was a long, uneasy silence, during which I made a few mental stabs at explaining, but I could never find the right words. Finally Michael said, "Okay, maybe tomorrow then," and hung up.

When I eventually climbed into bed, I couldn't sleep. One after another, in rapid succession, memories flipped through my brain, like a movie stuck on fast forward. And the bed that last night had been so warm and comfy, now seemed uncommonly cold. In the morning, when the gray light of dawn began leaking through the cracks in the curtains, I heard Anna pad down the hall to my room, where she slipped silently under the covers and nestled against me. In less than a minute, we were both asleep.

Anna wanted me to park the car around the corner from the school so that no one would be able to see her arriving in "that heap." She asked me over breakfast and then again as we approached the parking lot.

"Listen," I told her, "there are lots of children with families that don't even own a car. They're thankful if they can afford bus fare." Anna scowled and wiggled lower in her seat. "Some of them," I added, speaking slowly for emphasis, "don't even have houses to live in or food to eat."

She tugged at her sock and ventured one quick peek out the side window. "But *we* have a car."

Wearily, I parked—right smack in front of the school. When I'd assured her the coast was clear, Anna opened the door and climbed quickly out.

"Remember," I said as we walked into the building, "you're going home with Kimberly today because I'm going out with Daria after work. I'll pick you up as soon as I can."

"Mrs. Marsh has a nice car."

I kissed her, handing over her lunch box. "Have a nice day, sweetie. And if anybody asks, you can tell them ours is a special, magical car."

Outside I met up with Tina, who had just dropped off Zachary. "Did you manage to find a baby sitter?" she asked me. "I asked around for you but most everyone was full up."

"I've got a temporary arrangement with Kimberly's sitter, and once school is out Heather will be available."

"Sorry I couldn't help you out, I would have liked to. Be nice to care for a little girl now and then."

Given Anna's recent snooty drift, I thought a boy's boisterousness might be preferable. "That's okay," I told her, "I appreciate your looking."

We walked to the parking lot, where Tina stopped so abruptly I had to do a little shuffle to avoid running into her.

"What's the matter?" I asked.

"That car." She pointed to my colorful clunker.

"Quite something to look at, isn't it? But it runs well."

She pivoted quickly to face me. "It's *yours?*"

"Only for a couple of days, I hope. It's from the

shop; my Datsun needs a new engine. Given what it's going to cost to have mine fixed, maybe I ought to see about a permanent swap." I opened the door and climbed in. "I've got to run or I'll be late for work."

With Tina standing woodenly by the curb, I drove off, stopping by the bakery to pick up croissants and lattes to share with Daria. After considerable deliberation I'd made up my mind to say nothing about Jim's philandering. In the first place, it was over. Knowing about it would only hurt her. More than that really. Daria was the sort who would be destroyed by infidelity. Anyway, she and Jim were off to Mexico next week—Jim's idea—so maybe he'd decided to make amends.

Then, too, there was that little issue of casting stones when you, yourself, were not without sin, though I suppose it could be argued that since Andy had left me, my situation was a little different. Still, I thought I was hardly in a position to judge Jim too harshly. So it was business as usual, but that didn't stop me from feeling more than a little uncomfortable about coming face to face with Daria.

She seemed to notice nothing unusual, however. She greeted me with her usual warm but distracted manner. "How's the car-repair business?"

"Expensive."

"Isn't that the truth?" She finally looked up from the stack of papers she was sorting. "Oh, goody, I'm starved. You're such a doll to think of this." Popping off the plastic lid, she took a sip of coffee, licking the white foam with her tongue. "I feel so bad for you, as if you don't have enough to worry about already, and now this thing with your car."

"I'll manage somehow. At the moment, and much to Anna's chagrin, I've got your hand-me-down."

She looked confused.

"The multitoned clunker Jim had a couple of weeks ago when his car was in the shop."

"How did you know about that?"

"I rode in it, remember? When we went to the Guild Wine Festival."

"Oh, that's right, you did." Her mouth relaxed into a smile. "Seems like everyone in Walnut Hills has driven that car at one time or another."

I finished my croissant and tossed the bag into the garbage, then started for the back room where I was unpacking a shipment of hand-blown glass.

"I've been thinking," Daria said in that slow, deliberate way of hers, "maybe you should get serious about your painting. We could carry your things here as a start. That piece Sondra bought is really very good."

Daria did not hand out compliments readily, so I was pleased she liked the painting but wasn't so sure about the offer. "I don't know, I've never thought about painting professionally."

"Well, think about it. You've got talent, Kate, and that's rarer than you'd think." Standing, she ran her fingers through her thick curls and laughed. "In the meantime, you'll have to handle things here while I run into the city for a couple of hours."

As soon as Daria left, I placed a call to Michael who, it turned out, was "unavailable." Since the receptionist had asked for my name before checking, I thought perhaps he was angry with me, as he had every reason to be. But I left my name anyway and then set about addressing a stack of fliers while I readied myself to answer questions from customers.

But there weren't many, customers or questions. A middle-aged man with a cherubic face and carefully manicured nails bought a ceramic vase for two hundred dollars, but his only questions were "How much?" and "This *is* something you put flowers in, right?" When he left, two women entered—one about my age, the other a generation older. The older woman, who wore a turquoise polyester pantsuit, tittered and scoffed while her younger companion looked uncomfortable. "Look at these prices," she said. "Who in the world ever buys this stuff? Back home a place like this would be laughed out of town." The younger woman smiled blandly. "That's why you live in Kansas, Mother, and I live in California."

The person who asked the most questions was a young man sporting an American flag tattoo on one arm and a ponytail. He wanted to place a collection box and a small poster that read Drug-Free Kids by the door.

"I'll have to ask the owner," I told him. "She's not here at the moment."

"Can't you agree to something like this yourself? It's for a good cause."

"She might not like the idea."

"How can you not like the idea of keeping kids off drugs?"

"It's not that. She might think asking for change is . . . well, tacky."

"Tacky? She sells stuff costing hundreds and thousands of dollars, and she thinks asking customers for a quarter to fight drugs is tacky?"

"I didn't say that was what she thought, I merely said it was what she *might* think." And in fact would think, I was pretty sure. Daria had already said no to posting a sign about missing children. This was a gallery, she told me, not a convenience store.

The young man would have stayed around to badger me, which he seemed to enjoy doing, if Tina hadn't shown up and stood uncertainly by the entrance.

"Come in," I called to her as the young man shuffled past on his way out the door. "Can I help you find something or would you prefer to browse?"

She shook her head. "Actually, I came to talk to you."

"Is something wrong?" I thought instantly of dozens of things that could be. Some pretty horrible—stealing, drugs, child abuse; some not so horrible but still fairly disturbing. Maybe Anna was being mean to Zachary. Or mean to everyone. The terror of preschool. And nobody wanted to confront me with it.

"Are we alone?" she asked, looking around like a conspirator in a grade-B movie.

I nodded.

"That car you're driving . . ."

I nodded again.

"It's the car I saw that night."

"What night?"

"The night Mrs. Livingston was killed. Remember I told you about it that day in the park when Zachary scraped his knee. How I couldn't sleep that night because it was so hot, and how I went to the window for air?"

I did recall, vaguely.

"There was a car parked across the street by the Dumpster. The same car you're driving now."

"Are you sure?"

"I know it was the same car because I thought maybe it belonged to one of the workmen. It looks like the kind they drive, you know, beat up and all, and I was trying to figure out what it would be doing there in the dark of night. Then I saw someone come walking down the street, way off on the shoulder, step behind the Dumpster before getting in the car and driving off."

"What time was this, do you remember?"

"Oh, yes. I looked at the clock just before I got out of bed. It was one o'clock exactly."

"Did you see what this person looked like?"

"No, it was too dark, and the person stayed in the shadows. All I saw was a dark shape."

The day and hour of Pepper's murder. Her jewelry found in the Dumpster. The car in all likelihood was driven by the killer.

An acid taste rose in my throat. "Why didn't you tell the police?"

"I sort of forgot about it until I saw the car this morning." She stared at her shoes for a moment before continuing, her voice almost a whisper. "And I didn't want to create trouble. I'm only here on a tourist visa; I was supposed to leave months ago. If the police find out, I'm afraid they'll send me home. My family needs the money I send them." Her mouth quivered, and she looked as though she might at any moment break into tears. "But I should have said something before now, I know. I did rather like Mrs. Livingston."

I reached for her hand and gave it a squeeze. "It's okay, Tina. Sometimes it's not easy to know what's right."

She nodded.

"But you're sure it was the same car?"

"Absolutely."

I did some quick calculations, but I knew the answer before I finished. I knew who had the car that night—the same person who'd had it four days later when he gave me a ride to the Wine Festival. The same person who was hurt and angered by Pepper's refusal to divorce Robert. The man who'd been humiliated by the woman he loved.

You don't know for sure, I told myself. There could be a logical explanation. But I knew I would have to tell the police, and I also knew that I would have to tell Daria—at least enough so that the police wouldn't spring it on her from out of the blue. I owed her that much, friend to friend.

21

While I was sorting through my options, the phone rang.

"I have a message here that you called," Michael said. His voice was flat, and very businesslike.

"I wanted to apologize for last night."

"No need. You're entitled to your own life."

"But you're part of my life. An important part," I added, in what I hoped was an appropriately contrite tone. "It had been a horrible day and . . . oh, Michael, I don't know why I was so short with you, but I'm sorry. I feel awful about it."

I half expected a thank-you-for-calling kind of reply, pleasant but cool. Instead Michael laughed. A warm, rich, wonderful sound that made my skin tingle. "I was afraid you were calling to tell me to get lost."

"You're not angry then?"

"Just at myself. If I come on too strong, it's only because I'm crazy about you and I want you to feel the same way about me."

I do, I wanted to tell him. So much so that it scares me. Instead, I responded with one of those all-purpose, mechanical laughs and asked, "How about dinner tonight? I'm going out for a drink with Daria right after work, but I should be home by seven. No frozen pizza, I promise."

Michael sighed. "I've got a retirement dinner tonight—for a guy I used to work with in the city—but maybe I could drop by later. Unless you'd prefer I didn't."

"No, I'd like that."

He hesitated. "And I'm free all day tomorrow."

"Good," I said softly, "so am I." I picked up the paperweight from Daria's desk and turned it over in my hands. It was made of smooth, rounded glass, and inside were droplets of colored oil that drifted and curled and meandered in free-form patterns. "There's something else," I said slowly.

"Mmm."

"I think I know who killed Pepper."

"You what?"

I told him everything I'd learned, starting with Tina's remarks that afternoon and working backward to my visit to the Royal Arms Motel. "Pepper broke off with him a couple of days before she was killed. Apparently he was quite upset. It wasn't just some meaningless fling; he'd wanted to marry her."

"Where'd you learn that?"

"Andy told me. Seems he talked to Jim the Saturday before Pepper was killed."

"Andy, your husband?"

I bit my lip. "He called yesterday."

"I see."

My marriage was not a subject I wanted to discuss right then; murder was far less complicated. "Jim is such a gentle guy," I said, frowning. "I still can't believe it."

"This isn't easy for you, I know. But you've got to remember that killers come in all sizes and shapes; they buy groceries, drive cars, go to the movies. They have lives, even family and friends, just like the rest of us. Now tell me how I can contact this witness who saw the car by the Dumpster."

"I can't."

"What do you mean, you can't?"

"She's . . . sort of in this country illegally. She doesn't want the police to find her."

"Look," he said, his voice rising with exasperation, "we're a small, suburban police force, not the INS. You think I'm going to take her down to the dock and throw her on a boat? I promise you, the subject won't even come up."

"Still, I'll have to ask her first."

"Well do it," he snapped, "and get back to me ASAP." Then his voice softened. "And remember, we don't know anything for sure. It may turn out it wasn't Jim after all."

At Daria's suggestion we went to her place after work instead of out on the town. "It's such a beautiful evening," she said, "it doesn't make sense to spend it huddled in some crowded, smelly room. And I have a bottle of Kendall-Jackson chardonnay all iced and ready to go."

It *was* a beautiful night, warm without being oppressively hot, and the air was fragrant with the sweet scent of jasmine. But the real reason I agreed so readily was that I thought we would have a better chance to talk privately if we weren't yelling to be heard over the din of Friday night happy hour. And much as I dreaded it, I knew there were some pretty weighty things that needed to be said.

"Daria, I have to talk to you," I began as soon as we were through the front door. It was probably best, I thought, to jump in with both feet and get it over with before we got all cozy. "It's about Pepper's murder."

"Not that again!"

"It's important. I wouldn't be telling you this, except that you're my friend and I think you need to know." The words came in a rush, the way Anna's did whenever she was forced to confess her role in some transgression.

"Let me change my shoes first," Daria said. "My feet are killing me. Go get the wine. It's on the bottom shelf of the fridge, there's some brie in there too. We can sit out on the patio."

I found the wine and opened it, then got out two glasses. I was looking for the crackers when Daria joined me. She poured two glasses of wine, then took a sip of hers. "Now what about Pepper?"

"It's about Jim too," I said slowly.

She smoothed one eyebrow with the tip of her finger, but her expression remained unchanged.

"I think he may have been involved."

"Really? What makes you think that?"

I turned back to get the brie, hoping to buy time; choosing the right words wasn't going to be easy. How did you go about telling your best friend that her husband was unfaithful—and a murderer?

And that's when I saw the picture on the refrigerator door. It was in one of those clear plastic holders with a magnetic back. A photograph I'd seen dozens of times. Daria with her two boys, standing under the big oak in their front yard. Three fresh, smiling faces. Only this time I saw something I'd missed before, something that caused my blood to run cold.

"It's on the left," Daria said, "next to the milk I think. You can't miss it."

Slowly, I turned around to face her. "Oh, God, Daria, I was wrong. It wasn't Jim—it was you."

"What are you talking about?"

"You killed Pepper."

I waited for her to deny it, to laugh at me or get angry. But she stood motionless, without uttering a word.

"The earring the police found—it wasn't one of Pepper's, it was yours. I thought it looked familiar, but it didn't seem like the sort of thing Pepper usually wore, and until I saw this picture I'd forgotten you had them. And the scarf. It wasn't a tie that got caught in the bedpost, it was a yellow and black silk scarf, the one you used to wear all the time."

She took another sip of wine and gazed at me impassively over the rim of the glass. "My, you're clever."

I didn't feel clever; I felt sick. "But why?"

"I had to," she said simply. "Pepper was going to destroy everything I had, everything I'd always wanted and worked so hard to get." With a feeble smile, Daria picked up the wine bottle, "Come on, we might as well go outside and enjoy the fresh air."

I unwrapped the cheese, plopped it on the plate next to the crackers, grabbed my glass and followed her out onto the patio.

"She was having an affair with Jim, but I guess you know that."

"Only since yesterday."

"I found out a month ago when I discovered a note from her in Jim's shirt pocket. I hired a detective and had them followed. Got pictures and everything." She cut herself a wedge of cheese and then leaned toward me. "People like that," she said, in a tone somewhere between disgust and disbelief, "people like that make me sick."

"People like who?"

"Like Pepper. Rich, beautiful, selfish, used to get-

..ing their own way—they think they can just take whatever they want."

"You're not being fair, Daria; Jim had something to do with it too."

She shook her head. "No, you don't understand Jim. Oh, he went along with it obviously, but Pepper seduced him; beguiled him with her phony charm and empty-headed femininity. He would never have looked twice at another woman without some pretty strong encouragement."

I shut my eyes, willing things to be as they were not. The reality that faced me was incomprehensible. "At this point it doesn't really matter what Pepper did or didn't do. You killed her, Daria. You murdered someone."

Her eyes were fixed on something off in the distance, but I could see the glimmer of tears at their corners. Her mouth trembled.

"I know," she said, so softly I had to strain to hear her, "but I couldn't stand to lose Jim. To be one of those pathetic, middle-aged women with nothing." She began to cry in earnest. "Pepper had so much; it wasn't fair she wanted Jim too."

A numbing sadness settled over me like a heavy cloak, and I squeezed her hand gently, wishing there was something I could say. For some time we sat in silence, gazing at the hills behind her house, golden in the light of the setting sun. Good friends sharing a quiet moment, a bottle of wine—and a terrible secret.

Finally Daria dried the last of her tears. "It's odd," she said, "but nothing about that night seems real to me. I can remember what happened, but it's far away, washed in a pale light. Like a dream or something."

I poured us both a second glass of wine, figuring we could use a little dreamlike unreality at that moment. "How did you even get into Pepper's house?" I asked, thinking that maybe if I focused on the mechanics of the murder, the terrible reality of it would remain in the shadows.

"It was so easy. Chris had a key from the time Pepper and Robert were in Hawaii, when he watered their houseplants and fed their cat. He had the alarm code too. I knew if I turned off the alarm and opened a window I could make it look like a burglary. You know . . . warm night, window open, some drug addict wanders through, steals enough for his next fix, and in the process, kills Pepper."

"But Pepper always set the alarm. If Robert hadn't been drinking that night, he'd have remembered it wasn't on when he got in."

"I'm sure," she said in a voice heavy with sarcasm, "that even Pepper occasionally slipped up."

I ignored her disdain. "She might have heard you, though."

Daria picked at her nail polish. "That afternoon I dropped off some samples of the fudge I was planning to bake for the festival. I wanted her to taste them, tell me which ones she liked best."

The details Michael had told me that first morning came rushing back. "And you laced the fudge with sleeping pills," I said, finishing for her.

Daria smiled self-consciously. "Right. I even persuaded her to give Kimberly some, although it was a fight. You know how Pepper was about sweets." She ran a finger around the rim of her wine glass. "The only problem was, Pepper didn't eat enough of the stuff. God, she was such a freak about food, I should have laced her carrot juice instead. I expected her to be out cold, but when I bumped against the bed that night, she woke up and began fighting me. She was groggy, of course, and disoriented, but it was enough to throw everything off. It was supposed to be quick

..d clean—no commotion, no blood—just shove a pillow over her face and be gone."

Daria hesitated, and I waited for another round of tears as the memory of that awful night played again in her head. But instead Daria looked almost amused. "Maybe it's better this way, though. If things had gone the way I planned, Pepper would never have realized *I* was the victor. You should have seen her expression! For once in her life, somebody had gotten the better of her." Daria leaned closer and whispered, "She wasn't so beautiful, you know, without makeup. Her eyes were kind of small, and her skin was splotchy."

Instinctively, I pulled away, shrinking as much from the image of Pepper's vulnerability as from Daria's delight in its discovery. "So you hit her with that rabbit statue," I continued, for her, "and then hid it in Robert's closet."

"No. As I said, Pepper's being awake surprised me. It threw everything off. When I grabbed the statue I wasn't wearing gloves. I was afraid my fingerprints were on it, so I took it with me. But then when the police were running out of leads, and you mentioned Robert didn't have an alibi for that night, well . . . it just seemed to come together. I went back to the house and hid the silly thing in his closet. I washed it very carefully, of course, except for the blood. I wanted the police to be able to connect it with Pepper's death."

"No wonder Michael was upset that he'd missed it the first time."

She laughed, an odd, delighted kind of laugh. "I was hoping you'd persuade him to keep an eye on Robert, search the house again and stuff, but you did even better. Really, Kate, poking around in Robert's closet, that must have taken a lot of nerve. Weren't you scared?"

"Frightened out of my wits."

"Of course, turns out it was all a waste after all. Who'd have thought he'd pull in a bunch of queers as witnesses?"

Standing, she stretched her arms high above her head, as though she'd been seated for hours. "You know, I appreciate your help in discovering the rabbit, but I wish you'd left it at that. Everything would have been fine if you hadn't gone sticking your nose in where it didn't belong. This would have been one of those cases that fades quietly into history. The leads dry up, some new crisis hits and the police stop searching. Pretty soon no one even remembers." She turned and looked into my face. "You really screwed things up, Kate."

I caught myself on the verge of apologizing.

"It may still be okay, though. The police will have a hard time proving I did it. And if you tell them, I'll deny everything."

Just then a faint rustling came from the bushes at the side of the yard. Like young girls at a slumber party, we clasped hands and moved close to each other. An instant later, Michael emerged from the darkness.

There was a moment of absolute stillness during which we both stared at him, wide-eyed. Then a look of recognition flashed in Daria's eyes. She dropped my hand and swirled to stare at me, her face contorted with rage.

"You bitch, you traitor. You set me up! And here I thought you were my *friend.*"

Before I could explain, she reached into her pocket and pulled out a gun. A very small, surprisingly delicate-looking weapon that glimmered silver in the twilight. "Don't move, either one of you," she said sharply. "Now raise your hands above your head, Lieutenant, and step forward very slowly."

Keeping his eyes on Daria, Michael stepped onto the brick patio. "Are you okay, Kate?"

"I was until you showed up."

He managed a faint grin. "When I realized it couldn't have been Jim, I got worried about you."

"Keep quiet," Daria snapped, stepping around the edge of the table so that she faced us both. "Kate, get his gun. And don't even *think* of trying anything." When I hesitated, she added, "You do have a gun don't you, Lieutenant? Maybe even two."

"Just one," he said. "It's in a holster on my left shoulder."

"Go on, Kate, get it."

I looked uneasily at Michael.

"It's okay. And she's right, don't try anything foolish."

Was this some cryptic code for "Make a move, but make it a sensible one?" If so, we were in trouble. Maybe if I'd watched more of those macho shoot-'em-ups Andy loved I might have been able to come up with some plan of attack. But whatever cleverness and ingenuity I possessed had deserted me the moment I saw the gun.

Weak-kneed, I inched toward Michael and reached under his jacket. Even through the material of his shirt, I could feel the heat of his skin and the rapid beating of his heart. Apparently his fear was as real as my own, which did not do a lot to reassure me. Finally, I retrieved the gun, holding it away from me the way I might a dead mouse.

"Set it down over here on the table," Daria said evenly.

I did as she asked, then stepped back. "Someone saw your car that night," I told her, "by the Dumpster. The police will get you eventually. If you kill us it will only be worse."

"Shut up, Kate. You're the one who caused all this trouble."

Me? I thought. I started to argue with her, but Michael interrupted. "Take it easy, Daria. Think this through." His voice was soft, calm, almost as though he were talking to a recalcitrant child. I guess in the police academy they teach you how to hide your terror. "Pepper's murder was clever, but this . . . You're not going to be able to get away with this so easily."

"You don't leave me a lot of choices, do you, Lieutenant?"

"Cooperate with us. Don't dig yourself in deeper." He paused and offered her a gentle smile. "Why don't you at least let Kate go. She didn't set you up—she didn't even know I was anywhere near here. She only wanted to help you."

"Sure. You think I'm going to believe that? Anyway, it doesn't make much difference at this point."

"This is crazy," I squeaked. "There—"

Daria's eyes flashed. "Just shut up! I need to think." She bit her lips thoughtfully. "Get his necktie, Kate, and bind his hands behind his back. Better yet, tie him to the basketball pole." She shifted closer to watch my moves with an eagle eye.

I tied Michael's hands as loosely as I dared, but I knew it didn't really make a difference. She wasn't planning on leaving us unattended; she only wanted to curtail any sudden movement on his part. Michael never took his eyes off Daria and we didn't speak, but when I wrapped the tie around his wrists, he reached for my hand and squeezed it gently with his own.

When I was finished, Daria inspected my handiwork, then resumed her position across the table from us. I noticed that her hands had begun to tremble and she was breathing hard. I glanced at Michael, but he appeared as unruffled as ever.

"This is going to be kind of hard for you to explain," he observed.

Daria shook her head. "I'm thinking. I could always claim I mistook you for an intruder, sneaking up through my garden at night. There *has* just been a murder in town, don't forget. A lady has every reason to be nervous. Kate will be harder to explain, but I'll think of something you can be sure." The edges of her mouth turned up in a quiet smirk. "Maybe I'll even kill her with *your* gun."

I felt suddenly sick. "Daria, please, you can't do this."

"Want to make a bet?" With one quick, crazed, glance in my direction, she raised the gun and pointed it directly at Michael. I leaped for her arm just as she fired, but I was a fraction of a second too late. I heard Michael groan and then slump to the ground. "Damn you, Kate," she shrieked, kicking me in the shins. She wrenched her arm free and brought the gun down on the back of my neck, sending a wave of pain through my head. "You just couldn't leave well enough alone, could you?"

As we struggled, we knocked over a chair and I fell, scraping my mouth and cheek on a piece of jagged metal. But I held Daria's wrists tightly and pulled her down with me, hitting my shoulder against the hard brick. There was a brief period where we rolled and thrashed and clawed at each other. Then she heaved herself up and slapped me hard in the face. I tried to scream, but her knee was pressing hard against my stomach so that I had trouble even breathing. And then, in the soft evening light, I saw the dainty little gun just six inches from my face.

"I didn't want things to end up like this," she whispered.

Neither did I, I wanted to tell her. But I thought that

part was pretty obvious. Daria's face was flushed, her eyes dark and glazed. The expression on her face was unreadable, but there was nothing remotely familiar about it.

So this is it, I told myself. Poor Andy, he was going to end up having to be a responsible parent by default.

Just then I head a faint shuffling sound from over to my right. Daria heard it too, and in the instant that she looked up, I reached for the gun and tried to knock it from her hands. She pulled away, but her reflexes were too slow, and I was able to grab hold of her arm, shoving it sharply back against her chest. There was a loud crack and suddenly Daria went limp, slouching forward so that her head lay on the hard brick surface next to my own.

That was the last thing I remember until I heard the sirens and felt Michael's hand brushing the hair from my forehead.

22

I awoke the next morning with a pounding headache that seemed to reverberate through my whole body. Even my toes throbbed. I didn't know if it was the glasses of scotch I'd drunk when I'd finally got home, the hours of incurable sobbing that had followed, or simply the whack my skull had suffered when Daria had knocked me to the ground, but the pain was enough to make me swear off all three situations for the foreseeable future.

The hour was already late, I could tell by the yellow sunlight that splashed against the far wall. Anna had come and snuggled, and then gone off to watch Saturday morning cartoons no doubt. I'd heard her return every so often to stand quietly by the door and peer in. But I remained still, pretending I wasn't yet awake. What I wanted, really, was to lie there in my bed, shut my eyes and drift back into the warm cocoon of sleep. But the headache made that impossible. Besides, I had an appointment.

Strong coffee and a couple of aspirin helped, and the long, hot shower helped even more. But by the time the awful pounding had subsided, an assortment of other aches had begun screaming for my attention.

Michael had warned me last night, when I'd insisted

I was just fine. He'd warned me about the sore spots and bruises, the pulled muscles and scrapes, and about the pain deep inside that nothing but time could cure. He knew about these things, I suppose, except maybe the last. After all, Daria wasn't just some common thug; she was a friend—my best friend.

I dropped Anna off at Sharon's a little before eleven and then made my way to the Walnut Hills police department. I'd been there once before, on a nursery-school field trip, so I had no trouble locating it even though it's on the second floor of a Spanish-style building that looks more like a real-estate office than City Hall. But that's the way we do things in Walnut Hills.

The sugar-coated voice that greeted me was one I recognized from my phone calls to the station, and I experienced a momentary twinge of jealousy, just as I had on those previous occasions. Only this time there was a little resentment thrown in too. I was in no mood to exchange pleasantries with a voluptuous blonde, particularly one who shared the bulk of her day with Michael.

The body did not match the voice, however, and my ruffled feathers settled back into place. The woman was a skinny little thing with dull brown hair, frizzed on the ends, and a large mole on her left cheek. She might have had a great personality, but she certainly wasn't going to have Walnut Hills' finest jockeying for peeks down her blouse.

"Lieutenant Stone," I said, smiling magnanimously. "He's expecting me."

"Oh, so *you're* the one!" She gave me a wide, toothy grin which seemed to last for a full minute. It wasn't clear whether she was referring to my renown as hot-blooded lover or cold-hearted sleuth. Both roles made me uncomfortable. "Down the hall, second door on the right," she said. I could feel her eyes following me the entire way.

Michael was on the phone, but he hung up when I poked my head through the door.

"How are you feeling?" he asked gently.

"Shaky. Sore. How about you?"

"Right at this moment," he said, leaning forward to kiss me, "I feel terrific."

I stepped away. "We can't do that here. Are you crazy?"

"Crazy about you anyway." But he walked over and shut door. "Better?"

"It's your job," I quipped, wrapping my arms around his middle. Then we kissed, a long, lovely kiss better suited to a lonely stretch of beach than a busy office.

"I hated having to leave you last night," he said finally. "I almost called you when I finished here, but it was after two and I thought you needed the rest." He touched the raw, red skin on the side of my face. "Were you able to sleep at all?"

"Surprisingly well. I thought I'd be awake all night, reliving everything. Guess maybe I got it all out of my system before I went to bed."

"Maybe. Don't be surprised if it sneaks up on you again, though. Things like this take time."

"I'll be okay," I told him, so breezily that the artificial tone hung in the air even when I'd finished speaking. Then I hugged him, turning to rest my head against his chest. Michael winced and pulled away. "Sorry," I mumbled, quickly pulling away myself.

"No, I like it." A pause and a feeble smile followed. "Except for the blinding shot of pain, that is. But hey, I'm not complaining. If you hadn't knocked that gun from Daria's hands when you did, I might not be around to feel anything."

"What did the doctor say?"

Michael shrugged, but there was a gleam in his eye. "The usual—take it easy and make love often."

I brought a hand up to sock him in the shoulder and Michael winced again, before I'd even touched him. "No fair," he said.

I dropped my arm and smiled at him.

He smiled back, a slow, sweet smile that sent a prickly sensation across my shoulders and down my back. "You have no idea what you do to me," he said after a moment.

"Tell me."

"Here?" he mocked. "Are you crazy?"

"Tell me why you like me then."

"You're kind, funny, clever, brave . . ."

"Sounds like a Boy Scout."

"And you make me feel happy. Incredibly, wonderfully, indescribably happy."

"Likewise," I said, kissing him gently. Then I dropped down in one of the gray vinyl chairs across from his desk and stared hard at the carpet for several moments. "I'm glad you showed up last night when you did."

"I don't know; seems to me you handled things just fine. I couldn't even get my wrists loose until it was all over."

"But if you hadn't been there . . . well, I'm not sure I would have turned Daria in. I'd like to think I would have, but I'm not certain." I raised my head and looked at him. "That's pretty disgusting, isn't it?"

"Listen, Kate, what's done is done. There's no point beating yourself up over it."

I bit my lip. No point maybe, but that didn't make it any easier. "How is she?"

"Still on the critical list."

"It's funny how you can think you know a person, and be so wrong."

Michael pulled a chair close to mine and sat also, hunching so that his bad arm was nestled against his chest. His shirt was fresh, but he hadn't shaved and the hair by his temples sprang outward with a life of its own.

"If she lives," I asked finally, "what will happen then?"

"I can't say for sure, it's out of my hands. But even if she isn't convicted of Pepper's murder, there's still last night."

"Will I have to testify?"

"Probably, if there's a trial."

"And this morning, what do I have to do now?"

"Just read over the statement you made last night, make any corrections and sign it."

The wail of a passing siren from outside sent a shiver down my back. It was a sound I would never again be able to ignore. "She would have done almost anything for me, you know. And she isn't a bad person really; somehow she just slipped over the edge."

He must have read the uncertainty in my voice, because he picked up my hands and held them with his own. "Daria killed Pepper. It was premeditated, cold-blooded murder. Last night she tried to kill me, and she would have killed you given the chance."

I shivered, although the office was quite warm. "Is there any coffee around here?"

"It's pretty terrible stuff."

"I don't care, just so it's hot."

Michael left, returning in no time with two Styrofoam cups and a package of fig newtons. "The only thing left in the machine," he explained, dropping the cookies in my lap with an apologetic laugh, "It was a long night around here."

I took a sip of coffee, feeling its heat work its way down my throat. It tasted flat and bitter, but the effect was instantly soothing.

"Kate?"

I looked up. Michael was watching me, his soft gray eyes unusually serious.

"Last night," he said, "when I saw you and Daria struggling with that gun and I couldn't do a blessed thing to help . . ."

I squeezed his hand. "It's okay, it's over."

"But when I heard it go off, I thought . . ." He traced his finger along my bare arm. "I thought I would never have the chance to tell you what I feel for you."

"Don't, Michael. Not now."

Just as he started to say something more, the door opened. A youngish cop with short, close-cropped hair poked his head in. "We're ready for you, Mrs. Austen," he said. "Sorry it took so long."

He led me down the hall to a room with four desks lined in a row and pointed to a gray metal chair just inside the door. Then he seated himself at the desk opposite and handed me a clump of papers. "Just read through these and make any changes you want. Feel free to take as long as you'd like."

Quickly, I scanned the pages. They were my words; I recognized them. And they seemed to cover all the main points. But I couldn't tell if they made sense. It was like trying to read Balzac in the original after only one year of high-school French. I handed the papers back to him.

"Done already?"

"Everything seems to be in order."

"Nothing you want to add?"

I shook my head and signed at the bottom, where he showed me.

"Guess you'll have quite a story to tell your

friends," he said, flashing me a tight smile. "Claim your fifteen minutes of fame while you can."

My stomach suddenly felt scrambled, and I turned away. "Am I finished?" I asked.

"Just a minute while I check." The young officer scratched something on the back of my statement and then picked up the phone. Before he'd finished punching the number, Michael walked in and the young man dropped the phone back down. "Hey, Lieutenant, you want anything more from Mrs. Austen?" he asked.

"Yes," Michael said, sounding remarkably casual, "as a matter of fact, I do. Show her to my office. I'll be there in a minute."

"You free tonight?" he asked a moment later, when we were again alone.

"I am, and I believe I owe you dinner." Michael grinned and started playing with the hair at the back of my neck. "There's something else," I told him. "I'd like to see Daria."

He stopped his playing. "She's in ICU, under armed guard."

"But you can arrange it, can't you?"

"Kate, there's nothing to be gained."

"Please?"

He looked at me for a long, quiet moment, then sighed. "Oh, all right. I'll take you myself." Grabbing the phone, he punched the buttons hard and then barked into the receiver. It took less than a minute.

"Thank you," I said as we walked to car.

"I still think it's a lousy idea."

The invitation to the previous night's retirement dinner was on the seat. I tucked it into the pocket under the dash. "You never told me, how did you know it wasn't Jim who killed Pepper?"

"He plays poker on Tuesday nights," Michael said, pulling out of the parking lot and across four lanes of intersecting traffic. A move destined to end the rest of us up in traffic court. "And the game on the night she was killed didn't break up until the wee hours of the morning."

"How do you know that?"

"Jim said so, at the Wine Festival."

I was impressed. "My God, what a memory."

He basked for a moment in my wide-eyed admiration, then laughed. "I only remembered because I was envious. There I was putting in sixteen-hour days while some rich dentist lolled around all night playing poker."

"Jim could have left for an hour and then come back."

"Maybe, but he wasn't driving the loaner that night; he had the BMW." Michael paused and glanced pointedly in my direction. "Another point of envy. That left Daria as the most likely candidate."

"Impressive," I told him with a pat on the knee. "But what about the bruises? That wasn't Daria, was it?"

"No, that *was* Jim. We questioned him at some length this morning."

"Jim hit Pepper?"

"Apparently she was a real ice queen, started taunting him with stories of other men, and then when he begged her to divorce Robert, she laughed in his face. He struck her and she fell. His story, anyway. I never saw the bruises, maybe he struck her more than once."

I couldn't imagine Jim hitting a woman, but then a lot of things had happened that I could never have imagined.

"The irony of the whole thing," Michael continued, "is that Daria didn't have to kill Pepper. She and Jim were history by that point. And I imagine Daria might have looked pretty good to him after what Pepper had put him through."

"I'm not sure Pepper was as heartless as you think," I told Michael. "It might have been a tough decision for her, choosing to stay with Robert. A number of people, including Robert himself, have mentioned that she seemed agitated and upset during the last few weeks."

"Yeah," he said, looking directly at me. "I imagine having a nice guy madly in love with you can be pretty upsetting." He smiled, but without humor.

I turned my head and looked out the window at the green foothills in the distance.

We drove in silence for several moments, until Michael cleared his throat and said, "The other day you mentioned something about a call from Andy."

I nodded.

"He's coming home?"

I nodded again, keeping my eyes fixed on the hills.

"When?"

"A week or so. He didn't know exactly."

"And then?"

I thought of Anna, wide-eyed and hopeful, eagerly marking off the days to Andy's return. I pictured him swinging her through the air and regaling her with stories of his adventures. My place in this picture wasn't so clear.

Shifting my position, I tucked one leg up under me and turned to meet Michael's eyes. "I have to see what happens, I owe Andy that much."

"Owe him. For Christ's sake!" Michael's tone was explosive. "The guy walked out on you. I don't see that you owe him anything."

"He didn't exactly walk out."

"Close enough." Michael looked straight ahead, his mouth tight, his jaw rigid.

Why was I defending Andy? It didn't make a whole lot of sense, even to me. Maybe I was simply afraid to let go; afraid to relinquish my hold on the last vestiges of the cozy, picture-perfect life I'd thought we had. Or maybe I wanted to be able to tell myself that I'd tried, that I wasn't the one turning my back on seven years of building togetherness. There was also, I suppose, the possibility that somewhere deep inside, part of me still loved him.

"I'm just not ready to make any decisions," I said. "But that doesn't affect what I feel for you."

Michael turned his head, but not his eyes. "So where does that leave us?"

"How about lunches? I just *love* your lunches." I tried for a light, playful tone, but it came out uneven and squeaky instead. Hardly the voice of a seductress.

"That's not what I want."

Nor I, I wanted to tell him. But I couldn't, not just yet. So instead I nodded and said, "I know, but I can't promise anything more at the moment."

He smiled weakly, and we drove the rest of the way to the hospital in silence.

ICU was on the fifth floor, behind double glass doors. There was a cop standing in the hallway just outside, and another by the nurses' desk at the front of the ward. Michael pulled out his ID, mumbled something I couldn't understand, and we went in. He repeated the exercise for the guy inside, and then left, saying he'd wait for me in the hallway.

The room was stuffy, filled with the heavy rankness of hospital routine and stale bodies. I felt the sourness from my stomach rise into my throat. Hesitantly, I looked once again at the guard, who nodded but didn't smile. Then I took a deep breath and headed for the far corner he had indicated.

Daria was almost lost in the huge bed and the equipment surrounding her. There were tubes in her nose and arms, others snaking under the covers. Machines whirred, lights blinked, screens flashed zigzag patterns like abstract neon billboards. And in their midst lay Daria, her skin white and pasty, her hair tangled and flattened against her head.

I stood quietly by the bed for a moment, then leaned forward and touched her arm lightly. Her eyes fluttered open and she looked at me impassively, as though she could see right through me.

"I'm so sorry, Daria," I whispered under my breath. "I wish things had turned out differently." I blinked, but she didn't. "And I *am* your friend, even now."

Her eyes closed again, and remained closed. I brushed a wisp of hair from her forehead and stood a moment longer, listening to the blips and pings. Waiting, maybe, for some sign of the Daria I had known. But there was no acknowledgment at all, not a trace. Her body remained motionless, like an abandoned rag doll's. Finally I turned and left.

Michael was waiting in the hallway, just as he'd promised. He draped an arm around my shoulder, wincing with the pain of extended movement. "You okay?" he asked.

I nodded, feeling curiously at peace. Maybe that's what happens when you begin to let go. Things were never going to be what they had been, but then they were never what I imagined them to be in the first place.

"We still on for tonight?" I asked.

"I hope so. What shall I bring?"

"Just your toothbrush."

A strained smile flickered across his face. "I was

hoping there would be a day I might leave it there per-
manently. Along with my slippers and books, and my
collection of gourmet spices."

"Who knows, there may be."

He looked surprised. "Want to give me odds?"

"No promises, but I'd say the odds are in your
favor."

He grinned and kissed the tip of my nose. "Be fore-
warned, I've picked up quite a collection of dirty tricks
over the years, and I'm not above using them."

We locked hands. "I'm not sure you'll need them," I
said.

Please turn the page for
an exciting sneak preview of
Jonnie Jacobs' next Kate Austen mystery

MURDER AMONG FRIENDS

now on sale
wherever hardcover mysteries are sold

Mixing business and friendship is always something of an iffy proposition, even when you expect things to go smoothly. I had no such expectation where Mona Sterling was concerned. Not that Mona wasn't wonderfully sincere and warm-hearted, because she was, in spades. But she was also opinionated, self-centered, and sometimes downright insensitive.

Although Mona and I had been drawn together initially by the bond of divorce, we'd soon moved beyond discussion of marital termination agreements and child support guidelines to more cheery subjects such as dieting, age lines and PMS. Whatever the subject, Mona would invariably carry on at length and with mind-numbing conviction. As fond as I was of the woman, I sometimes found her a daunting companion.

When she'd called and insisted we simply had to meet that Monday, which happened also to be a holiday at my daughter's school, and then announced that she was available only between the hours of 11:00 and 1:00, I'd managed to shrug off my initial irritation. After all, I'd known that working for Mona was going to tax my patience. I was hoping it would also bring

me a slew of flush new clients. Mona was, among other
things, well connected with the monied elite of Walnut
Hills—and as a fledgling entrepreneur, I needed all the
help I could get.

I reminded myself of this as I stood at Mona's massive front door and rang the bell. A sharp, wet, Febru-
ary wind whipped strands of hair across my face and
tunneled down the neck of my old raincoat. After
seven years of drought, El Niño or the hole in the
ozone or whatever other mysterious force was responsible had finally shifted, and we were having one of the
coldest, wettest winters in California history. Like cod
liver oil, it might be good for us but it wasn't pleasant.

Shivering, I tried the bell again, poking it several
times in quick succession the way my five year old,
Anna, does when I don't answer instantly. I waited for
a minute, which is something Anna never does, then
sighed, brushed the hair out of my eyes and reached
into my purse for the keys Mona had given me.

"I might be a few minutes late," she'd told me. "Just
go on in and get started. I shouldn't be too long."
Mona was invariably late so I'd planned for the fact
and arrived almost twenty minutes after the hour myself. Apparently I'd still beat her there.

I fumbled around in my bag, stabbing my finger on
one of Anna's stray jacks before finding the keys under
the phone bill I'd forgotten to mail. There were two
keys. The rounded one for the top lock, the narrow
one for the bottom. Or was it the other way around?
I'd been dashing off to drive the afternoon carpool
when Mona had gone over it, so I'd only listened with
half an ear.

I tried the narrow key in the bottom lock. Wonder
of wonders, it worked. I stuck the other in the top
lock, preparing to turn it with my left hand while using
my right to depress the latch, the way Mona had

showed me. But the door opened immediately. All those instructions and she hadn't even bothered with the dead-bolt after all!

I pushed open the door and called out in case she simply hadn't heard the bell. No answer. No sound of running water or footsteps either. Propping the door open with my purse (Mona had warned me that it locked automatically when shut), I went back to the car to retrieve the lithographs, which were the primary reason for my being there that morning. I'm an art consultant, a business I'd sort of back-stepped into when Andy and I separated and a friend offered me a job in her gallery. I'm an artist too, but that's an endeavor which provides more pleasure than profit. Not that I make such a killing from my consulting business. I'm counting on the fact that things will pick up over time though.

I had two pieces with me that morning. One was a monochromatic abstract which Mona had purchased, with my help, several weeks earlier. It was back now from the framers and ready to be hung. The other was something I'd stumbled across at a new gallery in Berkeley. I was pretty sure Mona would like it, but I didn't know if the colors were right for the room.

The pictures were large (which is what Mona wanted) and heavy (which sort of comes with the territory when you're talking large). With the ground so damp and the wind gusting about the way it was, I decided it would be best if I carried them to the house one at a time. You drop a fifteen hundred dollar painting and you're liable to spend the rest of your life cursing your stupidity.

By the time I got them both into the house and unwrapped, it was 11:40 and Mona still hadn't shown. Grumbling, I carted the pictures into the spacious living room and propped them against the wall.

Mona's house is large and sprawling, unlike my own which is so cramped that people and furniture have trouble co-existing. Andy and I had planned to add on, but we'd never managed to save enough money to do more than dream. Now, with the impending divorce, money was even tighter. It wasn't that Andy was being nasty about it. Bottom line is, he's a pretty decent guy. Unfortunately, he's also unreliable as all get out and practically penniless.

The financial fallout from Mona's divorce was different. Her husband was a first class sleaze, but a rich one. Though he'd fought her tooth and nail over everything from the country club membership to the left-over Christmas wrap, Mona had wound up with a more than satisfactory settlement. She got the house and a sizable portion of their assets, while Gary got the furniture, Persian carpets, and china, all of which he was eager to install in the even bigger house he and his wife-to-be were building on the edge of town.

I'd only seen Mona's house once in its former, sumptuous state. It had been decorated to the nines with massive and, to my taste, overly ornate antiques. Impressive certainly, in a formal, heavy-handed way, but not the sort of place where you'd want to kick off your shoes and stretch out. At that time the walls had been adorned with gold-framed hunting scenes and pseudo Rembrandts. In forging her life anew, Mona had gone from one extreme to another. She was now into serious minimalism. The walls were white, the floors and windows bare, the furnishings sparse. Libby's was the only room that actually looked inhabited. And it was a mess. Exactly what you'd expect from the teen-aged daughter of a woman who'd elevated empty space to new heights.

I checked my watch again, then stood back against the fireplace to get a feeling for the two pictures together. I liked the effect, though of course Mona would have the final say. If she ever got there. I couldn't imagine what was keeping her. Or why she didn't at least call.

Damn her anyway, I thought. I'd arranged my whole morning around her schedule. Mentally giving her the what-for, I stomped off into the kitchen, newly refurbished in white and chrome, and put on a kettle of water for coffee. Mona had told me she had something to discuss, and with Mona this meant coffee. It would speed up the process considerably if the coffee was ready when she was.

And that would have to be soon or we'd never get to the conversation part of the visit, which seemed, from Mona's tone, rather pressing. She wasn't the only one with an afternoon commitment. I had a one o'clock meeting, a final planning session for the upcoming school auction, and I'd promised Sharon I'd stop by the bakery on my way over. God forbid we should have to do all that planning without the benefit of oatmeal bars and brownies.

The water began to boil. I measured the coffee and then pulled down the cups, taking care not to knock against the two crystal tumblers sitting next to the sink. They hadn't been emptied completely, and had that heavy, boozy odor you never notice until the next morning. I dumped the contents, then rinsed them carefully. While I was at it, I dumped the ashtray as well. Company and a late night, I thought, maybe that explained it. Mona had probably slept through her alarm this morning and had been running late ever since.

If that was the case, though, she probably hadn't had time to pull together the samples I'd asked for. We were looking for a large, horizontal piece to hang above the couch in the den. I wanted to measure the space and maybe take one of the throw pillows to use in matching colors. I poured the water through the coffee, and then while it dripped, went to complete the work myself.

The smell was what I noticed first, even before I reached the den. An indistinct, slightly rank odor, like rotting leaves or a garbage disposal that hasn't been run through. Inside the room it was stronger and more fetid. I gagged slightly, thought about opening a window, then decided against it. Mona was not the fresh air freak I was.

I was halfway to the sofa before I noticed a shape mounded at one end, and even closer before it hit me.

The shape was Mona.

She was slouched against the back cushion, sweat pants twisted around her outstretched legs, one arm flung out to the side, the other draped across her chest. Her tee shirt had ridden up slightly, exposing a band of bare skin across her middle, skin that seemed oddly tight and waxy. Her head had rolled back so that she was facing the ceiling, her expression frozen and mask-like.

I closed the distance between us in a flash, grabbed her arm and felt for a pulse. The flesh my fingers touched was cold. Clammy and lifeless, as I'd known it would be. The prescription bottle and half-empty fifth of scotch on the table left little room for doubt.

"Mona. My God, Mona, why?" My mouth was too dry to actually form the words, but inside my head someone was shrieking, and sobbing her name over and over again.

I stumbled back to the kitchen where I called the paramedics, although I knew there was nothing they could do. Then I hung up and placed a second call to Lieutenant Michael Stone.